# Divided Lives

# Divided Lives

K.R. MULLINS

*To Claudia who reads all of my work.*
*To Jonathan and Joshua, my best boys.*

# Chapter One

F lash!

"What was that?" Lottie asked as she tried to sit up in her bed. "Why is it so bright, is it morning?" She shook her head, trying to clear her vision. "Rose, did you hear. . ." she trailed off, looking toward her lover. Frowning, she saw something wasn't right. Rose's eyes were wide open, and there was blood on her face and chest.

"Rose!"

She grabbed her shoulders. There was no reaction from her. Lottie started to scream, but the sound didn't make it past her lips as her world tilted and went black.

The second time she woke, her vision was clear. A sudden memory made her look quickly to where Rose should have been. She was alone. "Rose," she called. *Where was she?* Sitting up, she struggled to remember the night before, holding her pounding head in her hands.

*I didn't think I had that much to drink.*

*Blood,* she thought suddenly, remembering. She jerked the sheets to her, and uncovered Rose's side of the bed. There was

1

none. *A dream*, she thought, falling backward onto her pillows. *Thank goodness*. Rose must have already gone. Breakfast wasn't something she normally stayed around for.

*What happened last night? Where did the evening start?* she thought, trying to remember. *With Patrick.* Her brother had arrived a few days ago. His home was in Chicago and he was in town to accompany their aunt and uncle to the steamship for their trip to France. Lottie and Patrick had met with them for dinner and the send-off.

---

### The night before after their dinner with their aunt and uncle

Their motorcar, a green Scout with the top folded down, bounced along on their ride back to the village. Patrick glanced over at her and asked, "Lottie, where shall I drop you?" When he was in town, they had dinner together but separated after to spend time with friends.

"The tearoom, please," she requested. She looked over at him and asked, "Will I see you tomorrow?" The next day was Friday; she knew he would be going home on Saturday.

"I have some meetings in Manhattan that will take up most of the day. How about Saturday morning for breakfast and a ride to the train station?" he suggested.

She thought of her calendar and said, "That would be lovely. Call me if your plans change."

"I will," he said as he pulled the car to a stop, narrowly missing a young man and woman who appeared inebriated. The couple hadn't noticed their near accident and continued across the road.

Patrick laughed at their antics as he jumped out and went

around to help Lottie out of the car. "See you tomorrow, sis," he said as he bent down to kiss her on the cheek.

She stayed where she was and watched him jog back around to the driver's side. The car bounced and rumbled as he pulled into the busy street. The evening was pleasant, a cool breeze moving through the area, and even the sidewalks teeming with people didn't bother her. She took a moment to look around before going in. Like most retail spaces in Greenwich Village, the Tearoom, where she would spend part of her evening, was located in a storefront on the bottom part of a redbrick building. The buildings on either side of it were different shades of red brick, rising to five stories. Each had a personality of its own. Different brick patterns, and awnings, some with large windows and some with none. This type of building stretched down the blocks in the village.

She maneuvered through the crowd to reach the entrance to the tearoom. The location had moved a few times but seemed to find a more permanent home here. The owner didn't have a second job, and sometimes the income from the business wasn't enough to keep it open. Most of the individuals living in the village chose to live in the area for the cheap prices and atmosphere of free speech; the tearoom provided both.

As she entered, she noticed the furniture. It could be called an eclectic mix. The tables were pieced together out of planks of wood and found chairs. Nothing matched in shape or design, but it was tied together with white paint. The walls were painted the same bright white; the difference was that the owner had asked a local artist to paint what they liked on the walls. It made for a colorful and sometimes garish look. It also fit the women of the tearoom perfectly.

The women at those tables wore unique clothes, some in pants, long flowing gowns or skirts, and shirtwaists. No one questioned what the others chose to wear; it was their outward expression of who they were on the inside. *I love that,* she thought. She looked down at her outfit and smiled. Her dress was conservative that evening with a high-neck shirtwaist, a long skirt with a petticoat, and dark stockings. *Definitely not an outward expression of me. At least, not tonight,* she thought and smile ruefully. She reached up to unpin her short hair and let it fall to her shoulders.

Drinks were being served throughout the space. It was called a tearoom, but few people drank tea; most preferred the harder options, usually whisky or vodka. The owner was not licensed to sell alcohol and those who drank were at risk of arrest by the local police. The owner seemed to have some sort of deal with them to limit the raids for a fee—a well-known system of graft.

Conversations drifted by as she passed the different tables. The first: suffragettes sat around their table loudly demanding more movement and more marches. They'd had a very successful one in May of that year. She waved at them when she saw Henrietta at their table. Though Hen had other interests, the vote for women was her current passion. She was involved with the parades, a new development in the fight for women's suffrage in the United States.

At another table, the ladies were discussing the village kids and Washington Square park. "They won't let our kids play there! A man stopped us and said we were allowed to be there." Phillipa worked as a teacher at the local village school and had limited space where the kids could play safely.

"What happened exactly?" Lottie asked, hesitating briefly at their table.

Phillipa looked over at her and commented seriously, "A man came up to me in the park and told me our kids were not allowed to be there." She had to take a deep breath before continuing. "He thinks we're somehow degrading the park. He also said loudly that he's on the Washington Square Association and demanded we leave and stay away until we settle the dispute." Her face crumbled with despair, and she asked, "Lottie, how can we destroy the character of the park?"

"You can't. The park is there for everyone. Phillipa, get me the information and I'll write a letter to the committee," Lottie said firmly.

"Could you do that for us? I can bring it over to your apartment."

"Just slide it under my door. I'll take a look at it tomorrow. Will that be enough time?"

"Yes, of course. Do you think that will work?" she asked hopefully.

"We might be able to delay any relocation of the children and propose a park here in the village. I don't have time tonight, but get me that letter as soon as you can."

The ladies liked that response and started volunteering to help put a letter together.

As Lottie walked off, Phillipa called, "Thanks for helping."

"Just get me the letter," she reiterated over her shoulder.

"We will," Phillipa said, looking around at the ladies at her table.

Lottie walked past another group involved in a discussion about the newspapers spread out on their table. The heated tone caused her to pause. The subject being discussed shouldn't have surprised her: Charles Becker. She had kept up with the case; it involved gamblers, police corruption, and the murder of an informant. Since she started working for Justice Goff, she knew to stay away from conversations involving cases going to trial. She might inadvertently say something that could put her in an uncomfortable position later. Though she didn't expect to have it assigned to her court; that type of case was normally assigned to the General Session.

She passed other groups talking about politics and the policies they wanted to have changed. Normally, she would have enjoyed some drinks and a lively talk with the various groups, but tonight, she hadn't come to drink or discuss liberal politics. There was a specific reason she was there and that reason was Rose. She spotted her toward the back. As she got closer, she saw that she was already occupied with another woman. Lottie recognized her. *Lily*, she thought. She watched the hand Rose had down Lily's shirt, caressing her breast.

Rose was looking around and spotted Lottie. She called her over. "Sit down, join me." She slowly pulled her hand out of Lily's dress, squeezing her nipple on the way. Lily moaned, trying to keep Rose's hand where it was. But Rose had other interests and, instead of putting her hand back where Lily wanted it, she used it to wave at her. It was her dismissal; she shot a glare at Lottie as she pulled her top together over her exposed breast and moved to another table.

"I hope I didn't interrupt anything," Lottie said in a low voice, not meaning it.

"No, not at all," Rose murmured back. She reached over and brushed Lottie's hair off of her face, a caress she used to show her interest. They had an on-again, off-again relationship. Casual sex had become something she looked forward to with Rose. Lottie leaned forward and kissed her softly, seeing how receptive she was. Rose returned the kiss warmly and murmured, "I was hoping to see you tonight."

"Were you?" Lottie asked coyly.

"Yes, would you like me to spend the night?" she asked.

Rose had always been forthright. When Lottie first moved to the village, she had never been with a woman. In a move very similar to the one she used tonight, Rose had walked up to her in the tearoom, pushed her hair aside, and kissed her softly.

"I would," said Lottie, leaning into her.

Rose returned the embrace and glanced over Lottie's shoulder, toward the door. She pulled back slightly and said, "I need to make a quick phone call first. Help me finish my 'tea' and we can head to your apartment."

Lottie nodded and watched as she stepped into the back where the phone was located. She drank quickly, gathered her things, and moved to the door to wait. Rose stepped out, took Lottie's elbow, and headed to her apartment.

———

### Present Day

Pulling herself into the present, she thought, *Dream, only a dream. Rose is fine. I know she is. She must have left.* She might sleep over, but she would often leave before Lottie woke-up.

# Chapter Two

Lottie got up to begin her day and made her way to the washroom to take a bath. After, she went to the closet to select her clothes. The outfit she normally wore to work was a long-sleeved shirtwaist, fashioned like a man's shirt with buttons down the front, and was worn with tailored pants. Her aunt Emma favored pants when she was working and had made Lottie several pairs before she moved to New York City. They were perfect for running around the village, but not for her day job working as a clerk for Justice Goff. The office required women to wear skirts at all times, with no exceptions.

The dream stayed with her, even as she was dressing. *I'll find Rose this evening and we'll laugh about this*, she promised herself. Rose didn't have to work, so she was probably at her apartment. *Though with her sexual appetite*, she thought ruefully, *that girl she was caressing last night might be what she needed to get to this morning.*

As she continued to get ready, she reflected on Rose's opinion of her job. Lottie, like many of the other women in the village, had a college degree. They lived divided lives. During

8

the day, using their degrees, they worked as teachers, lawyers, and other jobs; during the night, they put the day's worries aside and enjoyed themselves to the fullest. Lottie's degree was in law, from Chicago Tech. She had practiced for several years before moving to New York City.

She sat on the bed, pulling on her boots, thinking about the many fights she and Rose had about this topic. Rose never understood balance and appropriate behavior for working outside the village. Lottie had accepted that who she was outside of the village must be different than the person she was inside. That boundary was a necessary protection for them. And so far, no one had breached the trust on either side.

# Chapter Three

She grabbed her bag that was sitting on the chair by her bedroom door. Folding her skirt, she added her work shoes to it as she moved into the living room. The boots she wore would be changed out at the office for more appropriate shoes.

Her quick breakfast consisted of fruit and bread with butter, she thought longingly of her mama's breakfasts. Her family owned a bakery and all of the children were expected to put in time working there. Lottie had worked there when she was a teenager so she could bake, but she preferred her mama's cooking to her own. It would be a while before she went home for Thanksgiving and Christmas.

Walking to the bedroom, she slipped her blue bow tie around her collar on the high neck of her shirtwaist and tied it. Turning to pick up her bag, she swung it onto her shoulder and walked quickly over to the dresser to glance in the mirror.

*Oh my*, she thought. Her short reddish-blond hair was a mess; she picked up the brush and pulled it through. Retrieving her hat, she dusted it off before putting it on her head. It was a burgundy French military, turned up in the front, showing off her bangs, with a large dark burgundy ribbon wrapped around it. *It needs some color.* She looked on the dresser and found just the thing - colorful feathers. *They would be perfect,* she thought and tucked them into the band.

A knock sounded on her door as she was leaving. Frowning, she glanced down at her watch, and a feeling of dread washed over her. She forced herself to open it and was not surprised to see Danny standing there.

"What's she done now?" asked Lottie in exasperation, glaring at him.

Danny took off his hat and started to worry the brim. "She's in jail."

"Again?" She didn't have to ask who he was talking about; this was about his wife Henrietta, who was also her best friend.

"She got picked up at the rally last night," he explained.

"What rally?" she asked, confused. "The last time I saw her, she was at the tearoom."

"Well, the ladies got into their cups and decided to have an impromptu one. They had the signs from the May rally stored at the tearoom and went off on their own. She thought there should be another one as a reminder."

"Last night?" she asked incredulously.

"Yes," he responded quietly.

"Who else was arrested?" she asked, wondering how expensive this was going to be.

"Just her," he admitted. "The others ran off and left her with the signs. She continued to demonstrate; the local police picked her up."

"You didn't go?" she pressed, surprised. Danny supported Henrietta in all things.

"No, I had to do inventory at the store. Even if I had gone, I couldn't have stopped her. You know how she is; she is so passionate about her belief in change."

"What precinct?" she ask, resigned.

"The regular one. The 6th."

"Of course. Where else would she be." She took a deep breath and tried to stem her building anger. "What are the charges?"

"What she says they are OR what they say?" he asked wryly. "Disorderly conduct and talking back to an officer."

"Well, at least it was suffrage and not naturalism this time. She did have her clothes on, didn't she?" Lottie asked hopefully.

He nodded; being married to a free spirit could be trying. Some of Henrietta's causes were ridiculous, but she had made headway on several big issues. Before leaving Chicago, she'd had a successful campaign to reduce children's working hours in the glass factories. After that, she had gone to New York to participate in a demonstration and met Danny.

"It has been a busy year for her," she commented.

"Yes, I think she's looking for a cause to work on, that she feels there's something she should be championing." He shrugged, wishing he could help direct her energy.

As they started downstairs, Lottie looked over at Danny and said, "Her work in January with the Lawrence Mill Operatives was amazing."

He hesitated on the stairs. "It was. When we first heard about the wage cuts, she wanted so much to be a part of it."

"Putting the women in front of the picket lines, protecting the men, was brilliant."

He smiled proudly and said, "They were singing constantly, uplifting songs. That one thing kept the police and militia back; they didn't want the negative attention."

"It finally changed when Big Bill Haywood arrived," she commented.

"Yes, he listened to the people and the demonstrators. The pay was increased and people went back to work. Hen wants her days to all end like that."

"Not all can," she said.

"No," he acknowledged.

"We'll have to figure something out to keep her out of trouble. You know I'm going to have a hard time convincing the judge to keep her out of jail, with all of her other arrests."

"Please, do what you can."

"I'll stop by the police station on the way to work. Will you meet me there?" she asked.

"Yes, I have a cab waiting."

She nodded and they started downstairs again.

Her mind was on Henrietta. She was glad Danny reminded her why she had to occasionally bail her out of jail. Henrietta was a constant fixture in her life, especially since Lottie got her law degree. She had been pulling Hen out of the scrapes she managed to get herself into.

———

Three years before in Chicago, a call came at 2:00 am. Lottie heard it in her room and struggled to get up. Her robe was thrown on the end of the bed, she grabbed it and moved quickly down the stairs. *That thing would wake up the whole house,* she thought and reached the phone just as Papa joined her in the dining room.

Papa stood quietly, listening while she answered. "Hello? Yes, this is she."

A loud voice came onto the line and said, "You have to come get me!"

Lottie squinted and looked at Papa. "Henrietta, is that you?"

Papa shook his head; Henrietta had been in and out of trouble because of her ongoing activism. Hen wasn't related by blood, but they had taken her in when she was a teenager. Her home situation had become abusive. Lottie's family became her second family, helping her get an education.

"Yes. It's me." She didn't let Lottie talk and went straight into her next question, "You passed your bar exam, didn't you?"

"Just today! What've you gotten into now?" she asked, exasperated. Knowing Hen, it would be complicated. She listened intently and reassured her, "Okay, okay, I'll be there soon." Hanging up the phone, she slowly put her hands into her robe pockets, staring into space. She finally said, "That was Henrietta."

"Yes, I got that. What's she doing out this time of night?" Papa said as he brushed the thick red hair off of his head. He still looked much younger than his 43years; there was not an ounce of fat on him and his only wrinkles were those laugh lines around his eyes.

"She's been arrested."

"What does she want you to do?" he asked, fearing he already knew where this was going.

"With Emma and Jeremy out of town, I'm the only one she feels she can call," she explained. Her aunt and Jeremy had welcomed Hen into their family and they had remained close.

"You know we love her, but don't let her drag you into this business. You have a career you are starting here. You don't want to be connected to this type of incident." As he spoke his frown burrowed deep furrows into his head; she was so intelligent and had a big life in front of her.

"I know, Papa," she said softly, "but I want to help her." Henrietta had moved into their boarding house when she was twelve and Lottie was two. When she wasn't in school or volunteering for some cause, she entertained Lottie with stories.

"Little girl, you always had a soft heart," he said and ruffed up her hair. "Okay, if you must go, up with you now."

"Yes, Papa," she said and went upstairs to change.

As she made her way back downstairs, she found him dressed and waiting. "I called for a cab; they should be here soon," he said.

"Are you coming with me?" she asked, surprised.

"Yes," he said in a tone that didn't brook any argument. Lottie was his only daughter and, though she was 23, he was still protective.

She smiled and said, "Let's go." Outside, Papa helped her into the waiting cab and climbed in beside her. The ride to the station was done in silence.

Once they arrived, he helped her down and accompanied her up the stoop into the station. Lottie turned to him and said, "Papa, let me handle this." She had, as part of her degree, worked part-time at the police station to get experience in that part of the law. She knew the procedure and wanted to do this by herself.

He nodded. "I'll wait here." He moved over to the long benches on the wall and sat down, watching closely as she approached the window where the officer stood. From her vantage point, she could see many desks and officers behind him.

"Good evening. Can I have Henrietta Lawson brought up?" she asked the desk sergeant.

He glanced down at his books and said, "She was picked up nearby."

"Are there any charges?"

"Loitering," he said shortly. It had been a long evening, and that one had been loud when she was brought in.

Lottie frowned. "Then why bring her in? For an offense like this, she should have gotten a ticket."

"She was being given a ticket, and then she got belligerent with the officer. He brought her in, and I went to help at the door." He sounded angry and, when Lottie looked at him questioningly, he explained, "She didn't want to be brought in. That was when she kicked me."

He called to an officer behind him, "Hey Jim go get Henrietta Kimball."

The officer nodded and headed out of the side door. They waited a few minutes for him to bring her up from the cells.

"Can you keep her inline?" the Sergeant asked Lottie.

Henrietta was in time to hear that last statement. When she started to open her mouth, Lottie glared at her.

Hen got the message and said, "Sergeant, I'm sorry about this."

Lottie squinted at Hen, who continued.

"And I'm sorry that I kicked you."

He eyed her, trying to determine if she was sincere. Making up his mind, he said, "Okay, just this once. You shouldn't be out this time of night. We're having some issues with men attacking women with a piece of pipe. We don't need you putting yourself in harm's way. Do you understand?"

"Yes, Sergeant," she said contritely.

"You'll need to pay a fine," he said firmly to Lottie. "Then she can be released."

"How much?" she asked, giving Henrietta a sideways look.

"Ten dollars," he said and waited patiently.

Lottie pulled out the money and handed it to him.

"And here's your receipt."

She took it and placed it in her wallet.

"Can we go now?" whispered Henrietta.

"Yes." She looked over at the benches and asked, "Ready, Papa?"

Henrietta groaned and rolled her eyes. Lottie knew she didn't appreciate her bringing Papa to the station.

Papa said in a quiet tone, "Henrietta."

"Tim," she mumbled his name in return. She had hoped to avoid having to tell Tim and Dora about her arrest.

"Henrietta, let's go home," said Lottie, not wanting a confrontation in the police station.

They headed to the door and down the stoop. Papa hailed a cab, he gave their address, and they headed home.

Lottie started to settle back again when something occurred to her, she sat up abruptly and demanded, "Just why were you in that area this time of night?"

"I'd like to know the answer to that also," stated Papa, crossing his arms over his chest.

Henrietta grimaced and said, "Tim, you're no fun."

He just stared at her, waiting for an answer.

She said in a rush, "I just thought I could catch some of the groups using pipes on women and turn them in."

Lottie and Tim looked at her in astonishment.

Tim finally said, "One of these days, you'll regret being so careless."

# Chapter Four

## Present Day New York City

She shook her head, thinking how Henrietta had promised she would listen and try to be more careful, but since moving to New York, she seemed to be getting worse. A conversation would be necessary. They parted at the sidewalk and she went to the garage space located under the building. The motorbike, her transportation, was an Abingdon King Dick motorcycle from Birmingham, England. These weren't available in the US, but Aunt Emma had tried one out in England and immediately sent three back for the family's use.

―――――

"This is amazing," Lottie said, inspecting every inch of the bike.

"I'm glad you like it," stated Jeremy. He grinned at Lottie and Emma, then he went back into the next room, rolling out another bike.

"Two?" she asked.

He held up his hand and said, "Just a minute." He went back into the next room again and rolled out a third one.

"Three," she said. They seemed to be waiting for something and, when she realized what it was, she asked excitedly, "Is one of these for me?"

Emma smiled and said, "One for me, one for Jeremy, and one for you. This will allow you some independence in New York City." Her aunt valued transportation, having used bicycles before hardly anyone else.

Jeremy bent down and began to show her how it worked. "You have to hand-crank it to start." He held out a funny-looking piece of metal. "This is the key, and you must keep it with you or the bike cannot be started. Are you ready to learn? If you're going to keep this, you must know how to take care of it."

She had a serious expression on her face as she bent down next to him. "Okay, where do we start?"

He laughed, delighted to know this girl, and wrapped his arm around her shoulder. He and Emma never had kids, but they treated Lottie as if she were their own and were always there for her as she grew up.

———

### New York City—present day

Lottie walked the motorcycle out of the storage space and pulled her bag strap over her head to secure it. Bending down, she pulled out the hand crank to start it before mounting it. She revved it a few times and headed out. The neighborhood was made up of brownstones and its huddled buildings exuded a charm and character.

Mixed in among these were cheap apartments, empty storefronts, and carriage houses. She had to slow down her bike on the neighborhood's narrow streets; some of them curved at odd angles, making for a more hazardous ride when crowded with people.

The shopkeepers were opening their stores and waved as she rode by. The villagers had converted many storefronts into studios, bookstores, and little theaters. She had met so many people since moving there; artists, writers, and performers.

She continued through an area where tenements lined the streets. A voice called her name, "Lottie!"

Slowing the bike, she pulled to a stop, noting who hailed her and called back, "Hey, Jojo. What's going on?" She watched as the boy ran up to her. His request would be one she had heard before, but she loved the little guy and could be patient with him.

"Hey, Lottie, can I get a ride?" he asked, not looking at her, his dark eyes were focused on her bike.

She looked at him consideringly and asked, "How old are you now?"

"You know I'm twelve. Lottie, please!" he implored.

She took another moment and said, "How about this weekend? I have to get to the police station just now."

That information distracted him from the bike, and he nodded knowingly. "Hen again?" He and his mom were close friends with Lottie, Hen, and Danny.

"Hen again," she acknowledged. Hen was well known for getting into situations where she could be arrested.

He said, "All right, I need to get to school."

She knew he would hold her to that promise of the weekend. "Hey, wait for a second," she said as she reached into her pocket. "I was going to come by tonight. I have the name and addresses of people needing some household help. I thought your mom might want them."

Reaching over to take it, he said, "Thanks, but I think we're okay right now. Bye." He ran off in the direction of the school.

*That's odd. I didn't think Annabeth had found a job.* She'd lost hers when the person she worked for had passed away, leaving her without a reference. The job market in the service industry was more crowded than ever with new immigrants arriving daily from Italy. *I'll have to go by and see her.*

Greenwich Village was heterogeneous—African American, Irish, and Italian. Each group holding together based on their backgrounds, each forming a cultural section of the village. Scattered throughout the neighborhood were also new pioneers from elsewhere in the U.S., some from big cities and others from small towns.

The stories of the bohemian group she lived among were made up of individuals who had escaped wealthy families, and others from the middle class. She made it a point to get to know people in other cultures. The future would be an immersion of people with different backgrounds and choices- living and working together.

She started the bike and headed out again. On the way to the precinct, she passed the south end of the village. The area had a rundown appearance, with empty lots along Fifth Avenue. 'To Let' signs hung in storefronts and poor immigrants crowded into the old brick houses, new tenements, and sweatshops. The line that divided the bohemian village on the south and the upper-class socialites on the north was drawn at Washington Square Park.

She thought about the promise she'd made the night before to Phillipa. That park could be a point of contention between the classes. *I hope she sends the letter. I'd like to help keep this civil before any demonstrations are arranged. The people in the village wanted to be supportive, but sometimes demonstrations weren't the answer.*

The area continued to change as she made her way uptown, leaving behind only a few enclaves of stranded elegance like the row of beautiful Greek Revival houses on the north edge of the square. As she rode to work, her thought turned to her continued arguments with Rose. She didn't understand why Lottie wanted to work outside the village, with people who wouldn't accept her lifestyle.

———

"You have no reason to work there. You could work here, in the village," Rose accused.

"I choose to live in both worlds. You may not believe it, but I am a part of this community; I am open with my sexuality."

"Here, you are, but there, when your professional people are around, you're not."

"Rose, they wouldn't understand. It's easier to compartmentalize. That doesn't make me a bad person. What about the freedom of thought?" asked Lottie. "I have that no matter where I am."

"You don't participate in the demonstrations," Rose accused.

"I could say the same about you." She had the grace to look embarrassed. Lottie continued, "At least I do support them, using the law to help the people taken in."

The arguments never ended and would lead to weeks of them not talking. Eventually, they made their way back to each other.

———

### Police Precinct #6

The police station was in her view, and she increased her

speed, enjoying the feel of the wind on her face. Using one hand to keep her hat on her head, she passed the horse-pulled buggies and motor cars.

She sighed, this was not something she enjoyed. Here she was again, because of Henrietta. Everything usually came back to her.

---

## Chicago, 1910

Two years ago, she had accompanied Henrietta to the Chicago train station. As they exited the cab, Lottie asked the driver to wait. "I'll be back in a moment."

Henrietta got her bag and linked her arm with Lottie's, walking toward the train. As they got closer, Lottie stopped her. "You will take care of yourself and please try to not get arrested while you are in New York? I won't be there to bail you out," she warned, reaching over to adjust Hen's collar.

"I'll only be gone for a few weeks, I promise. I want to help the demonstrators set up the marches. I don't plan on any arrest," she said earnestly.

Lottie looked doubtful and said softly, "You never plan, but it happens."

Henrietta gave her a hurt look and said, "Trust me."

She acquiesced, saying, "Okay, I trust you. I don't want a phone call in the middle of the night telling me I have to go to New York to bail you out."

They kissed each other's cheeks and hugged. Henrietta walked off toward the train as Lottie watched her board and waved her off.

When the call came, it wasn't the middle of the night; it was midday. Lottie was sitting at the dining table eating lunch with her parents. Amy, the cook/housekeeper answered it. She looked over and said, "Lottie, it's for you."

Lottie set her fork down slowly, hoping it wasn't Henrietta. She made her way to the phone. "Thanks, Amy," she said as she took it from her. She knew her mama and papa were listening in.

"Oh, hello! Coming home soon? . . . No? . . . News? When! . . . Okay, okay. . . Let me write this down. . ."

She looked over at Mama and asked, "Mama, can you hand me a notebook?"

She got up and located some paper and a pencil from the sideboard. She handed them to Lottie and frowned at her. They loved Henrietta, but she was always pulling Lottie into her dramas.

Lottie nodded, smiling absently and taking the paper and pencil. She put it on the wall and said, "I have paper now, give me the address..." She jotted it down and said, "Yes, I have it... Yes, I'll book the trip today... Yes, I promise... You'll wait for me? . . . Good..."

Mama and Papa were staring as she hung up the phone. "That was Henrietta," she told them, tapping the pencil on the paper on her hand.

"We got that much. What's she gotten herself into this time?" Papa asked in a resigned voice.

"A wedding," stated Lottie.

"A wedding? She's staying over for that? Why do you need the address?" Mama asked, confused.

"The wedding is for Henrietta," Lottie stated simply, sitting back down at the table. She was already planning what she would need to do to get organized to make the trip. *Work*, she thought. *I have to get some vacation time scheduled. It should be fine.* There were no pressing trials for her to work on.

Mama and Papa both looked surprised. Mama said, "That

seems too conventional for Henrietta." She continued hesitantly, "Who is this man? Has she known him before this?"

"I don't think so, Mama. I think they met there," Lottie explained. She felt like she spent most of her life explaining Henrietta to her family. Mama and Papa were used to women being independent, but Henrietta was constantly stirring things up, making people uncomfortable.

"What does he do?" asked the ever-practical Papa.

"I don't know." Lottie laughed. "But I will find out. I'm going to New York, and I'll stay with her in the hotel until the wedding."

Papa knew Lottie would do anything for Henrietta and said, "I'll go to the station for a ticket. I'm assuming you'll want to leave in the morning?"

"Yes, thank you, Papa. I'll send a note over to the office and let them know I'll be gone for a while." When she saw the concern on his face, she said, "I don't have an active trial right now and there is some flexibility."

Papa nodded. He didn't say anything; he knew Lottie was responsible and he could trust her. Finishing his meal, he took his plate into the kitchen, then headed back into the dining room and leaned down to kiss Mama.

"I'll be back soon," he said, planning to take the cable car to the station.

Mama looked at Lottie and said, "I don't think we can go at this short notice."

"Mama, she knows that. She said it's small and she just wanted me there."

"Henrietta knows, if we went, we'd try to talk some sense into her," Mama said. She looked over at Emma and asked, "Will she notify Jeremy and Emma?" They had been her guardians and continued to be an important part of her life. Her real parents didn't show much interest in Henrietta except for her money. They had put her to work in the factories at a young age.

"I'll make sure she sends them a letter." Emma and Jeremy were currently traveling and wouldn't be available to attend.

She finished her lunch, placed her napkin beside her plate, and said, "I need to head upstairs to pack."

Mama nodded and stood, indicating the plates needed to be cleared and taken to the kitchen. Amy and her assistant did so as Lottie headed up to her room, with Mama following behind. She sat on the bed while Lottie pulled out her luggage, setting the open bag beside her.

"Will you be okay on your own?" Mama asked in a worried tone as she took out the clothes Lottie was throwing in the bag. She refolded them before returning them to the case.

Lottie looked over at her and said, "Mama, I'm 24 years old. I believe I can make it on a train and to New York without being killed." She pulled out a hatbox and started putting her hats inside.

"Young women traveling alone. I just don't like it," she said, continuing to adjust the items in Lottie's bag.

Lottie sat next to her, took her hands, and said, "Did you say that to Aunt Emma also?" Her aunt Emma did everything her way; she hadn't adhered to societal norms.

"I did," Mama admitted. "I'd like to see you settled here, married and with babies, but I understand there are other paths you might take."

"Right now, I'm not sure I want to be married. I haven't met anyone yet who has changed my mind."

"You have so much of your aunt Emma in you," Mama accused lightly, touching Lottie's face.

"She does follow her own path," Lottie acknowledged. She got back up and continued to pack for her trip.

That evening was quiet. Mama was still worried but stayed silent.

Early the next morning, Papa called from downstairs, "Lottie, you need to get moving if you're going to catch that train."

"Yes, Papa," she answered from the top of the stairs. She headed back into the room to get her bag. Mama walked in just as she was exiting. She stopped Lottie suddenly, putting her hand on her arm, and said, "Do you have the little pistol Aunt Emma got for you?"

"I do, Mama," she assured her, patting her pocket. "Now, don't worry."

"I will worry. It's my right," she said, hugging her close. They stood there for a moment and Mama pulled back, wiping her eyes, and said, "You have to go now. Your papa will only be patient for so long."

Lottie smiled and helped Mama dry her tears. She picked up the suitcase, she had set down and took Mama's arm in hers to walk down the stairs together.

Papa stood tall in the foyer. Mama's eyes misted again as she saw him, looking exactly like he did on their first date. She didn't notice the gray in his red hair or his beard. What she saw was his smile, so big it crinkled up his eyes.

Lottie could tell Papa wanted to go. She looked back at Mama and asked, "Are you coming with us?"

"No," she said, looking at her. "I am not. I have baking to do and accounts to review."

Lottie smiled and leaned forward to kiss her on the cheek. "This is just a fast trip. I'll be home before you know it."

"Of course, I'm just being silly," Mama said, wiping her face. "Oh, I had Amy put something together for you. Let me get it."

As Mama headed out of the foyer, Lottie looked at Papa.

She could tell he was worried but, unlike Mama, he didn't voice his feelings.

Mama came out quickly, carrying a box lunch, snacks, and a dress. "This should tide you over for a few days. Do you have pocket money for lunch and dinner?"

"I do," Lottie assured her. She looked curiously at the dress and asked, "Mama, is that your wedding dress?"

"Henrietta should have something nice to wear," she said gruffly, handing it to her.

"Oh, Mama," Lottie said, tearing up.

"Telephone me as soon as you arrive and confirm the number there," Mama directed.

"I will," she assured her, opening her case quickly to place the dress inside.

"Where are you staying?" Mama asked.

"At the Park Avenue Hotel, but I'll probably be with Henrietta most of the time."

Papa tapped his watch and Lottie said quickly, "Bye, Mama."

They headed out the front door, and he helped her into the waiting cab. As they made their way to the station, he asked, "Do you have everything? Your tickets?"

"Yes, Papa," she said, enjoying the quiet of the early morning. The ride to the station was without incident. She gathered up her food box with her tickets and waited for Papa to lift her out.

"You're in a private compartment, so you can sleep," he said as he set her down. "Don't open the door to anyone you don't know."

"Yes, Papa. I've been on a train by myself before this," she reminded him.

"But never to New York," he stated. "Keep your purse close. There are pickpockets you need to watch for. Do you have transportation from the rail station?"

"Henrietta's meeting me there and taking me to the hotel."

"Good. I'm glad there is a direct train now," he said. She would be taking the Pennsylvania Special, a plush train that allowed for a direct line. Before that, stops had to be made in Buffalo and a day trip to New Jersey.

"She also promised me dinner," she said.

"Knowing her, I just hope she's there to meet you."

"Where else would she be?" Lottie asked.

He looked over and raised his eyebrows at her. "You never know," he said.

She grimaced and said, "Hopefully, nothing else comes up to distract her."

———

### Present-day Police Precinct #6

*Fortunately, I didn't have to bail her out when I got there,* Lottie thought to herself, remembering that day. The wedding was beautiful and Henrietta was radiant.

She pulled to a stop in front of the police station. Looking around, she called to the officer standing by the stoop, "Is it okay if I leave my motorbike here with you?"

He walked over and looked at it, saying, "Sure, roll it up on the sidewalk. I'll be here for a while longer if you would like me to watch it."

"I would, thanks," she said gratefully. She rolled it up on the sidewalk, parked it near the building wall, and turned it off.

"Can anyone start it?" he asked, bending down to look at the motor.

"Not without this." She pulled the crank out of her purse to show him.

The officer watched her closely and commented, "Smart."

"Thanks, I shouldn't be long." She put it back into her bag, then headed up the stoop and inside the door.

The officer sat on a stool behind a half wall that was solid up to 4 feet and open with bars from there to the ceiling. He knew her by sight and called, "She's in back. Want me to have her brought up?"

"Please," Lottie said, looking around her to see if Danny had arrived yet.

She saw him walk around the corner. "You made good time," she noted.

"There was little traffic this early. I told the cab driver to wait outside for us." He pulled out his wallet and handed her forty dollars. She nodded and headed back to the officer. *It probably did Hen some good to stay in the cell for a few hours; she probably needed the time to cool off.*

She looked at Officer Bob King, whom she had gotten to know quite well in the last two years. He was about thirty, with a full head of hair, and was always cheerful. It was odd because she felt like the smile and cheerfulness were a mask. Lottie went out of her way to be extra polite; this was not someone they needed to anger. He stood between her and Henrietta.

Her feelings for him were also based on a weird run-in she had with him before.

---

### Greenwich Village—Bob King

Lottie had been coming out of the tearoom when she ran into him.

"Officer King," she said, surprised. She noticed he wasn't in his uniform. "Are you on your way somewhere?"

Instead of answering, he moved close to her and said, "Lottie, I've been thinking about you and wanted to ask you out."

She looked at him and started to move away, trying to keep some distance between them. She kept her voice calm and said, "I'm involved with someone right now."

He frowned, clearly not expecting that response. He was used to getting his way when he approached women.

At that moment, Rose walked out of the tearoom and took Lottie's arm.

He watched the move and the intimate touch between the two. An ugly expression crossed his face. "So, that's how it is."

"Yes," said Lottie quietly, not ashamed of her relationship.

King continued to glare and then stormed off.

"Who was that?" asked Rose, watching him leave.

"No one really," said Lottie absently, wondering how he happened to know she was there. She finally looked over at Rose and said, "Ready?"

"I am," she said, smiling slowly.

———

### Police precinct #6—present day

Since then, she had not been comfortable with Officer King. She tried to keep all of their interactions on a strictly professional level.

He continued to read Hen's file. "As far as I know, it was a peaceful demonstration, except for Henrietta."

*Yeah,* she thought, *Henrietta doesn't feel successful if she doesn't get put into jail by the end of the night.*

"Do you want to leave her in for a while longer? I can send her back," asked Officer King, giving her a long look.

Lottie considered that, but shook her head and said, "No, we want her brought up, please."

While they waited, Lottie asked, "How much?" She knew the bail money was only part of what she would give him. The receipt would say forty, but the actual amount given would be one hundred dollars. New York City operated on graft; she didn't like it, but she understood why she was paying it. She had Danny's forty and pulled out her wallet to get the additional sixty.

*Henrietta is affecting my budget this month*, she thought ruefully. She would have to see if she could get her to stay out of jail for a while. *At least*, she thought, *until I get paid*. She looked again at the money. *Hopefully after a few more paychecks.*

They brought Hen out, and she immediately went into Danny's arms. She looked like she always looked in these circumstances: dress wrinkled from being slept in and hair sticking up. Danny reached up to pat it down, speaking softly to her.

Lottie just shook her head, watching them. "Court date?" she turned and asked Officer King.

"They want to see her this afternoon. Could mean some jail time," he said in a vaguely threatening tone.

She glanced at him quickly and saw a smile. She looked away, toward Danny and Henrietta. *She will just love that*, thought Lottie. The last time she was locked up, she started a riot for better conditions. They wouldn't want that to happen again, so she would probably get off on a fine.

Lottie stayed silent as he handed her the receipt. As she reached out to take it, he took the opportunity to grab her hand. Her expression did not change as she pulled it forcefully out of his.

"Do you want your receipt or not," he taunted.

She reached over and tugged it from his hand, trying to not touch him.

"See you next time," King promised. His tone was light, but his eyes indicated a different meaning.

Danny walked up and asked, "Can we go?" He wanted to get Hen home.

Lottie turned, grateful for the interruption. "Yes, we're done here."

She didn't glance back as she walked with him to Henrietta. "Let's go outside," she muttered. They exited onto the stoop.

Danny murmured something in Henrietta's ear, and she turned to Lottie and started in a placating tone, "Lottie..."

Lottie interrupted, "Henrietta, I thought we talked about this."

"We did," she said, her tone changing to one of defiance, "but what's right is right."

"Right," she echoed and looked at her. "No one else got arrested in the group."

"No," Hen admitted.

"So, why you?" Before she could justify her actions, Lottie said, "Let's talk about what's going to happen next." She looked over at Danny and said, "You'll need her clean, dressed, and in court this afternoon. Understood?"

He could be counted on when it meant keeping Henrietta out of jail. He said, "I'll make sure she's there and presentable."

"Fine, I'll see you both this afternoon. You better hope they remember you're more trouble in prison than out. I have to get to work now." She started down the stoop.

Danny called behind her, "Thanks again." Henrietta had gone quiet, not looking at Lottie.

She stopped and waved without turning back to them. The frustration with Hen was almost overwhelming, instead of reacting she headed down to get her bike. "Thank you," she said to the officer and bent down to crank it, she let it run for a moment before climbing on. The engine idled as she took a moment to watch Henrietta and Danny walked slowly down to their cab, talking quietly.

*He's one of the best people I know.* As she made her way to work, Lottie thought about when she'd first met Hen's Danny.

––––––

### New York City, Henrietta's wedding

*I hope Henrietta's hotel has a shower,* Lottie thought. She was not the best when it came to securing amenities. Hen could be was easily distracted, especially now with the wedding. *Hen was getting married,* she thought wonderingly. *Was this the right move for her?*

As she stepped off the train, she saw Henrietta wearing a ridiculously large hat. Holding her hand was a tall, spindly fellow with a bow tie, black-rimmed glasses, and a hat. He kept taking his glasses on and off, his hand appeared to be shaking.

"Lottie!" Henrietta called and ran over, dragging the man with her. "Oh, Lottie, I'm so glad you're here!" She threw her arms around the other woman.

Lottie hugged her close and said, "Me too! I wouldn't have missed it for the world."

Henrietta stepped back and took up the man's hand again and said proudly, "This is Danny Landry."

"The fiancé?" teased Lottie looking him over.

"Yes," Hen said, looking at him lovingly.

Danny spoke up and said, "It's nice to meet you."

"You too," Lottie said sincerely, deciding she liked the look of him.

"Would you like to go to the hotel?" he asked.

"I would," she said gratefully. "When's the wedding?"

"Tomorrow morning," said Henrietta firmly.

Lottie noticed Danny squeeze Hen's hand and the soft smile he directed at her.

"I have a buggy waiting," he said.

As they walked to it, Lottie asked casually, "What are you wearing for the wedding?"

Hen looked over and said, "Probably just my church dress."

"Hmm," she said casually. "I guess I should have left Mama's wedding dress at home."

Hen stopped suddenly and said, "Dora sent her wedding dress for me?"

When Lottie nodded, Hen started to cry. Danny looked concerned. Lottie handed her a handkerchief and said, "I think these are happy tears. Aren't they?"

Hen nodded. Lottie said, "Now, tell me about how you met and everything that's happening in New York City."

# Chapter Five

## Present day New York City

On her ride to work, Lottie tried to shake off her anger at Henrietta. She understood she had strong beliefs, but the constant trouble Hen got herself into was wearing. The drain on Lottie's finances had to end soon; she couldn't save any money. She tilted her head back and felt the sun and wind on her face as she drove.

A horse's neigh reminded her she needed to concentrate on driving the motorcycle. This early in the morning, she would have to be careful around the delivery horses. Drivers still used them for milk trucks and other types of deliveries. She buzzed by them, keeping her distance, heading into Manhattan to the courthouse where her office was located.

Slowing her bike, she stopped at the newsstand. "Paper, please," she called to the man working there. Pulling out the money, she handed it to him and took it. A glance at the front page told her Officer Becker was still the main subject.

Folding it up, she put it into her bag, waved at the man, and continued to work. She reached the court and moved her motorcycle to the lower level. Space had been arranged with the building manager to store it while she was at work. Unlocking the door, she rolled it inside and parked it. Exiting the space, she locked the door behind her and headed up the back stairs to her office door.

*My clothes*, she thought suddenly looking down. The ones she was wearing would not be acceptable. She looked at her timepiece. *I hope I got in before the Justice.* Opening the door slowly, she stuck her head in and looked around cautiously.

The office belonged to Justice Goff. She worked as a clerk for him. Her grades, prior work experience, and the recommendations of her law professor had helped get her the job, it was an important step in her career.

*Some Justices could be mentors*, she thought, *but this Justice doesn't take the time.* The other clerk in the office, Chris Burnes, was her actual mentor. She was glad Chris had already been in the office for two years before she started there. He was someone she could go to for advice.

Chris saw her and teased in a low voice, "Looking for someone?"

"Yes," she said in a whisper. "Is he in yet?"

"He is," he confirmed.

"He is?" Her voice rose a bit in panic; she hesitated, still not coming into the office. "Why is he early?"

"A new case was assigned this morning and we need to meet and review it. It's a big one. If you hurry, you should be able to change before we meet with him."

"Why didn't you tell me sooner?" she asked rushing into the door and toward the closet where she could change into her skirt. Dressing quickly, she combed her hair and put a clip in to hold it back. The clip also acted as a hair attachment, that gave her the appearance of longer hair. The Justice was conservative and wouldn't appreciate her short hairstyle.

As she exited the closet, Chris answered her question. "I

didn't have time. We were just assigned this morning. Whitman has already been here and gone."

"Whitman?" Charles S. Whitman was the current District Attorney in Manhattan and was working on the Becker investigation. He had just gotten the indictments for those involved in the case. "What trial have we been assigned?" Lottie asked, hoping it wasn't the one she thought it was.

He started to tell her when he heard the Justice call out, "Let's review this together. Everyone into my office."

She looked over at him and muttered, "I guess I'll hear it from him."

Chris cleared his throat. She looked at him and he pointed to her shoes. She looked down at her mannish boots and whispered, "Dammit." She needed to change them.

She mouthed, "Thanks," and ran back to her desk, pulling on the other pair of shoes. The boots were put into her bag and stashed under her desk.

"Ready now?" Chris teased.

Lottie nodded and picked up her newspaper absently as she followed Chris into the Justice's chamber. She walked over to the end of the long rectangular table and sat down. When she placed the papers on the table in front of her, it unfolded showing the front page. She knew the Becker investigation would be the lead article but was shocked at what else the text said. *A state court was assigned? They knew before the clerks were informed?* she thought, frowning and looking closer. There had been no announcements at the courthouse.

Chris looked over at her and raised an eyebrow.

"Later," she mouthed.

He nodded. She folded the papers as the Justice walked over to them and sat down.

"What do we have on the docket this week?" he asked, his eyes gleaming.

"Charles Becker was charged with first-degree murder of Manhattan gambler Herman Rosenthal," stated Chris.

Lottie started. *That was the headline of today's paper!*

Chris saw her response and sent her a frown before looking back at the Justice.

"Chris, give us the high points of the case," Goff instructed.

The man nodded and organized the files quickly. He pulled his summary to begin the review.

Lottie knew from experience the Justice had already reviewed the case and had made his decision. This was something hard for her to accept; he was not impartial. Goff usually had his decision on how the trial would end before it had even begun. He used his influence throughout the trial and in his jury instructions to get the outcome he wanted.

She had worked for the man for the past two years and learned something new every day. This included court procedures and organization, but ethics were not included in the instruction with this particular Justice. Lottie continued to watch him as he deliberately stayed at the end of the long table, remaining apart from them. His face was set in cold hard lines; showing he wasn't open to opinions from his clerks. He just wanted the facts.

Chris started. "The person being charged with murder is Lieutenant Charles Becker, head of the Special Squad. The charge is that he conspired with the Lennox gang who killed Herman Rosenthal."

Lottie sat taking notes, trying not to show how shocked she was that this case had been assigned to their court. This type of case normally went to the New York Court of General Sessions. The General Session Justices would be more lenient and unreliable when it came to charging members of the police force with a crime.

*Why their court?* She looked over at Goff and wondered,

39

*Did Whitman handpick Justice Goff. If so, he also planned the guilty verdict before the trial started.*

Chris continued, "The Grand Jury has handed down indictments for the Lennox gang members accused of shooting Herman Rosenthal: Harry "Gyp the Blood" Horowitz, Francesco "Dago Frank" Cirofici, Louis "Lefty Louie" Rosenberg, and, Jacob "Whitey Lewis" Seidenshnerr. Becker received his indictment first, and this trial will only include charges to him."

Lottie had kept up with the case in the newspaper, *The World*, not knowing her court could receive it. *Someone in the press must have an inside man in the DA's office; they seemed to have access to files they shouldn't have.*

"Chris," she interrupted, "I heard that, originally, the conspirators were part of a larger group and that they confessed. That confession didn't include Becker." She looked at her notes and said, "These were, Harry Vallon, Sam Schepps, Jack Rose, and Bridgey Webber. Will they be included in the conspiracy charge with Becker? Or will they be charged with the gunmen?"

A noise sounded in the back of the Justice's throat. Chris hurriedly answered, "They're going to be part of the Becker trial, but as witnesses, they will not face charges."

*Witnesses against a high-ranking police officer,* she thought. The press on Becker before the Rosenthal murders made him out to be a hero. He led the Special Squad and worked to break up the Car Barn Gang. New Yorkers were said to feel safer as a result of the Lieutenant's work. She leaned in as Chris continued.

"Rosenthal was a small-time bookmaker and gambler who also ran casinos. He approached the DA with a complaint that Becker was collecting graft. He seemed especially upset that

Becker was demanding larger percentages of money to protect them from raids from the Special Squad."

Lottie made a note to check the actual complaint and the date it was made.

"Interestingly, this isn't the first complaint against Becker," Chris observed.

"Who made the initial complaint?" asked Lottie, interested in how this case came together.

"It was under a pseudonym, but the assumption is that it was also Rosenthal. Though it could have been anyone," he stated.

"What happened to it?" asked Lottie curiously.

Chris dug out the note on the first complaint and reviewed it aloud, "It went through the Commissioner and was sent straight to Becker to investigate."

"To investigate his own complaint?" she asked. "That's odd."

"As would be expected, Becker rejected it and sent it back," Chris said, looking at his files.

"Nothing came of it, no follow-up from anyone else?" she asked.

"No. Lottie, pull your evidence list; it should be there," said Chris.

She pulled the list out to review. "Yes, it's here. I see we also have his bank statement listed. How come? What are we looking for?"

"Graft," Chris explained.

"But the charge here is murder," she reasoned. "Presenting this evidence could taint the jury. It would be an error that would help with Becker's appeal."

"Yes, but the state will try to prove ..." started Chris.

"Will prove," interrupted the Justice.

Chris nodded in agreement so he could move on. "The

state will be providing evidence that the graft led directly to the murders."

She continued to frown at him, knowing this was incorrect and the procedure required that they not allow the graft in. The justice glared at her; she noted the problem and stayed silent.

Chris went on with the review. "The witness to look at will be Jack Rose. He has given testimony showing he was Becker's informant and that he acted as an intermediate to the gambling houses, delivering information and collecting money. He'll also testify that Becker contacted him to recruit the gangsters to murder Rosenthal."

"Does he have an offer of immunity?" she asked, suspicious of his motives. He wouldn't do this out of the goodness of his heart.

"Full," Chris confirmed.

"Full? For a person who has confirmed he was an active member of the conspiracy?" she asked, shocked. When she started to ask more questions, she could see Goff's face turning red, his foot tapping impatiently. She stopped and made a note to talk to Chris about this.

Lottie looked at the list of witnesses. There was Bridgey Webber, Harry Vallon, Jack Zelig, and Jack Rose. Their current location was listed in the file. She said, "Wait, these men are being held in the same place." She checked further down and saw something more. "Chris, these men are most likely in contact with one another, they're in cells in the same area. Shouldn't they be separated?"

"That's none of your business," the Justice stated brusquely.

She nodded, letting the topic go, and pulled her calendar. "How many months do we expect this case to go on?" She wanted to get the dates set.

"Days, not months," stated the Justice. Chris was silent.

"Days?" she asked, confused. "With so many witnesses? There must be over 80 people on this list for the prosecution and defense." A large murder trial should have taken three months minimum.

Goff added to the shocking news. "And we'll be starting on September the 12th."

Chris and Lottie looked at him, eyes wide. That was Monday of the next week. He avoided their glances.

"The defense attorneys, John McIntyre, Lloyd Stryker, and George Whiteside will try to get it pushed," Chris said.

*I can see why,* thought Lottie. *There isn't enough time to build a case.* She would block the month and put tentative next to it. "Is McIntyre the lead council?"

"Yes," answered Chris.

"Who's prosecuting with Whitman?" she asked, adding the names to her court chart.

"Frank Moss," supplied Chris.

Lottie glanced up sharply. Moss was a close friend of the Justice and had spent vacations with him.

"That's enough for now," the Justice said as he stood and walked to his desk.

That was their dismissal. They got up and went back to the outer offices. Chris shut the door softly behind them and reached into his pocket. He held out his hand, palm up and said softly, "You might want this."

She looked into his hand and saw her hair clip.

"Oh no," she said and set down her files on his desk. "Did he notice?"

"He didn't," he assured her.

She nodded gratefully as she arranged her hair and clipped the hairpiece back into place. Once it was secure, she took her files to her desk and sat down. She opened them and pulled out the witness list. "Chris, should Moss be allowed to be the co-chair?" They were both aware of how tight the two men were in their personal lives.

He didn't look up from his notes and said, "I asked about it, and Goff said he wouldn't ask him to step down."

Lottie waited for a further explanation and, when she received no follow-up, she continued to review the list. "The witnesses are a collection of minor gamblers and low lifes," she muttered. Her eye continued down the list. "Jack Rose, I can't believe he is the primary prosecution witness."

"Shhh," he cautioned, looking toward the Justice's door. He walked over to her and said in a low voice. "His testimony is supposed to be the link to pull all of it together."

"You said he got full immunity?" she asked suspicious of Jack Rose having any part in this case as a witness.

"Yes," said Chris, not sharing anything further.

"How can he be a credible witness? They've been given time to get their stories straight and provide the same testimony to take down all four of the gunmen and Becker."

"Did you notice their location? These men are being kept at the westside prison. It's also called *Whitman's Ritz*."

She was shocked. "And Becker?"

"Look at where he is," he said, indicating her files.

She checked and was incredulous. "The Tombs? A police officer's never put there. That place is terrible. Severe over-crowding, no windows, and generally a horrible environment. Who approved this?"

"Whitman wants Becker," he said simply. "He has political aspirations, and this is a splashy case."

She looked down again and compared the prosecution and the defense list. "Chris, Zelig shows up on both lists."

He acknowledged her statement with a nod. "The head of the Lennox Gang. Yes, both sides seem to think he'll be testifying for them. My theory is that he's Becker's man. The only people on his list would be people he trusts implicitly."

"Hmm," she said, tapping her pencil on the paper. "He'll be the one to watch. This is an odd case. If it were me, I'd be discrediting the conspirators and putting up Becker's character. A policeman against a mob guy should be an easy case."

"It should be," he agreed.

"But if they prove graft is a key element, that could tilt the issue," she said.

"Yes, the case hinges on the feeling of the jury for who's more trustworthy. People don't want to think that the men who are supposed to be protecting them are in cahoots with gangsters."

"The jury may overlook everything and go against Becker because they perceive him as being less trustworthy than the mob members," she said, mulling the information over. *The Justice's leanings against police corruption are going to be an ongoing issue,* she thought.

He moved to bring another stack of files to her desk. "This is all of them. You should now have a full set of case files to review."

She sighed, looking at the stacks, and said, "How's this going to work? We just don't have time to get through the material before the start of the trial. Why's this scheduled so soon and why's he saying less than a month on the calendar?"

"Whitman's pushing for all of it to be over quickly, including the separate gunmen trials, so he stays at the top of the headlines. He persuaded the Governor to move the dates forward."

Lottie mulled this over and thought, *There's a conspiracy here.* It wasn't Rosenthal she was thinking of. *This conspiracy involved Whitman—with political aspirations, Justice Goff— known cop hater, and the Governor.* She could almost see

Justice Goff's reaction to being included in this mess, practically rubbing his hands in glee at the prospect of prosecuting a corrupt officer.

She and Chris concentrated on the files throughout the morning. At about 11 am, she took a break and unfolded her paper. As she started to read the article about the trial, she saw details about Jack Rose's testimony; it listed the graft and his work with Becker. "Chris, who's leaking the information from the grand jury? They already know all the people involved before the trial even starts. This should've been under lock and key."

"I agree," he said, standing and walking over to her desk. He read over her shoulder. "It has to be Whitman. There's no other person who could get away with this. We'll have to make it a point to get a copy of *The World* each day. If the reporter is consistently the same, then Whitman's probably involved."

She was trying to remember the law about sharing witness testimony from the grand jury. "Aren't the rules about grand jury testimony a bit odd in New York?"

"Yes," he said absently, still reading the article. "The DA can release information, but the people who offered the actual statements can't correct him."

"He's deliberately contaminating the jury pool."

"Yes. There'll be trouble because McIntyre will try to use it to discredit the witnesses, especially if any of the statements are contradictory. Jack's confession's in there," he said, nodding at her pile. "It's 38 pages in length."

"Wow," she said, digging for it. She found it and pulled it out.

"Yes, the reason the rest of the files are so large is that 30 detectives were called out of retirement to help with the investigation. When you read through the notes, you'll see several statements that contradict each other, especially right after the event."

She started reading from her pile again.

Chris walked back to his desk, turning back to her before he sat down. "What kept you this morning?" he asked curiously.

"Hen," she said, not looking up from her reading. She was still exasperated by the morning's events.

"Will you need to go to court today?" he asked in a low voice, knowing she normally represented Hen in all her cases.

"Yes," she said in the same tone, looking toward the Justice's office door. "If you can get me out at about 1:00 pm."

"I'll make sure," he promised as he sat down. "Oh, and don't stress too much about the calendar."

"Why? I thought the Justice was set on starting on Monday."

"I don't expect the trial to start that early. Becker's lawyer should be pushing back against the schedule. That'll be an automatic appeal if he isn't given enough time to prepare."

She nodded, thinking. *It made sense.* Chris and Lottie wouldn't have enough time to get organized, much less the defense. She went back and kept reading, taking notes. Next, she pulled her witness and evidence list and started to compare the information.

"Chris, there's hardly any evidence here."

"As you look further, you'll see most of the evidence against Becker is based on his protection racket," said Chris.

"Graft," commented Lottie. "That seems to affect all levels of this trial. How involved is he in that?"

"He was in charge of the Special Squad. That would have allowed him to dictate who got raided and who didn't," Chris said.

"I don't see where they'll be able to present information

about it in court. Won't that be considered prior bad acts?" Lottie asked.

"Yeah, until they tie it into the motive. Otherwise, it'll be an appeal issue," supplied Chris.

"I've seen the Special Squad in the papers. They got a lot of good press for breaking up the Car Barn Gang," stated Lottie.

"They seemed to get a large number of arrests, shutting down various establishments based on gambling and drinking charges. That's what moved him to that position; the promotion was for him to crack down on gambling and graft," explained Chris.

"What happened. What made him change?" asked Lottie.

"Right place, right time. He entered a role that was probably already taking bribes and he just continued. The fees were for him to limit or stop raids on certain establishments," answered Chris.

"Where did the money go?" asked Lottie.

"Check your evidence list; bank statements and safety deposit boxes are there, though I suspect he probably kept it mostly in cash. As I understand it, he has a second residence that he may be funneling the money into," said Chris.

"Could it really have been all that much money?" Lottie asked, not clear on how much this could be.

Chris pondered that, tapping his pencil. "I would think so. With over 100 gambling houses in Satan's Circus involved, give or take, probably about 1.8 million in just eight months."

"These were the 'fees' they charged?" she asked incredulously.

"There were the 'fees' for stopping the raids, but other monies came from the raids that went forward on the gambling houses. Rosenthal testified that the monies turned in to the police were significantly lower than those taken at the time of the raids. So, they were getting paid at the front and back ends of the operation."

"How did they track this back to Becker? Surely, he's smarter than that."

Chris chuckled suddenly and said, "You aren't going to believe this. They got lazy and used checks."

"Checks?" she asked, bewildered. "You mean like from a bank?"

"Yes, you'll see copies of those in the files." He went quiet as he mulled something over. "You know, if you look at the number of raids this group has done since Becker took the lead, it seems odd that the ones getting protected were still being raided," explained Chris.

"I read in the paper that the Mayor was involved in the choices of locations. Maybe Becker didn't have the power to stop them all. I have to think the people paying him questioned what they were getting for their money," stated Lottie.

"So, this might be a protection racket gone wrong," said Chris

Essentially, it was a case where it was one group's word against Becker's. "Wow," she said. "Becker could lose his life based on this testimony."

"Yes," said Chris.

"Has no one come forward to support Becker from the political side of things?"

"Most are too scared of being pulled in. Any support for Becker could uncover things they don't want to be uncovered."

"Though," she said consideringly, "I am surprised Big Tim hasn't interjected himself into this." As a member of the state senate, Big Tim Sullivan had kept the piece for years between the police, politicians, and gamblers.

"I believe he would have, but he has health issues

preventing him from making any moves to help Becker. No one else is going to step up and admit to the graft."

"I get that. People are making money at all levels," she said, thinking of her constant cash outlay to Officer King. "Chris, I just don't see a conspiracy case."

"For the murder?"

She nodded.

"Agreed. We have plenty showing the graft, but the murder will be based on all witness testimony."

"Will Becker testify?"

"He'd have to come clean on the graft. Several things in his background could be brought up, so no, I don't think he will. His defense is that he wasn't part of the conspiracy."

"Wouldn't it be better for him to admit to past mistakes and show he's trying to be honest with the jury?"

He pointed his pencil at her and said, "That's exactly it. If I were his lawyer, that's the first thing I'd do. Go for some jail time based on that and maybe save his life. "

They both knew the paper was hinting the outcome of this would be death by electrocution. Chris went back to his desk and started reading his files. They had to complete as much of the review as they could in a short time. Lunch times would be limited and Chris set up their meal deliveries for the week. Reading through the investigation that brought in the gunmen, she saw Mary A. Sullivan was involved. "Chris, did you see a woman officer, Mary A. Sullivan, helped with the case?"

"I must have missed that. What role did she play?" he asked with interest.

"You know the four gunmen?" she asked.

"Yeah, Cirofici, Horowitz, Rosenberg, Seidenshner, and Lewis."

"That's right. Well, a female officer, Mary A. Sullivan, went undercover to gain Cirofici's girlfriend's trust. She was instrumental in their arrest, adopting the role of a boarding house housekeeper, and eventually met the wives of the other suspects. Sullivan investigated the men's habits and tailed the women when she wasn't with them. All three men were caught via wiretaps enabled by her work."

"Wow!"

"Agreed, wow!"

They both went back to work, breaking at around noon when their lunches were delivered. At 12:45 pm, Chris looked over at Lottie and said in a loud voice, "Lottie, I need you to go to the courthouse to deliver some papers. We'll be moving a few trials around to make room for the change in our schedule. These will have to be re-distributed to other courts."

She nodded and stood to retrieve the files from him.

"Drop them off after your court appearance," he murmured.

"I will," she said loudly. "It may be backed up over there."

"Just get back when you can."

She nodded and headed out.

# Chapter Six

Lottie hurried to the court where she knew Henrietta was going to be arraigned. She spotted Danny and Henrietta outside. He waved to her, and Lottie jogged over to them.

"Her case is coming up now," Danny warned.

Lottie nodded, grabbed Hen's hand, and hurried to the front of the courtroom. She laid her things on the defense table. Judge Patterson called Henrietta's name and asked her to approach the bench. He recognized her immediately and looked around for her lawyer. He spotted Lottie and waved her up to stand beside Henrietta.

"Mrs. Landry, haven't we been here before?" the judge asked as he looked down from his bench at her.

"Yes, sir," Henrietta answered. She'd been through this so many times; she knew Lottie wanted her to behave respectfully.

The judge shook his head, remembering her vividly. She was more trouble in jail than out; he was going to get creative with her this time. "Mrs. Landry, I'm not going to fine you."

Lottie heard a breath exhaled behind her and could almost feel the relief coming off Danny.

"But what I am going to do is require you to find a job." He could see she was going to interrupt and stopped her. "It doesn't have to be a paying job, but as I understand it, you have a college degree?"

"I do," she confirmed.

"Then I would like you to look around and find something constructive to do with your time where this court is not involved."

Hen pulled on Lottie's arm and whispered furiously.

"Judge?" Lottie asked.

"Yes, Miss Flannigan?" he asked patiently.

"Mrs. Landry would like to know for how long."

He looked directly at Henrietta and said, "That depends. If this keeps you out of my courts, we might need to think long-term. You'll need to submit where you'll be working, and I'll need to approve it. Understood?"

"Yes, sir," Henrietta responded.

The judge looked over at Lottie. She nodded.

"You'll have a week to submit, or be prepared to go to jail." He used his gavel and indicated, "Next."

Henrietta, Danny, and Lottie went outside.

"That was certainly a creative verdict," said Lottie.

"Can he force me to do this?" Hen asked incredulously. "Isn't that restricting my liberty?"

Lottie looked at her and said, with a frown, "You lost that privilege when you got charged."

"I think he's being fair, Hen," stated Danny.

She looked at him and accused, "You want this."

"I would like to see you involved in something positive that keeps you out of jail," he said simply.

"I agree with Danny." Lottie saw the hurt in Hen's eyes and

said, "We're not ganging up on you, but it is time, Hen. It's time to realize that you need to be doing something constructive with your life." She glanced at her timepiece and said, "I need you to talk to Danny and think of something where you can help people and not get arrested. And I'm sure a little extra money coming in wouldn't hurt."

Danny nodded and said, "It would be nice."

She glanced at her timepiece again and said, "I have to run. I have some papers to drop at another court." Though she didn't think they heard her. Danny and Hen were wrapped up in each other.

Danny looked at Henrietta and said, "Thank Lottie."

"Yes, thank you. I do appreciate it," said Hen softly.

Lottie gave her a quick kiss and squeezed Danny's arm before turning and walking quickly to the courts that would be receiving the cases. She delivered the envelopes to the appropriate Justice's clerks and ran back to her office. As she stuck her head in, she heard Chris say, "Come in, he's gone for the day."

As she entered, he asked, "Did Hen get jail time?"

Chris had known about Hen since the beginning. They met when she was in court, defending her in one of her first New York arrests.

————

### Court—New York, 1910

"Hello," Lottie heard a man's voice say. She paused, in her conversation with Hen and noticed the handsome young gentleman standing to her right.

"Hello," she responded, looking at him, noticing the golden blond hair and nice build.

"I'm Chris Burnes. I work for Justice Goff," he said, introducing himself.

"Nice to meet you. I'm Lottie Flannigan. This is Henrietta Landry," she said as she motioned to the other woman.

"Hello," Henrietta said. She looked back at Lottie and said, "Thank you. We need to get back to the bookstore."

"Will I see you both this evening?" Lottie asked.

"Yes." Hen walked toward Danny. He raised a hand and waved as they left the courtroom.

Lottie looked back at Chris and said, "Sorry about that. Would you like to step outside?" The court was on break, and they would need to vacate for the next trial.

Chris accompanied her outside to a bench. They sat and he asked, "How long have you been working as a lawyer?"

"The last three years. I started in Chicago."

"You graduated there?"

"Yes, from Chicago Tech."

"You took the bar here?" he inquired with a serious expression.

"I did. I had to," she said, thinking of Hen. She eyed Chris, wondering about all the questions.

"Are you with anyone at this time?" he asked with a serious tone of voice.

"Not yet. I'm looking," she said. Perhaps he could help with that?

He handed her his card and said, "Come by. We have a clerkship open. I think you might be interested in it."

She looked at the card and smiled slowly. "I'll do that."

She followed up the next day. The interview with Chris had gone well, and he made the recommendation to hire her.

When she accepted the job, he said, "I think you'll be a good fit for this office."

———

### Present Day

She collapsed in her chair and said, "We were lucky we got Judge Patterson."

"That's good. He has a reputation for being fair."

"Yes, well, Hen didn't see it that way." She explained the ruling on the case.

Chris laughed out loud. "He got Hen where it hurts. She'll have to turn in the position to the judge for approval."

"Yes," she said wryly. "That was Hen's take also. She believes it interferes with her liberty."

"I believe that was the judge's point," Chris pointed out with a grin.

"I do, too, and honestly, I think it's time for her to focus on something besides demonstrating."

"She has beliefs."

"She does, but lately she seems to believe in everything. Danny is on a ragged edge and we are both going broke trying to keep her out of jail. Thanks for covering for me."

"Any time," he said absently.

# Chapter Seven

"Are you all right with a long afternoon?" he asked about an hour later.

"Yes, I'd like to get through as much as I can," she responded, not looking up from her files.

He nodded and returned to his reading. They worked in companionable silence until 5:00 pm. Chris stood up and stretched. He looked over at her and said, "That should be enough for today. Are you ready to head home?"

She nodded and stood up, glad the day was finally over. First, she had to change from her skirt to her pants, she retrieved her bag and went to the closet to change. As she made her way out, she remove her hair clip and fluffed her hair.

Next, she organized her desk and got the files ready to be moved to the secure room. Once these were moved and the room was locked Chris would keep the key with him.

They returned to their desks and, as they wrapped up, Chris looked over and asked, "Dinner with Patrick tonight?"

"No, he's busy." She had mentioned her brother was in town.

"Going out with Rose?" he asked with a smile.

She smiled back and said, "No, I think she's busy." He knew about her relationship with Rose.

"What about you?" She didn't know much about his private life but knew he was seeing someone.

"I'm meeting a friend here in Manhattan."

"That sounds nice," she commented. "Are we working tomorrow?" They would both need to work straight through the weekend if they were starting the trial next week.

He shook his head emphatically and said, "No, I'm sure this thing will be delayed, and I hate to waste a whole weekend preparing." Chris didn't mention it, but he would work some on Sunday to prepare for the scheduled pretrial meeting with Whitman and the other attorney on Monday. He was counting on the trial being delayed, but he wanted to prepare, just in case.

She trusted his judgment, gathered up her bag, and said, "Are you ready?"

He grabbed his shoulder bag and said, "Let's go." They both headed downstairs.

As they walked out, they discussed the upcoming trial.

"It's not a clear-cut case against Becker," Chris commented. "The conspiracy is going to be hard to prove."

"Unfortunately, the graft is going to be easy to prove," she observed.

"His lawyer will have to present the good work he did during the reform movement of 1906. Use his good press and the reason he was he was appointed by the New York City police commissioner Rhinelander Waldo to the vice squad in 1911."

"Unfortunately, the appointment is what gave him access to the areas where graft was rampant," noted Lottie.

"Yes, from our evidence, that's when he began, allegedly, to extort substantial sums from brothels and illegal casinos," Chris confirmed.

"Chris," she said and stopped him in their descent. "I am concerned about Whitman and Goff's closed-door meetings. I don't think some of this is appropriate."

"I'm afraid we'll see more inappropriate behavior as the trial begins," he said, his mouth twisting unhappily.

They finished the walk downstairs, and she waved him on. "I'll see you on Monday."

He nodded and waved back. She watched him leave and thought, *He looks so unhappy. He must be struggling with Goff's attitude. The Justice is full of himself and drunk with the power of his position.*

Retrieving her bike from the garage, she bent down to hand-crank the motor before climbing on. She revved it a few times and pulled out of the garage, probably going a little faster than she should, and headed toward home.

*Friday already,* she thought. With next week coming up so quickly. *Monday will be a very long day if the trial begins.*

They had gotten out later than usual and, since it was coming on fall, the sun was already starting its trek down in the sky. She sped up wanting to make it home before dark.

# Chapter Eight

Walking up to her apartment, Lottie thought of staying in for the night. The new case was going to be very involved and, according to the schedule, she would be assigned to work in the court while Chris was in the office. Thinking of the court days, she knew Hen might be a distraction. *She needs to get that job*, she thought.

The courtroom where she was assigned, was located on the first floor of the criminal courts building, just in front of city hall. She preferred to work in the office, but she knew it was important for her to be in the court for observation and to provide assistance to Justice Goff.

It was not going to be a good experience. That particular court was horrible; the building sagged and had an oppressive air to it. There was little to no air movement; she would be hot and sweaty for the length of the trial. Goff would use the deplorable conditions against both the prosecutors and the defense to get the verdict he wanted.

Lottie opened her door and bent down to pick up her mail off the floor. There was a large brown envelope on the top. As she picked it up, she thought, *Good, Phillipa got the letter to me. I'll review it later.* She gathered them up and moved to the kitchen to drop them on the table.

Next, she moved into the bedroom and tossed her hat on top of her dresser, and left her shoes by the door. She went to wash her face in the bathroom and, as she finished, padded over to the kitchen to prepare something to eat. *Food first;* she wanted to eat before anything else. Making herself a quick sandwich and pulling out a beer, she moved to her chair in the living room. *This is what I needed, some downtime,* she thought. She ignored the pile of mail she put on the small table next to her.

She ate unhurriedly; it had been a long day. She drank the last of the beer, laid the bottle down, and reached over for her mail. Flipping through the envelopes, she noticed the familiar handwriting on one. *That one first,* she thought and reached for her letter opener and opened it quickly. It was from Mama and included family news and new wedding notifications. One of her many cousins was getting married. She loved the letter, even with the obligatory, "We miss you and when will you visit" at the bottom. She smiled and thought, *I'm going home for a visit after this trial is over.*

She flipped through the next few items, some bills, and ads. The large envelope, she assumed from Phillipa, was the last item. No postal stamp or address was visible on it. She shrugged and thought, *Phillipa probably just dropped it off. I'll have to look into it before the trial starts.*

She used her letter opener to cut open the top fold. Sliding her hand inside, she realized the items felt like photographs. She frowned, sat up, and placed the other mail back on the side table. *The table in the kitchen would be a better place to see what was inside this envelope.*

Walking to it, she tilted the contents onto its surface. As she looked at them, her heart pounded loudly in her chest and the room tilted. Bracing herself on the table, she leaned forward, trying to make sense of what she was seeing. They were photos of her and Rose; lying together, their breasts exposed. There was blood on Rose's face and body. It was the same as her 'dream'; Rose's eyes were also wide open, and she appeared to be dead.

She shoved the pictures off the table and started to back away. *Dead, dead! No! She can't be! What happened? What can I do? Where's her body? Why can't I remember?* Lottie stepped back to the wall and slid down to the floor. Shock gave away to tears and she began to cry until she couldn't move.

# Chapter Nine

Abruptly she woke and looked around, not understanding where she was. *What happened?* Then she saw them on the floor. The pictures...

*I can't, not just yet.* She averted her eyes, pulled herself up, and almost ran from the room. Once in the living room, she felt at a loss as to what to do next. *Bathroom,* she thought and made her way there. She stayed in there, washed her face, brushed her hair, and finally forced herself to admit that she couldn't hide all night. Straightening her shoulders, she forced herself to the kitchen. The rooms seemed to elongate as she walked slowly back through the living room. They were still there, scattered on the floor, an awful reminder that it hadn't been a dream. *I must,* she thought and forced herself to bend down to gather them up.

She placed them in a pile back on the table, pulled out a chair, and sat down. Her eyes were closed as she tried to calm herself by breathing in deeply. *Logic,* she thought. *I need to think clearly. If Rose is dead, where is her body?*

She opened her eyes and looked at the stack in front of her.

Resolved to examine them, she spread them out on the table. This time, she noticed there was a lot of blood but no apparent wounds or bruising. Oddly, the "dead" Rose also seemed to have adjusted herself in one of the photos. *Rose always did like her left side better,* she thought, almost smiling.

She picked them up and ran to her bedroom. Holding them up, she compared them to her room. *This was taken here! How was that possible? How could someone?* She looked around quickly, stopped, and examined the window. It was open. She would never have left it like that. She walked over and leaned out, examining the fire escape. *Was it possible someone had snuck in last night and taken the pictures?*

*Rose is not a small person.* Her figure was round in all the right places—breast, hips, thighs. If she weren't involved, she'd have to be carried out. That would've been a hard process to get her out of this window.

She scanned the room again, trying to understand how this could work. *Could Rose be involved? Is this a deception? She loved games and tricks. If this was one of those, it was a mean one. First, I have to find her.*

She glanced at her timepiece and thought, *It's too late to try to pull myself together tonight. Rose is all right. I know it. I'll plan on investigating tomorrow.*

She was exhausted from the emotional toll of the day. Hen, work, and the pictures. She would put off thinking about this until tomorrow. Pulling back her covers, she climbed into her bed and tried to forget her evening.

# Chapter Ten

She woke with a start and realized the sunlight was streaming in through the window. *What's today? Saturday,* she thought and absently glanced at her clock. *Dammit, I need to go to breakfast with Patrick.* She pulled herself to the side of the bed. Glancing down at her rumpled shirt and pants, she remembered the events from the prior night.

There wasn't time to dwell on that this morning. She ran into the bathroom to take a quick bath and wash her hair. *I'm glad it's short; it's much easier to handle,* she thought as she used a towel to dry it briskly. A dress would be required for their breakfast in Manhattan. She grabbed a one from her closet, pulled it over her head, and hurried to get her things together. Patrick would arrive any minute to pick her up.

*The pictures! I have to hide them.* She didn't want to show them to Patrick; they were too personal. Running back into the kitchen, she picked them up and placed them back into the envelope. *Where to hide them?* The kitchen had few places where something could be hidden. *The icebox*, she thought and went over to drop the envelope behind it.

A knock sounded at the door and she called, "Come in."

The door was unlocked, she had left it that way, antici-pating Patrick's arrival. Brushing her hair over her ears, she exited the kitchen and saw him standing in her doorway.

"Why do you have some many locks on this door if you don't use them?" he scolded.

"I knew you were coming at this time," she explained.

He just shook his head. "Keep it locked at all times. For me?"

"For you, I will," she promised.

He looked around and into her bedroom. Walking back into the living room, he said, "You shouldn't leave your window open, especially the one with the fire escape. It was chilly last night; did you get hot?"

"No," she said. After seeing the pictures she'd forgotten about the opened window.

"I'll go close it now. Are you just about ready to go?"

"Just about, thanks," she said absently, carrying her hat to the mirror. She brushed her hair, placed it on her head, and asked, "Where are we eating?"

"My hotel, they have a breakfast set up."

"Nice," she said approvingly. She grabbed her jacket and pulled it on. "Ready."

He nodded and waved his hat for her to proceed him out of the door. As they stepped into the hallway, she started to walk down the stairs. Patrick cleared his throat and looked pointily at the door.

"Oh, yes. Patrick, I really do keep it locked. I'm just distracted this morning," she said as she moved back to the door and took out her keys to secure it.

"Can you tell me what's on your mind?" he asked.

"Not now. It might be nothing," she said.

"Is it a work thing?" he probed.

"No, it's personal."

"If it becomes something, you call me. Okay?"

"Yes, of course." They started down the stairs and she tried a change in topic. "You mentioned you had a meeting yesterday."

"Yes," he said noncommittally.

"Something you can talk about?"

"Not just yet."

Lottie looked over and teased, "If it becomes something, you call me. Okay?"

He laughed, delighted with how her brain worked. "Okay."

She understood that he sometimes worked as a liaison for the Chicago Police Department on confidential projects.

"What about you? How is work?" he asked.

"We're starting a high-profile case; it could start as early as Monday. I can tell you the name of the person involved once we're in court."

"That Becker trial is in all of the papers," he commented, watching her carefully.

"It is," she agreed casually.

He sent her a glance and said, "I saw in the paper that Justice Goff was listed as the presiding Justice."

"Have you?" she asked evasively. Those damn papers seem to know everything.

"Yes. And don't you work for him?"

"Patrick, you know I can't comment on that."

"I know," he said, and let the topic go- *for now*.

They exited the building and Lottie saw the same car he had the other evening, parked at the curb. "Still have it?" she asked. A friend loaned him the car while he was in town.

"Yes, just until breakfast. He'll pick it up from the train

67

station." He held her door and then went around to the driver's side to take the wheel. "Hungry?"

She nodded, looking forward to eating out. The opportunity didn't come up very often. There should have been enough money to enjoy restaurants and movies, but Hen cut into her pay. Patrick or her parents would loan her some, but she wanted to do this on her own.

They arrived at the hotel and immediately went to the dining room. As they waited for their breakfast, Patrick asked casually, "Have you seen Joseph?"

She looked surprised and commented, "Not since we broke up. Why do you ask?"

"You seemed serious about him," he continued, without answering her.

"I was, but he wasn't," she said with a grimace.

"Do you know what he does now?"

"For money?" she asked. She watched as he nodded. "He's in his father's business. They do very well. At least, I think so. His house is big and beautiful."

"Any idea what the business is?" Patrick asked while he pursued the menu.

"Why all the questions?" she asked, suspicious. She'd been raised in a house with detectives.

"No reason," he assured her. "I am just protective of my little sister."

Lottie smiled at him and asked him about home.

He wanted to ask more questions, but he could see the topic bothered her. The conversation turned to Mama and Papa.

Breakfast was delivered and, before she knew it, she was at the train station dropping him off. "You need to come home soon," he said, taking her by the shoulders.

"I know, I miss everyone so much. I'll try to get there before the holidays. It just depends on this trial. I'd like to be there for a few weeks after this one is over. I'll need the break."

"Will Goff allow that?" he asked, knowing his control of her schedule.

"He has a vacation scheduled and won't move it. I'll work it out," she promised.

"I hope so. You know, it might be time to start your own practice."

She nodded. "I'm thinking that way also. Especially given how my current trial is going and how the Justice is already behaving."

He watched her and said, "Let us know when you're ready. We can help set it up."

"I know, Patrick. Thank you." She thought, *It might be the right time to ask him a question. He is leaving town and won't be able to interfere.* "Patrick," she said, not looking at him. "If someone was missing or you think they might be missing, what would you do?"

He frowned. "First, I'd go to their home and see if they were there. I'd look for things they would always have with them."

"Then?"

"Then I'd find out who'd seen them last and try to retrace their steps."

"Okay then," she said, thinking about what she should do next.

"Lottie, is someone missing? Do I need to stay and help you?" Patrick asked. He was ready to stay if she needed him.

She thought about those pictures and knew she had to do this on her own. "No," she assured him. "I'm sure this person is at home. I just didn't think to check."

They heard the train call. She looked at him and said, "You need to get going."

"Yes, my friend will pick up the car, take a motor car home," he said and gave her a quick kiss on the cheek. He grabbed his bag and headed off to catch his train. Pausing briefly on the stairs, he turned to wave goodbye.

She waved back and watched him board the train. Making her way slowly out of the station, she motioned to a motor cab to take her back to the village.

*Rose's apartment is where I need to go next.*

# Chapter Eleven

L ottie gave the driver Rose's address. "The junction of Fourth and MacDougal Streets, please." As they made their way into the village, she thought about the types of housing available. Part of the charm for the artists living there was the small rooms used as apartments for as cheap as three dollars a month—no electrical lights and unfurnished.

*That is not the type of place Rose lives in,* she thought as they pulled up to old mansion that had been converted into apartments. After paying the driver, she made her way inside and up the first set of stairs, stopping in front of Rose's door. She reached up and pulled her necklace out of the top of her dress. A key was hanging from it and had been given to her as a token of their friendship. When Lottie received it, she had tried not to read too much into it. She tended to believe that people meant more than they said. With both Joseph and Rose, she had made wrong assumptions about their level of commitment to her.

As she pushed the door open the sheer expanse of Rose's

apartment struck her. She owned the entire floor of the building and it was filled with her things. The wall coverings were made with fabric and the hard floors were covered with large luxurious rugs. Her view also overlooked Washington Square Park. Her parents had disowned her because of her life-style, but her grandmother had been close to her and provided for her with an extensive inheritance.

She looked around and thought, *Anyone else entering the apartment would have said there'd been a break-in.* Rose didn't like to pick up after herself. Lottie had to nudge newspapers and magazines to be able to move about the room.

*Patrick said I'm looking for something she would never leave behind.* She kept searching and went into the bedroom; it was in the same disarray. Going to the dresser, she moved things around and saw the one thing she was looking for; a necklace. It was one that Lottie had given to Rose. She picked it up slowly, letting the light hit it. It was one of the times when they were a couple and happy.

――――

### *Artisan fair*

The two of them had been strolling through a local fair. The area artisans had set up booths to display their wares. The jewelry booth caught Lottie's eye. She left Rose's side to walk over and ask the vendor a low question, pointing to an item.

He picked it up and looked over at her, smiled, and said, "Yes, of course. Come back in an hour."

"We will," she promised and walked over to Rose, putting her hand in the crook of her arm.

"What was that about?" asked Rose curiously.

"A surprise," said Lottie with a small smile.

"Hmmm, for me?" she asked coyly.

"Maybe. You'll have to wait and see," she teased.

They walked on, enjoying cookies and looking at the other wares being offered. They waited the hour and made their way back to the jewelry booth. The merchant brought out the item and held it up for both to see. He had taken the letters L and R and had them intertwined into one design.

"This is for you," Lottie said and handed it to Rose.

Rose rarely showed raw emotion, sarcasm being her main method of communication but at this moment, she saw her face go red and her eyes teared up.

"Baby, I didn't mean to upset you," said Lottie, putting her hand up to Rose's face.

Rose brushed the tears away and said, "Help me put it on."

She turned and Lottie fastened it around her neck. Turning back to her, she said softly, "Thank you, lovely girl." Then leaned in to kiss her.

When Lottie and Rose turned around, Lottie saw that the artisan had stepped away to give them some privacy. She inquired, "Sir, how much?"

He told her the price and she paid him. "Thank you."

He smiled and said, "Come back again."

"We will," she responded.

———

### Rose's apartment present day

Rose hadn't removed the necklace since that day. Even when they were on the outs, she continued to wear it. *The pictures*, thought Lottie. *I need to check them.* The necklace was clasped tightly in her hand as she did a final walkthrough of the apartment.

Exiting the door into the hallway, she locked it behind her and took the stairs two at a time in her rush to get home. She exited onto the street and walked swiftly to her apartment a few blocks over. When she entered, she went to retrieve the pictures and dumped them onto the table. *Thank goodness.* She slumped down in relief when she saw Rose was wearing the necklace in the pictures. The chain was long enough to fall between her breasts. Her finger traced the necklace in the picture. That meant she was alive when the pictures were taken. But why would she do that? And why would she leave the necklace in her apartment?

*I'll need to talk to the ladies at the tearoom.* She checked her watch and realized it was still hours before she could do that. *Henrietta,* she thought. *She or Danny might have seen her after she left my apartment.*

She picked up the necklace, opened the clasps on the chain, and put it around her neck. Patrick's warning stopped her in the hallway and she turned to lock the door behind her before she headed downstairs. The bookstore would be her next stop. She left the building and headed there.

A bell jingled as she entered. "Danny, Henrietta!" she called. There was movement in the back; she paused and waited for them to come out. Smiling to herself, she had an idea of what was happening when Henrietta came out first, her hair mussed, buttoning up her dress. Danny followed close behind, and he looked just the same as always.

He straightened his glasses and said, "Lottie, you're out early this morning."

"Yes. I had to take Patrick to the train station."

"Oh! He left already?" asked Henrietta, disappointed. "I'd hoped to have you both over to dinner."

Danny moved to the desk and was documenting the books that had come in the day before, leaving them to their conversation.

Lottie answered, "He promised next time will be a longer trip."

"Did Emma and Jeremy get off okay?" Henrietta asked. She and Danny had gotten to spend the prior morning with them. She was glad they embarked on their trip before her arrest. They would not have reacted well to it. There had been a promise made last time they had a discussion, and she had not kept it.

———

### Prior visits with Emma, Jeremy, Danny, and Hen

There had been long conversations, both in Chicago and New York City, about Hen's activism leading to arrest and prison time. "Henrietta, you have strong beliefs," said Emma and looked at Jeremy. He nodded in agreement. "But you need to direct these beliefs into a task that will move you toward something positive."

She looked down at her hands and said, "Yes, I understand."

Jeremy said, "You also rely on Lottie to bail you out each time you get into trouble. I am concerned you might also be affecting her job. Doesn't she have to leave her office each time she has to represent you in court?"

That made Henrietta think; she'd always relied on Lottie to get her out of trouble. "It's time. I will take it seriously."

"That's all we ask," said Emma.

———

### Present day bookstore

"Yes," said Lottie. "They're off to their next adventure in

Paris. Aunt Emma enjoys her teaching assignments for the French police."

"It would be so fun. Can you imagine Paris?" Henrietta said dreamily.

"I can. I hope to go there one day. I heard there are sections there much like the village here," said Lottie.

Henrietta looked at Danny. "Wouldn't it be amazing?"

"It would be," he replied softly.

Lottie couldn't wait any longer and asked, "Danny, did you see Rose yesterday?" She knew he worked early hours and might have been in the store when Rose left her apartment.

He cocked his head at her, adjusted his glasses, and confirmed, "I did. She was coming from your apartment."

"Do you know what time that was?" she asked.

"Yes," he said. "It was early, around 6:00 am. I had just gone down to the store to unbox some deliveries and had pulled the shades up."

*So, she was alive. The pictures were faked. Why?* "Was she alone?" she asked.

He frowned and said, "At the time, I thought so, but as I think about it, a man was walking a few feet behind her."

"Did he look threatening?" she asked intently.

He took a moment to think about that, leaning back against the counter and folding his arms. "No, I would have noticed that. In fact, she did turn toward him a few times and appeared to be laughing."

"I need to go," Lottie said, turning around.

Henrietta stepped toward her. "Has something happened to Rose?"

Lottie turned back to them, frowned, and replied, "I am not sure, she might be playing a game with me."

Hen frowned, she didn't like the sound of that. "What type of game?"

Lottie hesitated before saying, "I am looking into it, I will let you more later."

Danny stepped forward taking Hen's hand, he wanted to stop her before she voiced her opinion on Rose. "Let us know what we can do."

Hen understood and nodded without commenting.

"Thanks, Danny, Henrietta. I love you both."

She turned and headed out, walking quickly to her apartment. Just outside the building, she stopped and looked toward the bookstore. The angle was what he could see from their business. Thinking about that, she turned back and headed to her apartment.

The locks on the door took a moment to open. Once it was unlocked, she entered, and looked down at the floor. Another envelope had been delivered. Frowning, she reached down and picked it up. *Was it here this morning? Did I miss it?* Turning it over in her hands, she couldn't find markings on either side. It was also much smaller than the previous one. *No pictures this time,* she thought, bending the envelope slightly.

She opened it quickly and sat down abruptly when she saw what it contained. It was a note: "The photos will be sent to Justice Goff and your family if you do not do as we say. We will send further instructions once the trial has begun."

*A dangerous game, blackmail. For what purpose? No confirmation that this involved the Becker trail? It had to be it. What could she give them, no one else could?* The threats were real and would need to be considered. Lottie knew her family would support her, but it was Goff's reaction and the eventual firing that worried her. She pondered Rose's involvement, she is not political and didn't involve herself in things outside of the village. Someone would have to go to her and offer her something she couldn't turn down. *What have you gotten into? Are you in over your head? Was leaving the neck-*

*lace part of the ruse?* she thought, fingering the LR between her breast.

Examining the letter, she turned it over, looking for any additional information, and found nothing. *A waiting game,* she thought. *I have to wait for them to ask for the first thing and see how far I am willing to go to protect my family and my job.*

# Chapter Twelve

tarting to lean back on the chair, she thought, *Jojo. I promised him I'd stop by today.* Sitting up abruptly, she took the note to the kitchen and accessed the larger envelope that held the pictures. The note was placed inside and returned to its hiding place. Lottie grabbed her hat, and went downstairs in a rush, taking them two at a time. Inserting the key into the lock, she went into the store room and retrieved her motorcycle. Once it was on the sidewalk, she locked the door and bent down to hand-crank it. It started smoothly, and she climbed on, rolling it onto the road toward Jojo's apartment. She knew he would hold her to the promise, and she didn't want to disappoint him.

On her way there, she waved at several people she recognized. The bike rolled easily on to the walkway just outside of Jojo's apartment building. It was shutoff and she patted her pocket to check for her hand crank. The bike would be safe there, and she knew Jojo would want to ride it immediately. She headed in, looking at the well-maintained building. Some parts of the village were not being kept in good condition. She found their door, quickly knocked, and waited. It swung open and revealed Jojo.

"Lottie! You came!" he shouted.

"I promised, didn't I?" she chided, waiting to be invited into the apartment.

"Ma, Lottie's here," he called back over his shoulder.

"Bring her into the kitchen," Jojo's mother called back.

"On our way!" he shouted again.

He waved at Lottie to follow him in, and they made their way down the short hallway. Jojo pushed open the door for her and then followed behind.

The door opened to a galley kitchen. Large pots cooled on the stove and assorted items spread out on the counters.

"I could have found it on my own. That lovely smell just draws you in," Lottie said, leaning over to breathe the fumes coming from the pot Annabeth, Jojo's mother, was stirring.

Annabeth made fragrant soap and candles using herbs from her small garden. *She must be toward the end of the soap/candle-making process,* thought Lottie. From the wonderful smells, she could tell this was the final step prior to pouring the material into glass jars and molds to shape the soaps/candles. She could see they were already lined up on the counter, waiting for Annabeth to fill.

Lottie was happy to be present for the scent addition rather than that of fat. Fat was integral to the making of soap, but the smell wasn't pleasant. It came from the local butchers and was mixed with caustic and lye to complete the soap-making operation. She noticed the protective goggles and gloves nearby; it could be a dangerous process.

Annabeth continued to chop up her herbs and flowers to add to her different products. Lottie waited patiently and, when Annabeth finished her task, she hugged her.

"So nice to see you. Jojo mentioned you would be by today."

"I'll bet," Lottie commented, looking around at him.

He smiled brightly and shrugged.

Annabeth leaned over and whispered in her ear, "Did you ride it over?"

Lottie answered in a whisper, "I did."

They grinned at each other.

Lottie sobered suddenly and said, "Annabeth, I'm worried about you and Jojo. I sent some addresses over with him a few days ago. Were you able to contact them?"

Annabeth went back to her pot, stirring. She looked over and smiled suddenly. Her long black hair was pulled back, showing her ebony skin and high cheekbones. "I've found another way to make money." She nodded at the pot containing the fragrant material.

"Is there enough in that kind of business for you to survive?" Lottie asked, not knowing much about it.

"Initially, I was worried, but once I started talking to the people in your group to try my soaps, I had so many sales, I couldn't keep up."

"My group?" she asked, wondering who Annabeth was referencing.

"Yes. I approached a few shop owners first. They tried the product and liked it. Some of them told me that the packaging was the problem. They wanted something more decorative."

"What did you do?" she inquired.

"They referred me to several artists in the area to work on the packaging."

"Artists?"

"You know the ones, always carrying their drawing pads around. They always look like they need haircuts."

"Yes," said Lottie, covering her smile with her hand.

"I met with them, explained what I was selling, and bought the designs I liked. They're over there," she said, pointing to the counter behind Lottie.

Lottie turned around and saw the labels. They had lovely flower patterns. She turned them over and saw they had adhesive backs. "Who'd you get to print them?"

"I got with the local pharmacist to see who he used," Annabeth said proudly. "I'd noticed the bottles he used had labels like I wanted."

"Soap and candles pay well?"

"It does okay. I hope I can get into shops in Manhattan."

"Oh, Annabeth, that's wonderful!" Lottie thought for a moment and asked curiously, "New business requires an influx of money. How did you do it?"

"Now, that is a story. I was interviewing the different artists for the soap labels, but all they wanted to talk about was drawing or sculpting me. Another wants to tell my story in a book."

"Your story?" asked Lottie.

Annabeth explained patiently. "How we came up from the south, our family. My background and how the family was torn apart during the slave days."

Lottie reached out and placed her hand on Annabeth's arm and said, "That is a story that should be told. I'd love to hear it."

"Thank you, dear."

"Sculpture?" she asked contemplatively.

"Yes, I have to sit and be patient with sketches and then I am there for the actual work."

"What type is it? Stone, clay?"

"Stone and very noisy," Annabeth said, shaking her head.

Jojo's patience ran out. "Can I get my ride now? Please!"

Lottie and Annabeth laughed. She took his hand and said, "Of course. You'll have to hang on. Can you handle that?"

"I can!" he shouted.

Annabeth said, "Wait, you must come back and have some coffee with me when you're done."

"That's a deal," Lottie agreed.

Jojo was so happy, that he almost floated outside with her. She bent down, cranked the motor, and got on. While she revved the engine, she looked over and reminded him, "The seat is small, so hug me tight."

He nodded and she put out her arm to help him climb on. "Watch your legs," she said; the pipes could burn him through his pants.

Once he was safely behind her, she called over the noise of the engine, "Are you ready?"

"I am," he said, his voice breathless.

She could feel his arms around her waist. As they took off, she took extra care, knowing he was with her. They toured the entire village and when she started to head back, he called out, "More, more!"

Lottie was enjoying herself and said, "Ok, just a bit more, around Washington Square." *And*, she thought, *around to Rose's apartment.*

She turned the bike, carefully watching out for Jojo, and made her way there. The sidewalks around Rose's apartment were mostly empty. There was one person that caught her interest, it was Joseph. She frowned and said out loud, "Why is he here?"

Jojo said in a muffled voice, his face buried in her jacket, "I've seen him around here before."

*Near Rose's place?* she thought slowing down. She didn't want to be seen, so she cut through a nearby alley. They went down a few more streets and headed back to his apartment.

Once they arrived, she turned off the bike and helped him down, reminding him, "Watch your legs."

"Remember, Ma wants to see you," Jojo reminded her.

"I remember." She climbed off and rolled the bike onto the sidewalk, parking it against the wall. "Jojo?"

"Yeah?" he asked. He had knelt to look at the engine. Mechanical things were fascinating to him.

She said, casually not looking over at him, "You said you'd seen Joseph in the area?"

"Yeah, he hangs around there sometimes."

"Have you seen him with Rose?" she asked.

He looked over at her and shrugged. "I think so."

They started to go in and Jojo warned, "You might roll it inside. It's getting dark."

He was right. The area changed at night, with more people coming there for the local bars and brothels.

"Thanks for the reminder," she said, thinking about Joseph and Rose as she rolled the motorcycle in behind him.

He looked over his shoulder as he opened the door and said, "Ma won't mind. Leave it in the hallway." As they entered, he yelled, "Ma, we're back!"

"Come into the kitchen!" Annabeth yelled.

Lottie parked the bike in the hallway, careful not to scuff the walls, and followed him. The door had been left open by Jojo, Annabeth had been busy, her jars and molds were filled and cooling. The wicks poked out of the tops of the candles.

"Jojo set the table," she instructed.

He ran back into the kitchen and moved around Lottie to pick up silverware and dishes. As he dashed about the table, Lottie noticed three places set.

Annabeth said, "I have coffee and lunch laid out. Sit, sit."

"Annabeth, I can't take your food," Lottie protested, though the smells made her mouth water.

"We have enough," the other woman said firmly. She gestured with her hand. "Sit down."

Lottie hesitated a moment and said, "Only if you and Jojo will come to my house to eat soon."

"You can cook?" asked Jojo, not believing her.

"I do," she confirmed. "Well, at least, I bake well. I learned the skill when I worked in the family bakery. Have you ever had strudel?"

"What's that?" asked Jojo.

"That's a wonderful pastry that has apples and sugar," supplied Annabeth.

"Yum," he said.

"Yum, indeed," said Lottie.

Jojo picked up his fork and his mother reminded him, "Prayers first."

"Okay, Ma." They bowed their heads. "God bless these people and this food. We are thankful for you every day. Amen."

"Good," said Annabeth approvingly. "Now, where did you ride to?"

"All around the neighborhood, Ma. We went fast."

Over his head, Lottie mouthed to Annabeth, "Not too fast."

Annabeth nodded, grateful she was careful; Jojo was her only family. Her close relatives had passed away and her other family members scattered after the war until there were none in the area. She and Jojo had had to make a go of it on their own.

"Have you seen Rose lately?" asked Lottie casually.

Annabeth answered first and said, "No, not really. She occasionally buys my soap, but we don't socialize much."

Jojo said, with his mouth full, "I have."

"When was the last time you saw her?" asked Lottie.

He wiped his mouth and responded, "Yesterday."

"Was she alone?" asked Lottie, surprised.

"No, she was with a man," he said as he continued to eat.

"Did you recognize the man?" Lottie asked, wondering if she'd finally gotten a lead on who had accompanied Rose.

"I've seen him before." He looked over at Annabeth and said, "Ma, I think you sell soap to him."

"Was he from the village?" Annabeth asked, thinking of her male customers.

"No, Ma, he's that odd bugger, you know the one. He seems scared of women."

Annabeth made a face when she heard that comment. "Oh, him. Yes, I know his name. It's Jacko Griffin. He doesn't live in the village, but he's close by."

# Chapter Thirteen

L ottie stood with her bike outside Jacko Griffin's shop, located at the bottom of a four-story redbrick building just outside the village.

She leaned into the glass window of the small photography shop. *How should I approach this?* she thought. It appeared to be empty; she could see a long counter and what appeared to be a curtain leading to a back room.

Annabeth knew of him because he'd tried to work an exchange of pictures for soap. She told him that pictures don't put food on the table and to come back when he had money. Annabeth had warned her that she hadn't felt comfortable with him. "That one is odd. He seems afraid of women, but I also didn't want to be alone with him."

Lottie took a deep breath, opened the door, and rolled the motorcycle into the small shop. She parked the bike to the left of the counter, where it was fairly well hidden. Silently, she continued to look around until she spotted the dark curtain behind the desk. She slowly approached it and called, "Jacko?"

A voice called back, "Don't come in here, I'm developing film! I will come out.

She waited by the curtain, tapping her foot, knowing she might have found the man she was looking for.

When he finally walked out, Lottie saw he was just about her height and age. He was so thin as to be gaunt.

"Are you Jacko Griffin?" she asked in a firm voice.

He hadn't gotten a clear view of her face; he was polishing his glasses as he exited the back room.

"I am," Jacko said as he slid his glasses back on. He finally got a good look at who was asking for him; his face went deep red. The embarrassment was too much for him, and he started to retreat from her into the back room.

Lottie saw immediately that he recognized her and had taken the pictures. She followed him into the room and unbuttoned her blouse quickly, exposing her breasts to him.

"What? You don't want to see them while I'm conscious? You prefer the people you're taking pictures of to be unaware you're there?"

She continued toward him, pushing him into a corner. He looked petrified, and she didn't care.

Just then, a voice came from the curtained doorway behind them, "Why don't you put those away and we can all have a civil conversation." Lottie whipped around and gave the visitor a good view of her breasts. "Not that I mind, of course, but it might make it easier for Jacko to function."

She angrily grabbed parts of her shift and pulled them together, buttoning them up.

"Now, can you tell me what this is about?" the stranger inquired, looking at the extremely attractive young lady.

Lottie glanced back to make sure Jacko was still in the corner, then turned to the new man. He was taller than her, about 5'10", and solidly built. He was dressed in a suit, well pressed, buttoned-up, with a nice tie in place on his collar. She got a good look at his face; it was solid and attractive, and his hair, though trimmed short, seemed to have a wave running through it. *His eyes*, she thought, *are direct.*

"What business is it of yours?" she asked belligerently.

"None," he acknowledged. "Except that you were seemingly threatening Jacko here. Albeit with your breasts."

"Yeah!" said Jacko, who had finally gathered up enough confidence to say something. He took a step out of his corner.

She gave him a threatening look; it cowed him back. Turning, she glared at the intruder. "Why would anything I might do to Jacko be a problem for you?"

"Well," he said, pulling out his wallet. "This might explain a few things."

A police officer's badge! Her eyes went wide. She didn't know who to trust; it could just as easily be an officer behind this whole thing. Instead of answering, she said, "I need to have a private conversation with Jacko about some pictures he took."

He frowned, but not at Lottie this time. "Jacko, what have you gotten yourself involved in this time?" the man asked, exasperated.

Lottie almost smiled at the tone; it was one she used on Henrietta all the time.

"Honestly, nothing, Frank," he whined rubbing his hands together nervously. "I don't know what she's talking about."

"Do you want me to open my shift again?" she asked, lifting her hand to the buttons of her shirt.

"Nooooo!" He looked frantically toward the officer and yelled, "Frank!"

"Yeah, let's not do that." He looked at Lottie and said, "You tell me. What pictures are you inquiring about?"

"I don't have any of her pictures," Jacko tried again.

"Let me get my set," she said, running out to her bike,

where her bag was located. She pulled them out, re-entered the backroom, and laid it on the counter with a thump.

"Let's take a look," the policeman said, motioning toward the envelope.

She opened it up and let the pictures spill out onto the table. She was not embarrassed by them; she just wanted to know why they were taken. He'd also just gotten a pretty good view of her breast already.

He looked at the pictures and said, "Jacko, I recognize your work." He eyed the other man with a heavy frown on his face. "What's your involvement here? Is this woman dead?" His voice rose with the last question.

"Frank, those aren't mine," Jacko said, but he didn't sound as sure as he had previously.

Frank just frowned at him and turned to Lottie. "Do you know if this woman is dead?"

Lottie said, pushing her hair from her forehead, "I don't think she was at that time. Some friends saw her and I believe Jacko exiting my apartment after the pictures were taken."

He continued to watch her and finally said, indicating the pictures, "You can put those away now."

She piled them up and slid them back into the envelope.

Frank looked at Jacko, taking a step toward him, and said forcefully, "Okay, start talking."

"Don't tell Ma!!" Jacko fairly screamed.

*Brothers.* She looked from one to another and thought, *They look nothing alike.*

Frank walked closer to him and said, "That depends. Spill!"

"I was told it was a game," Jacko said, moving out of the corner to sit in a chair located more in the center of the room. He slumped down, trying to make himself smaller.

"Who contacted you about this 'game'?" asked Frank.

"Rose," he mumbled.

"So, you do know her," said Lottie.

"Yes," he admitted. "She sometimes set up pictures of the women she was dating."

"You've done this before," pounced Frank.

Jacko nodded and said, "But normally, she isn't made up like she is there."

"You mean like she's dead?" asked Frank.

He nodded and mumbled, "Yeah."

Lottie demanded, "How did you get into my apartment?"

"So, breaking and entering also?" Frank asked, wondering how many charges this could lead to.

"NO! I didn't break anything!" He continued in a lower voice, "Rose left the window open for me."

"And that made it okay?" Frank asked.

"We never got caught before. This is all Rose's fault," he said miserably.

"Why?" Lottie asked.

"She changed the game. I normally just take the pictures. This time, she told me to give them to you."

"It was you who delivered them to me. Jacko, is Rose alive?" she asked.

"The last time I saw her she was," he said miserably.

"When was that?" she asked quickly.

"The morning after we took the pictures. She saw them first. I left a copy with her and placed yours under your door."

*Nothing more there*, thought Lottie.

"Why did she want her...?" the officer asked. Before she could answer, he said, "I just realized I don't know your name."

"Lottie. Lottie Flannigan," she supplied.

"Jacko, why did Rose want Lottie to have the pictures? Why was it different this time?"

"I don't know. Rose can be odd," responded Jacko.

Frank looked over at Lottie and asked, "Why do you think she had these sent to you?"

"My first thought was to blackmail me. I think someone is trying to set me up," she said, thinking of the note from that morning.

"But you still cared enough to look for her," said Frank, wondering about her and Rose's relationship.

"As you saw, we are very close," she said, tapping the envelope on the table beside her.

"Are you together now?" he asked casually.

Frowning briefly, she wondered about that question but answered honestly, "We have an agreement. We're casual."

She heard Jacko mutter something and looked over at him. "What was that?" asked Lottie.

"It was just different this time," said Jacko.

"Was there a note in the envelope?" asked Frank, wondering about the reason the pictures were given to her.

"Not in the first one, but there was one this morning," she said.

Frank's reaction to the comment was to glare at Jacko.

Jacko took offense at this and said, "Hey, I only put one envelope under the door."

Frank ignored him and asked, "Can you show me the note?"

She pulled out the handwritten paper and handed it to him, the threat to expose the pictures to family, and mentioned a trial.

"Which trial are they referencing?" Frank asked.

"I'm not supposed to say," she said.

He considered her words; the only trial that might have people working to change a verdict would be the Becker one. Instead of pressing her, he asked, "What do you do that they think you could help them with?"

She could share this information. "I'm a clerk in Justice John Goff's office."

"You're a lawyer?" he asked, looking a bit shamefaced when he realized how the question sounded.

"Yes, they do let women do that now," she said with a slight mocking tone.

Frank realized the blackmailer was aware of her job and her relationship with Rose. He moved on to the next subject. "Someone has the originals and is using them to threaten you," he said. He looked over at Jacko and asked, "Where's Rose?"

"I don't know," he said miserably. "I went by her apartment, but she wasn't there."

"I checked there also," commented Lottie.

"Did you go into the apartment?" Frank asked her. He wondered if Rose was there, hiding out.

"Yes, I went in and looked around, she's not there," said Lottie firmly.

"How do you have access?"

"I have a key. I used it to go in," said Lottie.

"Did you find anything out of the ordinary?" Frank asked.

"Just this," she said, showing him the necklace. She reached up, took it off, and handed it to him.

"Is this special to her?" Frank asked, looking at it closely before handing it back to her.

Lottie nodded and put it back on.

"Was she wearing that in the pictures?" Frank asked.

"Yes," said Lottie quietly. "After I gave it to her, she never took it off."

"Do you believe she was taken?"

"I don't think so, she seems to be an active participant in at least part of this. Did it get bigger than she could handle? Was that the reason the necklace was left? I don't know. We also may only have a limited time to find out."

"Why limited?" Frank asked.

"The trial is only expected to last less than 30 days. These threats seem to know the timeline. I think the demands will start when it begins."

"Isn't that odd timing for a murder trial?" he frowned, thinking about what the note said.

"Right now, it's soon. Motions are supposed to start on Monday." She let the assumption about the case involving murder go by. They were all avoiding Becker's name.

"Monday? Isn't that fast?"

"Yes, but I expect the defense attorney will push back."

"Will it work?" he asked curiously.

"Not for long. The Justice wants this trial to begin soon," she commented.

"These threats aren't clear about which side they're coming from?" Frank asked.

"I'm not sure which side is trying to apply pressure on me," she admitted.

"What could you do for them? Either side?"

"I don't know," she said, bewildered. "I'm just a clerk. I just don't have that kind of influence."

"So, we wait for further instructions.

"I need to be looking for Rose in the meantime."

He nodded and asked, "Can you show me her apartment?"

"I can," Lottie agreed.

Frank closed his notebook and suggested, "Let's go over there now. One second." He looked over at his brother and asked, "Jacko, where are the negatives?"

Jacko looked away and didn't say anything.

"Do you want me to call Ma?" asked Frank threateningly.

"No," Jacko whined, standing, he stomped to a cabinet. He unlocked it, pulled out a file, and handed it to him.

"And..." Frank prompted.

Jacko mumbled as he reached in and took out another file, handing it to him.

He looked over at Lottie and explained, "He always keeps another set of copies just in case."

"He does, does he?" *Interesting*, she thought. She would file that information away for now.

Frank had turned and was pulling the curtain back. "Are you ready to go?" he asked her.

"I am," she responded and walked into the main room. She didn't immediately go to the door. Instead, she went to the side counter and rolled out her motorcycle.

"Is that yours?" he asked, distracted for a moment. He walked over and bent down to look at it. "It appears to be in good condition."

"Yes," she said. "My uncle had me take it apart and put it back together before he would let me have it."

He stood up and said, "I'll follow you over."

"Do you have an auto or a buggy?" she asked curiously.

"Auto," he said simply.

*Not a beat cop*, she thought and worried that a cop's salary didn't lend itself to personal automobiles. She covered by smiling and said, "I'll watch my speed for you.'

"Please do. I'd hate to get a ticket," he said thoughtfully, taking in the dashing picture she made in her pants and short red hair.

"Of course."

Lottie rolled the bike onto the street, bent down to crank it, and got on. She revved it a bit. She watched him hand-crank his auto and, once both were going, they were off.

On her way to the apartment, she thought about this man. She didn't know much about him, but she needed help. If it was a cop behind this, could it be him? He knew Jacko and Jacko knew her and Rose. She would keep an open mind.

She was conscious of him behind her as she pulled to a stop in front of Rose's apartment. As he exited his auto, she turned off her bike and walked it onto the sidewalk, parking it against the stoop.

He was watching her and asked, "You have your crank with you?"

"Yes. I know most people here; if we were downtown, I'd be concerned about it. I do have secure parking there."

As they headed up and onto Rose's floor, Lottie said, "Could you wait here?" She went around, pulled the key out, and opened the door. Tucking it back in her blouse, she called, "You can come around now."

He did so, not questioning the additional security. She turned the knob, opened the door, and he immediately went in. Newspapers, magazines, and other debris blocked his path. Looking back at her, he said, "I thought you said nothing was different. This place looks like it was tossed."

Lottie smiled slightly. "It may look that way, but this is how Rose lives."

He looked at her incredulously but moved forward into the room.

She noted his response seemed honest; he didn't appear to have been here before.

"Okay then, for this room, the large living room, did you find anything unusual?" he asked.

Lottie looked around the room again and said, "No, this is typical."

"Are all these her clothes?" Frank asked, noting the mounds laying haphazardly on stuffed sofas and other furniture. He moved things around, noting the newspapers and magazines scattered about. He turned over the newspapers and looked at her.

"Looks like she took an interest in the Becker case," he

observed.

Lottie frowned. "Rose didn't normally involve herself in politics. Magazines, yes, for fashion, but not politics."

"I thought most people living in the village followed politics closely. A certain side anyway."

She laughed suddenly. "That's true, but I would say, out of our group, Rose and I were the holdouts."

They finished their review of the living room and headed to the bedroom. Lottie indicated the dresser.

"That's where I found the necklace."

He walked over, moving things about. "Did she have any other jewelry that was taken or is still here?"

"She had a few rings and bangles. Nothing of much value. I think the good stuff is with her family."

"Who are they?"

"Rose never told me; I do know they were well off."

"Can you tell me about your relationship with her?"

"Rose? That's involved. I thought we were serious, but it turns out it was a casual relationship. Over time, we would get together when each of us was free."

"Are you...?"

"Bisexual?" she asked, not taking any offense.

He nodded, having heard the term used previously.

"I like both men and women," she confirmed, looking him in the eyes. "I tended to get too serious about relationships when I first moved here."

"Not just with Rose?"

"No, also with a man." That made her think of Joseph. *Why was he in the area?*

"Is he still in the picture?" he asked, his voice neutral.

"No, he's married now," she said softly. "Is my sex life important to this case?"

"It might be," he said honestly.

"I keep thinking that it has to be someone who knows Rose and I have a relationship. They'd have to know her pretty well to know she'd go along with a game like this."

"Who else do you think might be involved?" Frank asked, taking advantage of Lottie's analytical mind.

"Someone who knows Rose and I are involved and that I'm a clerk in Justice Goff's office," she said, connecting the clues.

"Do you know who might fit that bill?"

"I'll need to think about it, but I could make a list."

"Please," he replied.

"Can you give me your contact information?" she asked.

He took out a notepad and wrote his number and address. He handed it to her.

She looked at it and asked, "Address?"

"In case," he stressed. "Where's your apartment?"

"Near here, a few blocks," she commented.

"Can I see it?" he asked in a strangely flat voice.

"Why?" she asked curiously.

"I'd like to see the windows. What floor are you on?"

"Why would the floor matter?"

"Jacko's afraid of heights."

"Girls and heights?" She chuckled and said, "He's a mess."

"Yeah, Ma babied him."

"Is he that scared of her?"

"He is," he confirmed. "She can control him."

"Is he dangerous?" she asked, suddenly nervous.

"No, but the people using his photography skills can be. He deals with an element I'd prefer him not to."

"Would you like to go now?"

"If you don't mind."

"No, I don't. Let's go."

They headed out and he watched as she got the bike

started. Once she was on it, he moved to crank his car, calling, "I'll follow you over."

It was a quick trip, and she moved the motorcycle to the storage place under her building. She stepped out and locked the door behind her.

He was studying the outside of the building. Neighborhoods like SoHo, Greenwich Village, the East Village, and the Lower East Side were developed in the late 19th and early 20th centuries when fire escapes first became ubiquitous in New York. Walk through these neighborhoods and you'd see fire escapes in every color of the rainbow.

She looked up at the building and asked, "Would he have used the fire escape"?

"I don't think he would by himself. Someone helped him."

"Rose," she commented softly.

He nodded. "Yes, I believe so. She'd have to be involved." He finished his sweep and asked, "Can I see the apartment?"

"Of course," she said and led the way.

He commented, "Did you see the flash?" *The camera's flash should have woken her up.*

"Funny you should mention that," she said as she got out her keys to open the multiple locks.

The locks distracted him for a moment, and he asked, "Have you always had that many locks on your door?"

She confirmed, "Yes, my brother and father were firm. I couldn't live here unless it was secure."

"Now you just have to make sure your windows are locked," he teased.

"Yeah," she said, sarcastically.

They walked in and she led him to the kitchen. She opened the icebox and asked, "Coke?"

"That would be nice, thank you."

She handed him one and took hers to the living room. He sat on the settee, facing her chair.

"You mentioned something as we were coming in?"

"It was the flash," she said as she sat back and looked toward the ceiling. "I had been in a deep sleep after Rose and me . . ."

"Had relations?" he supplied.

She smiled, amused and said, "Yes, relations. I don't know what woke me, but I did wake up and found Rose 'dead' beside me."

"What happened next?"

"I don't remember," she said, feeling helpless.

"What was the next thing you do remember?"

"Waking up the next morning—no Rose, no blood, and a headache."

"The headache, what did you drink that night?"

She shook her head. "I've thought about that. I had dinner with my brother; we had wine, but I only had half a glass."

"Where did you go after?"

"To the tearoom, to meet Rose."

"Did you drink anything there?" He knew the tearooms were notorious for drinks other than tea.

"Just one. I finished Rose's beverage, but it was almost empty."

"When was the next time you drank anything?"

"At my apartment, as soon as Rose and I got here."

"What was it?"

"Tea," she supplied. "Actual tea," she quantified.

"Who made it?"

"Rose," she said, getting up to move restlessly around the room. "She wanted to do something special for me."

"Did you drink all of it?"

"I did."

"Did Rose drink hers?"

Emma frowned. "No, I don't think she did. Also, the next morning, there were no dishes to clean up. We had left them there," she said, indicating the sink.

"There was no occasion where she would clean up by herself?"

She gave him a side look and laughed shortly. "You've seen the way she keeps her apartment."

"It may have been a drug. How long did take to affect you?"

"It didn't affect me quickly, I do remember getting up for water, after our ... relations."

His mouth quirked up at her response and he continued, "What did you do next?"

She turned a bit red and said, "We went to bed and to sleep."

"What was your next memory?"

"I woke up twice. The first time, the flash startled me, but I wasn't awake long. When I woke the second time and saw nothing, I thought it was a dream. I discounted it, given there was no evidence."

"Until the pictures arrived?"

"Yes," she confirmed.

"How did you connect Jacko to them?"

"He was seen with Rose, near my apartment and I was able to find his shop based on that information," she explained.

"You think Jacko was who woke you up the first time?"

"I do," she confirmed.

"You probably scared him out of his wits."

"I wasn't up long," she said.

"That must be the reason you're in two different poses in the pictures."

She pulled them out and looked at them. She decided she couldn't be more embarrassed.

He understood and tried to keep his comments clinical as he asked questions. He checked his watch; he had to go on duty that night. "Can I come by tomorrow?"

"I'll have the list ready for you," she confirmed.

He nodded, stood, and said, "Tomorrow, then."

"Yes," she said softly as she watched the large, quiet man leave. She locked the door behind him, and leaned back on it, thinking about that list.

# Chapter Fourteen

A little while later she pulled herself up and made her way to the kitchen, absently getting out bread, ham, and cheese for her dinner. *It's been a long day*, she thought, and she was no closer to finding Rose.

*If she is an active member of the blackmail, why leave the necklace? What's going to be my role in this?* She ate, chewing each piece slowly. Who was in this with Rose? It would have to be someone who knew both sides of her life. Her conservative law life and her bohemian life within the village. The wording of the note also indicated they knew about her family.

*They don't know my family well enough to know that, no matter what, they would support me, even my current lifestyle.* She hadn't told them, but she felt she could at any time.

She laughed; she wasn't the first free-thinking individual in her family. Her aunt never married but her friend Jeremy had lived at the boarding house for Lottie's whole life. Their rooms were next to each other, and she had seen how the bookcase in both rooms opened between the two.

Even though her family would accept her, she didn't want

them to have to deal with the disruptions the news could cause in their lives. She needed to figure out who was behind this scheme. *The list,* she thought, and picked up a notebook from her side table.

Mulling it over, she jotted down everyone in her life since moving to Greenwich. When she finished, she saw the time and noticed it was getting dark. She crossed the room to look out her window and noticed someone standing on the corner. *Who was that?* Squinting, she tried to see more details. A man appeared to be looking up at her. He watched for a long while, then seemed to lose interest and walked away.

She leaned her head against the window frame for a long moment, then straightened. *I need to get out, not stay here and dwell on this.* The first thing she did was go to the kitchen to turn on the stove and heat her hair iron. Next, she headed to her closet and pulled out a dark blue dress with a lace insert. Stockings were next, along with a chemise and lace drawers. Her corset would be different than the one she wore to work. This one was silk and much lighter on her form. Lastly, a light covering to smooth the corset and sat to add her matching shoes.

She moved back to the kitchen and picked up the hot iron, it had to be handled carefully as she twisted the hair around it. It added a nice curl to her face. When she finished, she carefully laid the iron down and went to the mirror in the living room. She dragged the brush through her hair and thought, *What I need is something festive.* Looking through her things, she found a decorative lace band and pinned it around her head. As she finished, she added her makeup, rubbing some rouge into her cheeks and lips.

Rose was involved in this, she was sure. She rarely got tangled up in something she wasn't in control of. *Could any of the ladies in the tearoom be a party to this? I might as well head over there and see what I can find out.*

She went to the dresser and got out her purse. Opening it, she confirmed the small gun was still inside. Clicking it shut, she grabbed her coat and headed downstairs. The tearoom was a few blocks off and could easily be accessed by walking. The way there was through a quiet part of the village and, normally, she didn't expect trouble. She did glance at the corner where she'd seen the man standing. He wasn't there, and she breathed easier.

She strolled down the street, closer to that corner. Slowing as she neared it, she glanced down the alleyways, the shadows suggested sinister activities were taking place. *No alleys tonight.* As she continued, she realized she had picked up a follower. Footsteps echoed behind her; she sped up and ducked into a nearby doorway; her hand on the gun in her purse. The steps got closer and a shadow could be seen first, it continued past her and she sank back until the form was illuminated by the streetlight.

"Frank!"

He started at hearing his name and looked over at the doorway where she was standing.

"What are you doing?" she asked, her voice going hard.

"I was in the neighborhood," he said.

"Just walking by a quiet street?" she paused, thinking. She looked at him sharply and demanded, "Was it you I saw on the corner?"

"Why?" he asked, not answering her question.

"Just answer the question."

He gave her a long, steady look and asked, "What time was this?"

"About 8:00 pm."

"I was at the station until 8:30 pm. I can give you a name to call and check up on me." When she didn't answer, he said quietly, "Lottie, it wasn't me."

"Okay, not you," she said haltingly and let her grip on the gun go loose. She was having a hard time knowing who to trust, but she felt this man was on her side.

"Thank you for believing me." He thought of something and said, "Hey, if you saw someone and thought they were following you, why are you out?"

"I won't be controlled by anyone, especially whoever is involved in these shenanigans," she said closing her purse back with a snap.

He admired her nerve but had to ask, "What if I had bad intentions?"

"I know how to protect myself," she said confidently.

"You do? What can you do?"

"Self-defense. I know some nasty moves to make a person back off."

"Really?" He laughed.

"Yes, would you like me to demonstrate?" she said, stepping toward him.

"What? No, that's okay." He grinned, putting his hands up. "Who taught you?" he asked.

"My aunt," she said, not mentioning her name. Aunt Emma was rather famous in law enforcement circles.

"Hmm," he said, not doubting her words. "Well, how about I accompany you? Where are you headed?

"To the tearoom," she said. "I don't need the protection, but the company would be nice."

Frank offered her his elbow; she took it, and they started off together.

"Why are you in the area, if you're not stalking me?" she teased.

He sent her a side glance. "I am looking into the different

bars in the areas. Tonight, I will be at McSorley's. Do you know it?"

"I've been there," she acknowledged.

"You have?" He looked surprised. That bar is rough.

"Yes, I didn't like it much. The crowd was more than I could handle."

As they got closer to the tearoom, he said, "I'll have to leave you here. I'm expected back soon."

"It was nice to see you. Thank you for accompanying me," she said.

"Any time," he murmured as he watched her turn and walked to the entrance of the tearoom.

Once she opened the door, she looked around for Hen and spotted Lily. The woman was frowning heavily at her. Lottie recognized that look; she'd had the same one when she found out Rose was sleeping with other women. Patience would be required on her part. She knew what was about to take place.

Lily marched up to her and put her face inches from Lottie's. "Where's Rose?" she demanded. "Were you with her?"

"No, Lily," Lottie said quietly. "I haven't seen her today." That was the truth; there was no reason to remind her she had been with her the night before.

"Your lying!" she screamed.

Lottie stood her ground and said, "Why do you think that?" All conversation had stopped in the room and the two of them were the center of attention. She took Lily by the arm and moved them to a corner.

Lily shook out of Lottie's hold and said, "I was supposed to meet her this morning and she didn't show up."

"That doesn't mean I was with her," Lottie reasoned.

Lily looked confused about what to do next. When she finally made her decision, she went for Lottie with her claws drawn, like a cat. Given Lily's unstable nature, Lottie had expected this and used the side of her hand to hit her in the neck.

Lily went down like a rock, gasping. "You bitch."

"Yeah." She completely disregarded her and walked over to where Hen was sitting.

The ladies let Lily pull herself up; they didn't offer her any help. They weren't there to mother this girl. If she was going to make it in the Village, she had to be able to take care of herself.

Hen was laughing as Lottie moved to her table. "What's funny?" she asked, sitting down across from her.

"You. One and a half years ago, that was you," Hen pointed out.

"I don't think I attacked anyone," she said thoughtfully.

"No, but you realized, rather abruptly, that Rose likes options. Lily hasn't figured that out yet."

"She's so young," she said, watching Lily move to a nearby table to sit by herself.

"Really no younger than you," said Hen.

"Really?"

"She's just not mature. If she wants to be a part of this community, she'll develop a tougher skin." Hen looked around and asked, "Did you find Rose? It isn't like her to miss a Saturday night or a willing young woman."

"No, no, it isn't," she said, looking down.

"Is there something you need to tell me? Something you've found out?" she asked. She knew Lottie so well.

"Maybe later," Lottie suggested. "Why not enjoy the evening and talk about other things?"

She shrugged. "Sure."

"What about you? Have you found something to do that the judge will approve of?"

Hen sat forward, looking earnest, and said, "I'm working on something. I'll let you know soon."

"Remember, we have to report to the court in another week."

"I will have something figured out soon," she promised.

Lottie took a moment to look around at the familiar faces and asked, "Hen, how many people know I'm a lawyer?"

"Out of these ladies?" she asked, also looking around.

"Yes," Lottie said simply.

Hen took a moment to consider. "The table over there—the suffragettes—they know because of me." She looked around and said, "You've done law work for many people here. I think nearly everyone knows about your work."

*That doesn't limit the list,* Lottie thought.

"Does this involve Rose being gone?" Hen asked in a low voice.

"It might," she admitted in a similar tone.

That comment made Hen go silent, she studied Lottie for a long moment and suggested, "Can you come by tomorrow? My Danny's good with puzzles."

"That might be the thing." She looked up and saw a server and asked, "Can I get some hard tea?"

"Sure, gin or vodka?" the server asked.

"Gin, please," Lottie responded.

Hen raised her eyebrows at her. "You don't normally drink gin."

"Today has not been normal. I'd like some tonight."

Hen watched her closely and decided she would stay and make sure Lottie got home safely. *There has to be more to this than just Rose being gone,* she thought. Rose was notorious for going away for a few days and turning up with a new dress or a new girl. She tended to be careless with both. Hen would be patient and wait for Lottie to tell her what was troubling her.

Lottie drank the first cup and immediately ordered a second. Hen watched and didn't stop her; she needed to make her own mistakes. As the evening wore on, Lottie started to lean over in her chair. She tried to set her cup down and would have missed had Hen not taken it from her.

"I think I'd like to go home now," said Lottie, slurring her words.

"I should think so," murmured Hen. As she watched Lottie struggle to her feet, she grabbed her and Lottie's purses and put them under her arm.

Hen almost laughed; Lottie wasn't aware that she walked several times toward a wall before eventually finding the door. She shook her head and headed forward to escort Lottie home. Catching up with her outside, she found her leaning on a man Hen didn't recognize.

"Hey, stop that! She's in no condition for that type of thing!" Hen said rather indignantly.

Frank looked up and said, "Got into her cups, right?"

"I know him," Lottie slurred. "He's helping with Rose."

"Well, that's fine, but you don't need to be with him tonight," commented Hen, concerned for her safety.

"I'm fine," Lottie slurred. "I'm just..." She trailed off and made a distressed sound, glancing around quickly.

"Back up," Frank said to Hen. She backed up as he helped Lottie bend at the waist to throw up. When she finally stopped, Frank wiped her mouth with his hand-kerchief.

She leaned on him and said, "I don't feel well."

"No, I don't think you do," agreed Hen.

"Why don't I help you get her home?" suggested Frank.

Hen looked him over, unsure she should take him up on his offer of help.

He saw the look and pulled his badge.

"I'm not sure that is a positive thing," said Hen, thinking of the current corruption on the front pages of the newspapers.

She decided to trust him and said, "You take one arm, and I'll take the other."

After they started walking, Frank looked at her over Lottie's head.

"I'm Frank Griffin."

"I'm Henrietta Landry," she replied.

"Is this a normal Saturday activity for her?" he asked.

"No," she said thoughtfully. "She's normally reserved." *Is this Rose or something else?*

They got Lottie up to her apartment and leaned her against the wall. Hen looked over at Frank and said in a firm voice, "I think we have it from here."

He took the hint. "Okay. I need to head back to work." He looked at Lottie, tilted his hat, and said, "Good evening."

Lotte raised her head. "Thank you."

He looked at both of them before going back down the stairs.

Hen eyed Lottie and said, "We need to get you inside and into the bath."

Lottie leaned back against the door, waiting for the world to settle. "Thank you, Hen."

"You've been there for me more times than I can count. You looked like you needed to blow off some steam tonight," she said using Lottie's keys to open the multiple locks.

"I did," Lottie commented. The color drained out of her face and her eyes widened. "Hen! I think I need to get in NOW!"

Hen got the final lock opened, rushed her through the door, and ran with her to the bathroom. They got into the room and over to the toilet. Lottie hesitated, then said slowly, "No, I think I'm okay."

Hen didn't trust her, but cleaning up would be easier in here. "Then into the bath with you." She turned on the bathwater and, while it filled, helped her undress. She moved the dress to the sink.

"Did I ruin it?" Lottie asked, slumping to the floor beside the tub.

Hen looked down at it and said, "No, I'll take a wet cloth to it. It should be fine." She laid the dress down on the sink. She went back over to Lottie and pushed Lottie's hair off her forehead. "I'm glad your hair's short."

Once the tub was half full, she pulled Lottie up and helped her step in. Once she was settled, Hen said, "I need to go make you some coffee and I need to step into the hall to call Danny. Will you be okay?"

"Yes." She sank back and let her hair get wet. "Another reminder of Rose," commented Lottie as Hen was leaving the room.

Hen hmphed as she was leaving.

Lottie laid her head back and thought about that day.

———

### *1 year and a half ago—Rose*

She had been so excited that morning; walking and enjoying the lovely spring day. Her long hair pulled into a ponytail, bounced on her back as she walked. Reaching up, she brushed an errant strand off her forehead, thinking only about Rose. The scent of flowers stopped her. She turned to the small flower shop and thought, *A bundle of flowers would be beautiful in Rose's apartment.* She stepped closer to the shop, picked one bunch up, and breathed them in.

"Would you like those?" a small woman stooped over with age asked from the doorway.

"I would," Lottie said, giving her a great smile.

"They are lovely. For someone special?" the woman asked

curiously, slowly making her way over. She thought the village girls were interesting, and she had fun watching them.

"Yes," Lottie said softly, fingering the petals. She paid and carried them with her. Rose was who she spent all of her time with. All she could think about was Rose and being in love for the first time in her life. Everything about her new life in New York was working out for her—a new job and a new relationship.

She thought dreamily about how they'd met. It was her first time in the tearoom. She went in with Hen and stood in the doorway, looking around.

———

### Meeting Rose for the first time

Hen and Lottie entered the tearoom. Immediately a lovely woman with short, wavy chestnut hair and a rounded figure caught Lottie's interest. The woman called over and said, "Won't you sit down?"

Lottie looked around and saw Hen already engaged in an animated discussion with a group of ladies.

She walked over and said, "That would be nice." She sat, watching this woman and wondering about her.

"My name is Rose," the woman said leaning over, running her fingers through Lottie's hair and down her face to her chest, stopping just above her cleavage. "What's your name?"

Lottie had felt physical attraction before this, but now she couldn't catch her breath. "Lottie," she said. She didn't know why she did it, but she leaned forward and kissed Rose softly.

"My," Rose said. "We will have to get to know each other." Rose was very beautiful, and Lottie just stared at her rounded body and breasts pushing out the top of her dress. Lottie was fascinated, her eyes soaking up every curve.

Lottie placed her hat on the table and said, "That would be nice."

Rose asked, "Have you ever been with a woman?"

"No," she said haltingly.

"Would you like to?" she said, quickly getting to the point.

Lottie didn't think. She responded based on what she was feeling, "I would, but I'd also like to get to know you."

"I think we can arrange that," Rose said as she sat back in her chair. She seemed to come to a decision. "Can I escort you home?"

Lottie was feeling the same way, though she thought it was fast. Maybe it should happen that way. She nodded and softly said, "Yes. Let me tell Henrietta we're heading out."

"Why don't you do that and meet me outside?" she suggested softly.

She nodded and went to where Henrietta was standing; Lottie leaned toward her and said, "I'm leaving."

Hen turned, looking contrite, and said, "I'm sorry, did I leave you alone for too long?"

"No. I just met someone I'd like to spend some time with."

Henrietta looked from her to the door, where Rose waited. She squinted and said, "Careful with that one. She's volatile."

"I just can't help myself."

Henrietta nodded. "Okay, have fun. Talk to me tomorrow."

"I will," Lottie murmured and headed out to join Rose. When they stepped out of the tea room, Rose held out her hand and Lottie took it. They walked along for a block when Rose pushed her against a wall and kissed her deeply, grinding her hips into hers; she put her face in her cleavage, licking it lightly. Lottie let out a small moan.

Rose looked satisfied at the response and said as she pulled back, "Where do you live?"

Lottie's legs felt like jelly, and she had to make herself talk.

"Just up here to the right, second floor," she said, indicating the brick apartments a block down.

They entered Lottie's apartment, staying close together. Rose took the lead and turned Lottie into her arms, continuing to give her long, drugging kisses.

Lottie tried to mimic Rose's moves. When she started to undress her, Lottie did the same to Rose. It felt natural to Lottie to see her without her clothes. Rose ran her hands slowly down her chest, rubbing her nipples lightly at first and then more roughly. With one hand still on her nipples, she moved the other one between Lottie's legs. Lottie almost collapsed with all the sensation running over her body.

Rose moved them to the bed and bent her over with Lottie's feet still on the floor. Her mouth went to her nipples, sucking lightly at first, then strongly. At the same time, she moved her fingers lightly between Lottie's thighs. Lottie felt her body swelling in response as Rose moved to the other breast.

Lottie started to respond and rubbed Rose's breasts, enjoying the rounded curves and femininity

When Rose first penetrated her with one finger, then two, Lottie bucked back on the bed, lost in the response. She'd had sex before, but those experiences were nothing like this one.

She felt Rose's fingers between her legs. She felt Rose's lips slide down to where her fingers were located. When her mouth moved to the same place, Lottie felt like her body exploded from the inside out.

Rose moved up to kiss her and placed the heel of her hand on her femininity. It felt so lovely, that pressure.

Lottie moved her hand down to help and rubbed the hand rubbing her. Rose moved them to their side and moved Lottie's hand between her legs. Lottie rubbed Rose's swollen flesh and penetrated with her fingers. Rose responded with a strong shutter as she peaked. Lottie leaned over and licked her nipples. She rubbed her breasts against hers and slid her lips to give her the same treatment. Her moans showed she had been successful in getting her to orgasm.

She kept her fingers there, rubbing and stroking as she moved further up her body to her mouth.

Rose responded in kind as they lay breast to breast.

Small orgasms ricocheted through her body as they lay there, touching each other.

Rose pressed her forehead against Lottie's. "Wow. Your first time?"

"I'm a fast study," she murmured.

"Yes, you are. I'll want to spend a lot of time with you."

"I feel the same."

The next few weeks kept Lottie in a sexual haze. They didn't leave Rose's apartment much and spent time getting to know each other. She thought it would last forever.

---

### On the way to Rose's apartment

Lottie continued to Rose's, smelling the flowers in her hand. Tomorrow would be her first day of employment at Justice Goff's office. Life was working out; she was so happy. She fairly floated as she made her way into Rose's building. Her good mood continued as she climbed the stairs quickly.

Trying the knob, she wasn't surprised to find it open. Rose hardly ever locked her door, and Lottie wanted to surprise her. The knob turned easily she pushed it open and walked in quietly. She took the flowers to the kitchen, found a vase, and moved them to the living room. The bedroom door was closed; *she must be in there.* Before she entered, she pulled out her hairband, fluffed her hair, and pushed it open.

What she saw made her freeze, as she took in the scene in

front of her. Rose was with another woman. The woman's face was buried between Rose's breasts, and they were both nude.

*Crash!*

Lottie stared down at the vase, now shattered on the floor. She looked up again. The scene had not changed. As she turned to leave, Rose yelled at her, "Lottie!" She pushed at the girl on top of her and said, "Get off me, you cow!"

Lottie didn't hear her; she was crying and running down the stairs. She slipped down several steps, grabbed the rail to steady herself, and exited the front door out of the building. Rose was close behind and had stopped only to grab a robe. She grabbed Lottie by the arm, swinging her around. "That didn't mean anything."

"No?" Lottie asked, sniffing, she met her gaze. "I find that very sad, for her and you."

"You weren't here," Rose said defensively.

Lottie's laughter had a shrill tone. "Really, this is my fault?"

"Yes, if you were here, this wouldn't have happened. If you hadn't gone to work..."

Lottie thought about other times she had been away. "What about a few weeks ago when I went to Buffalo to pick up some papers?" she asked suspiciously. "What about then?"

Rose turned away from her and didn't answer.

Lottie stopped being hurt and started being angry. "Look at me!"

The tone in her voice forced Rose to turn back to her.

"Yes, you cheated then also," Lottie said, taking in her silence. She gave her a look that took in Rose's lack of clothes. "I think you might want to go in. That's a bit much, even in the village."

Rose angrily pulled her robe together and glared at the other woman before stomping back into her building.

Lottie walked slowly back to her apartment and allowed

the tears to fall. She dashed them away and thought, *I'm so independent. I can sleep with women and men and not care. What a laugh! I want something steady, someone who only has eyes for me. And that isn't Rose.*

Had she known Rose was sleeping with other women? She didn't think so, but she was so wrapped up in her, almost anything could pass her by. Continuing to walk home, she tried to stop crying. She was nearly successful until she saw Henrietta had come up behind her on the stairs.

"I saw you pass the bookstore. You look upset. What happened? Are you okay?" Henrietta asked, concerned for her friend.

"Me?" she asked, and the tears fell harder.

Henrietta took her in her arms. "Why don't we go in?"

Lottie fumbled with the keys and finally got them into the multiple locks. They went in, with Henrietta supporting a still crying Lottie.

Hen guided her to a chair.

"Sit down, let me get you some water." She went to the kitchen and came back quickly with a glass. "Now, drink this and tell me what happened."

Lottie took a long drink, put her head back on the chair, and said simply, "Rose."

"Did something happen to her?" Hen asked, concerned.

"No," she said. "Nothing happens to Rose that she doesn't want to happen."

"So, what occurred?"

"I found her with someone else."

Henrietta frowned and said, "Oh." She sat down across from Lottie. "Did you think you were exclusive?"

"I was. I guess I thought she was also."

Hen shook her head regretfully and said, "I should have warned you, but you were so happy. Rose takes an

118

initial interest and then moves on to the next girl." She stood up and walked around, thinking. She came to a conclusion and asked, "Lottie, what are you doing tonight?"

"What do you mean?" she said, wiping her face. "I'm staying here."

"Crying and feeling sorry for yourself?" she asked.

"Yes," she said stiffly.

"No, you're not." She went to the freezer and got out some ice. She placed them in a cloth and brought them to her. "Put this on your eyes. You are going out tonight."

"Out?" Lottie asked, doing as she was told. "Why would I do that?"

Hen said determinedly, "Because Rose will be there. She'll be with another woman, and you want to show her this didn't affect you."

"But why would I do that? Why the games?" She could hear the whining tone in her voice, but she couldn't seem to stop it.

"Lottie," Hen said as she bent down and cupped her face with her hands. "You're going to have to toughen up if you want to live here. Not everyone is going to be your friend and not every relationship will last forever."

"You found Danny here," Lottie reminded her.

"Yes, I did, but I was lucky. Did you think it would be that easy?" she asked, dropping her hands and placing them on her legs.

Lottie squinted. "You and Danny met and were married within two weeks."

She smiled slightly and said, "I forget how young you are, Lottie. Danny and I didn't know each other at all when we got married. We fought constantly because of that."

"I didn't know."

"No, I kept it between us. We also were on the same page and wanted to stay married."

"I haven't found someone like that for me," she said tugging at her hair and frowning.

Hen nodded and said, "I'm glad you realize that." She stepped back and looked at her consideringly. "You know what? You need a change."

"What kind of change?"

"Your hair," she said decisively.

"My hair," Lottie said weakly, raising her hand to it. "What do you want to do with it?" Was it too much to hope that she wanted to put it up?

"You'll see," Hen said and walked out to the kitchen, returning with scissors.

Lotte saw what she was carrying and said weakly, "I'm just going to close my eyes."

Hen laughed. "You do that."

She started working on Lottie's hair; Lottie jumped as she felt the strands hitting her legs. Trying to relax, she listened to the other woman humming and the scissors snapping.

"Just a second, don't open your eyes," Hen said as she hurried off.

Lottie peeked down and saw piles of her hair on the floor. She quickly shut her eyes tight and waited. Hen's shoes clicked and a brush was pulled through her hair.

Hen said, "Open your eyes." She handed Lottie a mirror.

Lottie looked, expecting the worst, and saw the shorter style looked shiny and had a bounce to it. She ran a hand through it, not saying anything.

Hen watched her and, for the first time, got nervous. "Do you like it?"

Lottie turned suddenly and hugged her. "I love it."

"I'm so glad," she sighed, relieved.

"But what about work? I don't think this will be acceptable."

"I'll make you a hairpiece for the office," she said decisively.

———

### Present-day—bathroom

Lottie sat up slowly, trying to determine if she could wash herself. *Soap, I can handle,* she thought. Reaching for it, she scrubbed herself clean and drained the water. Once the tub was empty, she turned the water back on to wash her hair.

Hen came in as she was finishing and said, "You had more energy than I expected. Let me help you out." Lottie stepped out and Hen handed her a large towel to dry off.

"Sit down," she directed.

Lottie secured the towel around her and sat on the small stool while Hen took a smaller towel to dry her hair. She rubbed her scalp as gently as possible and threw it on the sink.

"You're not planning on cutting my hair again, are you?" Lottie asked, her tone droll.

Hen smiled slightly at the question. "Brush your teeth, put on your night clothes and I'll move you to the bed."

Hen stayed in case she was needed. When her friend had finished, Hen walked her to bed, pulled back the covers, and helped her climb in. The coffee was on her side table. Hen reached over to hand it to her, watching her take a sip.

"Thank you," Lottie said gratefully, resting back against her headboard.

Hen studied her for a long time. She finally said, "I know you say it's casual with Rose, but this is the second time you've gone to pieces because of her."

"I didn't go to pieces," she defended. "I just blew off some steam."

"Really?" Hen waited a long moment. "I'll let that one go."

"Thank you," she muttered.

"I'd like you to take some advice and step back from this relationship. It's toxic."

"I don't know what you are talking about..." Lottie wished she could get out of this conversation.

Hen gave her that look again; she knew her friend. "You know exactly what I'm talking about. You always rebound back to her."

"I was serious about Joseph..." Lottie insisted, thinking about the breakup. And then their final day.

———

## *Joseph*

"Leaving? What do you mean?" Lottie asked, starting to cry. "I thought we were going to live here. Get married."

"Lottie, you know my father's ill. I have to go home to take over the business."

"No, I don't understand. Why can't I come with you?"

They had been living together for a year.

Joseph looked over at her and said, "As soon as I'm settled, I'll send for you."

"You will?" she asked, having hope for the first time.

He tilted her chin and kissed her softly. "Of course, I will."

Lottie started rubbing against him and said, "Do you want to one last time before you leave?"

He looked at his packing and said, "Regretfully, I need to get this organized."

Cold air blew over her as she stood there, stunned. He had never turned down sex with her before this.

He left, and the days turned into months. There hadn't

been any communication between them but Lottie waited for him. She had not seen anyone in that time, not even casually.

Hen saw Lottie come into the tearoom and called her over. The conversation was mostly coming from Hen. She finally asked, "Are you still preoccupied with Joseph?"

"I need to find out if he's okay," Lottie said.

Hen frowned. "Do you think he's being held against his will?"

"I think he might be," she admitted. "He promised he would send for me and he hasn't."

"Why not do the romantic thing and go rescue him?" suggested Hen, loving the drama of the idea.

"Me?"

"Yes, you. You're a smart, brave lady. Let him know your true feelings."

"I'll do that," she said decisively and left the tearoom to head home.

"Hen," called Rose as she watched Lottie leave. "What was that about?"

She told her.

"Hmm," said Rose. That relationship with Joseph had gone on far longer than she'd expected. *Considering this development*, she thought, *it looks like I'm going to be able to start spending time with Lottie again.* She smiled broadly and headed back to her table.

"What are you so happy about?" asked the other woman at the table. She was not happy that Rose's attention wavered from her.

"Nothing at all, Daisy dear. Where were we?" Rose reached over and placed her hand between the other woman's legs. "Here, I believe."

"Now I remember," Daisy sighed as Rose leaned over to

insert her fingers into her and kiss her deeply, swallowing her moan.

―――――

**Present-day**

"And then you went back to Rose when that imploded. You do understand Rose doesn't have it in her to have a monogamous relationship. I also don't like how she treats you like a possession," Henrietta said.

"I know I'm being manipulated, and I can't seem to find my way out."

"What about this game you mentioned?"

"It is bigger than that now," she muttered.

"Can you tell me more?" Hen asked, concerned.

"Right know I can tell you she isn't around.

She didn't remind her that Rose had been gone without notice before this. Instead, she asked, "What are your plans?"

"I'm going to look into a few more things, I am concerned she can't be located. I'm also planning to stop there if I don't find anything."

"I'm glad," Hen said simply.

"Thanks for looking out for me."

"We look out for each other. Now, drink your coffee," she directed.

Lottie sipped, looked at Hen, and said, "You'll make a good mom."

"Well, that's good to know," her friend said, rubbing her tummy.

Lottie sat up abruptly, jostling her coffee. "Hen, are you...?" She let the question hang in the air.

"I am," she confirmed. "I'd planned to tell you tonight."

Lottie moved her cup to the nightstand and grabbed the other woman's hands.

"Oh, Hen, I ruined your surprise. I am so sorry." Tears welled up in her eyes and threatened to spill over.

"Now, nothing to be worried about. You need to lie back and try to sleep this off," she said, tucking the covers around her. "After that, plan on coming to our place tomorrow, no later than 1:30 pm. I need to hear all the facts. You're my family and we take care of one another."

"Yes, Mom," Lottie mocked lightly.

"That's right. Mom," she said consideringly as she left. "I'll lock the door on the way out." She exited quickly, wanting to share the evening's events with Danny.

Lottie decided sleep was better than dwelling on the last few days. She laid back and let herself relax.

# Chapter Fifteen

The pounding in her head woke Lottie up. She held her head in her hands and thought, *This is similar to how I felt the morning Rose went missing.* Continuing to hold it, she got out of bed to locate some aspirin in the bathroom. When she reached to open her cabinet, she saw her wrinkled fingertips. *Dehydrated—water first, then a bath.* She filled a tall glass and drank it with some aspirin.

She stood for a moment, trying to decide if it was going to stay down. When the water didn't come back up, she breathed deeply. *What time is it?* she thought blearily, pulling on her robe. She remembered what Hen had said about a baby. Some good had come out of last night.

She moved to the sink to set the glass down and her eyes found the clock. They widened abruptly. *1:00 pm? Oh, I'm so late!* Hen wanted her at her place by 1:30 pm

Lottie made her way to the bathroom, turned on the water, and watched as it filled the tub. Bathing quickly, she dried off, wrapped herself in a towel, and made her way to the kitchen. She opened the refrigerator, took out some ice, and wrapped a kitchen towel around it. Placing it on her neck, she sat down for a few minutes. The ice helped with her headache, and she was able to get up from the table and move into the living room. A knock on the door caused her to start.

She walked over, still holding the ice to her head, and asked, "Who is it?

"It's Frank," he called through the door.

Frank!

"I'm here to pick you up. Hen and Danny are expecting us."

"Did we have plans?" she asked, leaning on the door. She was having trouble remembering the conversation from last night.

"Why not open the door? I'd rather not yell the rest of this conversation," he said, looking down the hallway to the strange little man who stuck his head out to see what the ruckus was about.

"Okay." Lottie started to open the door, then stopped abruptly when she looked down and realized she wasn't dressed. "Frank, I'm going to unlock it but wait until I call for you to come in."

"All right."

He waited until he heard her call and reached out to open it. As he walked in, he noticed her apartment had a warm, comfortable look to it. *And*, he thought dryly, *it's also very neat, unlike Rose's place.*

He called out, "Feeling better, I hope?"

"I am," she answered.

"Do you do that often?"

"What?" she asked, sticking her head out of the bedroom. "Drink?"

"No." He smiled. "Drink to excess."

"No, not usually, but it's been a stressful few days." She

finished dressing, then walked out. "How did you end up invited to Danny and Hen's today?"

"That's a funny story," he commented.

Lottie looked at him quizzically.

"Henrietta must have called every precinct in the area to find me."

That made her laugh out loud. "That's Hen. Once she wants something, nothing will stop her."

"That's what I thought."

He wasn't angry at being tracked down, especially not when he got to see Lottie again. He walked around the apartment as he waited for her to get organized, looking at her art. Pointing to one vibrant picture, he said, "This is wonderful. Where did you get it?"

She walked over, sliding on her long coat and pulling her brush through her hair. She nodded at the picture and said, "That's a fee a local paid for some legal services."

He raised his eyebrow at that statement.

"We use a barter system when money isn't an option," she explained.

"Hmm." He looked around and observed, "By the looks of this place, you look like you do all right."

Lottie laughed again, thinking she liked how she felt around this man. "I do okay, but this apartment is because of my family. Originally, I showed them the artist studio I had picked out and Papa said a firm no."

"Were they upset you wanted to move so far away from them?"

"More concerned, I would say," she said, thinking of that time just before moving to New York.

———

## Chicago 1910

Lottie sat on her bed reading. She heard a knock on the door. "Come in," she called. The door opened and she saw it was her aunt Emma.

Emma entered and sat on the bed. She looked concerned about something.

"Lottie, I hear you want to move to New York, specifically Greenwich Village."

"I do," she commented warily, wondering if Mama had sent her to talk her into staying in Chicago.

Emma took a deep breath and began, "You know I was there a few months ago."

"Yes."

"The investigation I was involved in, the missing girl? Dorothy Arnold."

"I remember that one."

She reminded her of the facts of the case, "She was similar to you Lottie, college-educated, wanting to see more of the world, out on her own for the first time."

"And she disappeared," Lottie finished for her.

"Yes," Emma said. She was sad they hadn't found any leads.

"That won't happen to me. I won't take any unnecessary chances. And you taught me how to get away from such a situation." Emma had a few nasty tricks that would allow her to incapacitate any attacker.

"Yes, that's true. I'll still worry."

"Henrietta's there. She's married and doing well." *Except for the arrest*, thought Lottie ruefully.

"Your father and Patrick are helping you pick a location to live?"

"They are," she confirmed.

She mulled that over. "All right, but if you ever need anything, don't hesitate to call me."

Emma started to get up, but Lottie stopped her. "There is one thing I would like to discuss with you."

"With me and not your mama?"

"No." She chuckled. "Not this topic. I don't think Mama would approve."

Emma looked intrigued and sat back down on the bed.

Lottie blurted out, "Sex. How do I protect myself from getting pregnant?"

Emma was at a loss; her generation hadn't spoken so openly about this. She'd had similar questions, at an age younger than Lottie was now, but she'd had a friend she could go to.

"There are ways," she said thoughtfully. "The one method I found that worked for me was honey and herbs to prevent pregnancy." She explained how to use it. "Am I to understand that you've had some experience already?"

Lottie wasn't embarrassed and said, "Yes."

"Then I don't need to explain how all of this works," Emma stated, somewhat relieved.

"No." Lottie laughed. "We figured it out together."

"He wasn't someone you could see yourself with long-term?"

"No, it wasn't that. I just wanted to experience other things."

Emma didn't delve too far into what that meant.

They talked quietly into the late afternoon.

Lottie spent the rest of the week getting organized. One bag and two trunks would be taken. One of these was packed with clothes and one heavy with her law books.

Papa, Lottie, and Patrick made the trip to New York together. They toured the first apartments that Henrietta and

Lottie had found. Papa turned down each one. One was not safe; another no water; still another, no steam.

"Papa, you're looking for a perfect place," Lottie protested.

"No. I'm looking for a place you can call home. If that home doesn't have basic needs, we agreed you'd come back with us," he said firmly.

Lottie sighed. "Okay, Papa." She looked down at the list of rooms and apartments she wanted to show him.

He was patient with the next few, taking a look at the one-room locations, and said, "These won't do. What else is on your list?"

"Well, more of the single rooms and a few two bedrooms," Lottie admitted.

"Let me see the paper," he said, holding out his hand expectantly.

She handed it to him and watched as he reviewed it.

He focused on the listings with two bedrooms. "We'll go see these," he said decisively.

They were in the area she wanted to live in, so she couldn't complain about the location. The rent was also reasonable. They entered and found high ceilings, a smallish kitchen, a living room, and two bedrooms.

"You can use one as an office," said Papa as he exited one of the bedrooms. "And we can add a bed for when we visit."

"That would be lovely, Papa," she said sincerely, running over to see the room he mentioned.

After looking around and testing everything that could be tested, Papa rubbed his hands together. "Now, let me find that manager and work this out."

The paperwork was signed and some small repairs promised to be completed before she would move in. Papa walked around and looked at the walls. He turned a contemplative look at Lottie and Patrick and said, "We need to paint first."

"Agreed," they responded at the same time. They laughed and went out to get the paint and supplies.

They spent the next few days getting the rooms ready. They decided not to paint the floors. Lottie liked the original wood. They added a rug, beds, and other furniture they found at a local antique dealer. The mattresses were bought new. Mama had sent everything to outfit the kitchen.

When they were finished, they stood in the doorway and Lottie said, "It looks like home."

Patrick made his way to the sofa and sat. "I'll have to visit soon. This turned out nice."

"You're welcome any time," she said sincerely.

———

### Present-day

Frank laughed; he had seen some of those rooms, often rented by the week. "I understand why your father said that. Those are barely livable."

"Yes," she said. "Papa was right. Lawyers don't need to be miserable to achieve success."

He gave her a long look and nodded.

"Ready?" she asked, grabbing her shoulder bag and jacket. "Do you know where we're going?"

"Henrietta mentioned a bookstore about a block from here."

"They live above it," she confirmed and held the door for him to exit. "Shall we go?"

She locked the door and turned toward him. Frank offered her his elbow and she took it as they descended the stairs. They exited onto the street; the weather was warm and she opened her jacket to get some air.

She looked over at him and warned, "Hen will want to know everything that's happening."

"Do you want to share everything?" he asked, willing to limit the information if she asked him.

"Yes," she said quietly. "They're my family."

He nodded, understanding.

It was a short walk to the store; Lottie saw the closed sign in the window. She peered through the glass and knocked lightly.

Hen was waiting for them and came to the door quickly. "Come in," she said, swinging the door wide. "Head on up. Danny's waiting on you." She locked the door behind them and followed them to the back of the store and up the stairs.

The door to the second floor was open and they went in.

Lottie called out, "Danny!"

He came in from the kitchen, carrying a tray of cakes. Looking toward Lottie, he said, "If you want to get the tea, it's ready in the kitchen."

She headed that way and commented over her shoulder, "I will. Danny, this is Frank Griffin."

She heard Frank and Danny exchange pleasantries as she gathered up the teapot and cups. Placing them on the waiting tray, she carried them back out to the living room.

Hen came up and set down a few books she was carrying. She directed everyone, "Let's sit."

Danny moved close to the low table that held the tea and cakes. "Tea?" he asked everyone.

"Yes, please," said Frank.

"And me, also," said Lottie.

Before she handed out the cake, Hen gave Lottie a long look and asked, "Are you up to eating?"

She nodded, understanding she was asking how she was feeling. "Hen, don't worry. I'm fine and I would love some cake."

Hen handed it to her and asked, "How's your head?"

She took the cup and grimaced slightly, reaching up to touch it. "It's better. I put some ice on it this morning." She paused and looked at her and then Frank. "Thank you both for the help last night. I was not myself."

Danny smiled suddenly. "Hen was happy she could be there to help."

"You've always done so much for me. It was nice to be the one helping this time," Hen said.

Frank waited for them to finish before commenting, "I didn't do much."

Lottie touched his hand and smiled softly. Hen saw the move and wondered about this man. *Who is he to Lottie?* Continuing to watch them, she handed out the small plates to Frank and Danny, taking one for herself.

Lottie looked at Frank. "Hen has been close family from when I was a baby. She moved in with us when she was about twelve. She is the reason I looked at law as a career."

Frank asked, "Now, why would that have been?"

Lottie looked at Hen, then back at Frank. "You don't recognize Hen's name?"

"No, I'm sorry, I don't think so." Frank frowned, looking at Hen.

Danny sat back and said, "Have you read anything about child labor laws?"

Something clicked and he sat forward. "But that was Henrietta Lawson."

Hen said, "That is my maiden name."

Frank was very impressed; this was a brave woman. "The law changed with your efforts. Children's lives were made better. Do you stay involved in the same things here?"

Hen's cheeks went red. "Yes."

Danny and Lottie laughed. Lottie answered for them, "Yes,

she's still involved." She glanced at her friend, and a thought raced across her mind. "Oh, Hen, did you do what the court asked you to do? I'm sorry I haven't followed up."

Danny spoke up and said proudly, "She's going to start teaching at the village school."

"Hen, that's perfect!" Lottie exclaimed. *That will also keep her out of trouble for a while*, Lottie thought to herself.

Hen went to the desk set up in the corner of the room. She opened a drawer, pulled out a file, then returned to the group and handed it to Lottie. "This is the paperwork."

Lottie read through it quickly, looked up, and said, "Great. I'll see if the judge can approve this without another court date."

"Thank you."

"Hen, I'm very happy you're doing this."

"It's the right time," she said, looking at Danny. He held out his hand to her, she took it and held it for a long moment.

Frank looked on, aware he was missing something, but he let it pass.

"That's enough about me," said Hen abruptly, directing the conversation toward Lottie and Frank. "Tell me the situation with Rose." She turned her steady gaze to Frank and said, "Danny and I are aware that she is gone."

Dropping back against the settee, Lottie sighed. "I'm honestly confused," she said, sounding defeated. She told them about the pictures, threats and the fact of Rose's involvement.

"She IS this isn't she? She's always working an angle," Hen said, pounding her fist on the arm of her chair.

"I think she may have been initially. What bothers me is the necklace. I took it as a clue that she needed help. Though with all the other facts we have now, I'm not sure what her role in this is," Lottie said.

Danny took off his glasses and began to clean them when

he inquired, "You indicated you also received a note with the photos?"

"Yes, I have it here," Lottie said, pulling it out of her bag.

"Can I see it?" he asked, putting his glasses back on.

"Of course," she said and handed it to him.

Lottie said to Hen, Frank had seen the note the previous day, "It threatens to send the photos to my family and my place of business if I didn't follow their direction."

Hen looked nonplussed. "Whoever wrote this note doesn't know your parents at all. Dora and Tim would support you no matter what."

Lottie explained to Frank, "My parents would understand." She knew they would support her, but their businesses might suffer and she didn't want that.

"Most families wouldn't feel that way," commented Frank. He had known parents could disown their children for choosing the bohemian way of life.

"Yes, most would abandon them," said Lottie, stating Frank's thoughts. "That's what happened to Rose. She was lucky her grandmother provided her with an inheritance." She frowned. "No, the main issue is work. I wouldn't survive that scandal."

"But what do they want from you? Why send the note?" Hen asked.

"I don't know," said Lottie. "I have a trial coming up that might be the reason, it is the only thing that makes sense."

They didn't ask which one, they all knew it was the Becker trial and that Lottie couldn't answer direct questions about it.

Danny folded the note, handed it back to Lottie, and asked, "We know Rose is part of this; but this seems bigger than just her. Who else is behind this?"

"I'm not sure. I think it would be someone with knowledge

of Rose and my life inside and outside the village. That being said, it could be the police. Sorry," she said, glancing at Frank.

"No offense taken. We're trying to clean out the graft and violations ongoing in the department."

"Who also might be involved?" asked Danny.

"Gangsters, of course," said Frank, helping to fill in the gap.

*Both sides are very dangerous,* thought Lottie.

"So, what are we going to do?" asked Hen. She was ready to be part of the plan.

Lottie looked at the group and said, "Wait on their demands. They're in control. There's nothing to do but wait."

"What about Rose?" asked Danny.

"I'm afraid that, until we figure out who's behind this, we don't have much to go on," Lottie said.

Each thought about that as they finished their tea and cake.

Frank looked over at Lottie. "Did you compile the list I requested?" he asked.

"I put it together before going out last night." She reached into her pocket and pulled out a folded piece of paper.

He was curious. "Where did you start? Who knows you're a lawyer and about your relationship with Rose?"

"I thought about that a long time. I spoke with Hen last night and most people here in the village know both sides of my life. I'm not worried about them; most have the same setup I do. Their day job is conservative and they would have the same worries as I about our personal lives being exposed."

"Why don't you start," he said, pulling out his notepad.

She started at the top. "First, Chris Burnes, he works with me at the Justice's office. He's the senior clerk."

"Do you know him well?" asked Frank as he wrote down relevant facts.

"Yes, he recommended me for the job after meeting me in

court. I was defending Hen at the time." Lottie smiled over at her.

Hen commented, "Yes, that was when we first moved here."

Lottie continued. "Chris arranged an interview and coached me in the Justice's quirks. He's been my mentor all this time. He also covers for me on a routine basis if I need to run to court."

"Court? Why would he need to cover for that? Isn't that your job?" asked Frank.

"She means for me," muttered Hen. She realized how much she had put Lottie's job in jeopardy.

Frank let that go and asked, "Do you socialize with him outside the office?"

She shook her head. "He doesn't live in the village. He lives in Manhattan and his social life is there. We do talk about everything together, though."

"So, he knows about Rose?" Frank inquired.

"Yes. I have mentioned her." She grimaced. "I voiced my frustrations with her behavior more than once."

The look on her face made him pause. He asked, "And . . ."

Grimacing again, she said, "Well, I probably told Chris almost everything about mine and Rose's relationship."

"Hmm. You said he lives in Manhattan. Have you ever seen him in the village?" Frank asked.

"No, I haven't," she confirmed.

"What about you, Hen or Danny, have you seen him here?" he asked as a follow-up.

Danny looked at Hen. "We know Chris, but Hen and I haven't seen him here."

Hen nodded in agreement.

"Okay. Who's next?" prompted Frank.

"Bob King," Lottie stated firmly.

He looked surprised when he recognized the name. "The clerk at the 6<sup>th</sup> precinct?"

Hen and Danny looked surprised also.

"Yes. Do you remember me mentioning Henrietta and court? I'm in that precinct regularly bailing her out for any one of her causes."

"Why is he on the list?" asked Frank.

"He knows me as a lawyer," said Lottie.

He asked, "What is there about him that might be a concern?

"He appears to be pleasant, at least at first. It's the graft that gets annoying."

"Graft?" Frank asked, confused. He knew graft was occurring at all levels, but how could that be applied here?

"Yes, Hen's fines are supposed to be 40 dollars and he's been making me pay an additional 60."

Danny protested, "Lottie, you didn't tell us about that!"

She looked over and said kindly, "I didn't want to tax your income. I've been able to handle it."

Hen reached over and took her hand. "You won't have to now. I'll be limiting my arrest."

"I would appreciate that," Lottie said and leaned over to kiss the other woman on the cheek.

"What does the extra 60 buy you?" Frank asked. He wondered why she paid it.

Lottie shrugged. "Usually, an earlier time in court and a lenient judge."

"Does she get jail time for her offenses?" asked Frank.

That made Lottie laugh out loud. "Just the once. But she stirred everyone up so much. Now, they just fine her."

"What happened?" asked Frank.

"The prison conditions are just awful. I had to do something," Hen said, remembering.

"What did you do?" Frank asked, fascinated by this family.

Danny answered, "I believe there was a food fight in the cafeteria. Then she organized everyone to sit in the yard and not move until conditions were changed."

"There are more prisoners than guards. They couldn't move us easily," Hen explained.

"Did anything change?" he asked. He knew the prison system was big and corrupt. The main issue was no one cared about what happened to the criminals.

"Not a lot," Hen admitted, "but we did call attention to it."

"I understand there's a reason to stay out of court?"

"Yes." She looked over at Frank and said, "We're having a baby."

"Congratulations," he said quietly.

"Thank you," Hen said.

"Does Bob know Rose?" he asked Lottie, wondering how the policeman could have met her.

"Well, that's another story. Rose and I were broken up." She caught his look and said, "Yes, it is a normal occurrence. Her relationship, after ours ended, was with a very adventurous girl she uses to fill in her time with."

"What happened?" Frank asked. He was curious about Rose.

"The lovely lady she was with liked to have sex outside," Lottie explained.

"Outside?" echoed Frank. He was fascinated with these women pushing boundaries.

Hen spoke up. "The location they picked was near the 6$^{th}$ precinct."

"On purpose?" he asked incredulously.

"Evidently, fear of getting caught is also part of the appeal," Hen replied sardonically.

"Not something you have an interest in," he commented to her.

"No." She laughed, not offended at the question. "That's one of the few things I like to keep private." She squeezed Danny's hand.

"So, what happened?"

"Bob was the one who caught them. He barely gave them time to dress before hauling them in. The other woman, Daisy, called me to bail her out. The price was much steeper and Rose was hard to control. We had a tough time with her, she wouldn't cooperate with me or the police. The court date was a fiasco, but at the last minute, the judge released her and Daisy and dismissed the charges."

"Why the change?" Frank asked.

"I don't know what happened. It was odd. I thought she'd be getting some jail time. The charge for resisting arrest was the worst of them. It wasn't a judge I know very well; his court normally handles more criminal matters."

"How did it end up in that court? Was Officer King involved?"

"In the past, he was involved in getting the court assignment," Lottie admitted.

He made notes to look into King, even if he wasn't involved in this. He was a dirty cop and abused his power. "Anything else?"

Hen looked over at Lottie and said, "Tell him."

"Tell me what?" Frank inquired.

"I don't think it's related." But she finally relented upon seeing Hen's heavy frown. "Bob has shown up in the village."

"In spots where Lottie happened to be," commented Danny.

"Did he speak with you?" asked Frank.

"Yes," Lottie admitted. "He asked me out."

"What did you say?" he asked.

"I told him I wasn't interested."

"Did it end there?" he felt the anger building in him at Bob's behavior.

"No, he saw Rose come up and take my hand."

"What was his response?"

"Mean," she admitted. "His tone was nasty."

"Did he threaten you?"

"No, but he used a few names I won't mention here, and our interactions at the station now have an underlying tone."

She stopped talking about it, so he went on to the next suspect. "Who else is on your list?"

"People from the tearoom. I don't think they're involved."

He nodded and went on to his next question. "You work for Justice Goff. Is he aware of your life here in the village?"

"Goff? No, that would require him to be interested in my life," Lottie said dismissively.

"So, no knowledge of Rose?" he commented.

"No. I wouldn't have a job if he knew who I was involved with. He's very conservative."

"Close-minded is what he is," muttered Hen.

"Yes," agreed Lottie.

"Could Chris have told him?" Frank asked.

"No! He wouldn't do that. We're very close. He goes out of his way to make sure I'm not exposed."

He nodded and took that down. "What about D.A. Whitman?" he asked. He was still thinking about the legal side of her life.

"Whitman? That man doesn't know I exist much less what I do in my personal life," said Lottie.

"But he comes to the office where you work?"

"He does," she conceded, "but he only deals directly with Chris. I'm invisible."

Hen said, "Lottie, Joseph should be on that list." Danny nodded. They were both very familiar with Joseph and his treatment of her.

"Joseph, I believe you mentioned him previously," said Frank. "Where is he now?"

"With his wife," she muttered, looking away. These questions were hitting too close to home.

"Are there still feelings between you?" he asked, trying to keep any sort of emotion out of his voice. "No, no. It was over a year ago."

"What happened? Did he stumble on you and Rose together?"

"NO!" She calmed a bit and continued, "Rose and I had broken up again when Joseph and I met."

"How did you meet?"

"At the bookstore," Danny spoke up. "They met here."

"How long were you together?"

"Almost a year."

"Why did you break up?"

"His family, or so I thought," she muttered.

"Was it serious?" he asked.

"I thought it was. We'd planned to get married and live in the village, where he'd write books."

"How conventional," he teased.

"It didn't start that way, but it moved toward it quickly," she admitted.

"A year is a long time. You mentioned you were on and off with Rose. Did you see her at the same time you saw Joseph?"

"I was 100% committed to Joseph during that time. I didn't see anyone else."

"How did Rose feel about that?"

"She didn't like it," Lottie admitted. "She doesn't believe in monogamy."

"Did she say or do anything to let you know that?"

"Yes," she mumbled. "We had some confrontations." Their relationship had started up again after Joseph moved back home. The jealousy she'd exhibited hadn't been seen again.

"Did Rose know Joseph?"

"I never saw them together, but they knew of each other."

"Did you see Rose, personally, during that time?"

———

### Lottie, Joseph, and Rose

Lottie had been spending more and more time with Joseph and hadn't been to the tearoom in weeks. They had been lost in their sexual haze, concerned with nothing but each other.

She heard a knock on her apartment door. Lottie glanced at Joseph, who was still asleep. She got up and pulled a loose robe over her naked body. As she made her way to the door, she pushed the hair off her face.

"Who is it?" she asked.

There was no answer; Lottie opened the door. It was Rose. Lottie put a bright smile on her face and said, "Rose. Well, it's wonderful to see you."

"Is it?" the woman asked and pushed Lottie aside to enter the apartment.

"Yes, of course." Lottie watched her, wondering why she was upset.

Rose said, her tone accusing, "He's here, isn't he?"

Lottie frowned. "Rose, lower your voice. Yes, he's here. Is that why you're so upset?"

Rose looked a little lost for a moment and said, "I thought it was a fling. That you'd get tired of him." She walked over to Lottie and ran her hand down her face and into the deep V of her robe, and said, "I thought you'd come back to me."

144

In the past, that had been true. Lottie had always made her way back to Rose. The sexual attraction between them had always been strong, and she still felt the pull of it. She started to lean in, but caught herself and took Rose's hand.

"Rose, I'm with Joseph now. I want to see where this goes."

"Okay then, if that's the way you feel."

"It is."

Lottie started to turn to show her out when Rose pushed her back against the wall. She grabbed the edges of Lottie's robe and pulled them aside, baring her body. She moved to place her mouth on an exposed breast. As she sucked, Lottie caressed her head. She responded to the caress longer than she should have. She used her hands to gently push Rose away.

As Rose straightened, she ran her hand between Lottie's legs. Rose drew her hand slowly away, feeling the other woman was wet there, and smiled.

"Come see me when it ends." Rose slammed the door on her way out.

Lottie slowly pulled her robe back together, closed her eyes, and took a deep breath. *That was exquisite, she thought.* Their sexual attraction had not lessened in the time she had been with Joseph.

She heard a noise and looked up. She was shocked to see Joseph standing in the doorway.

He slanted her a look she couldn't read and said, "Do I need to be concerned?"

"No," she said. "What we had was casual."

"To you, yes, but to her?"

"She never implied anything different," Lottie explained softly.

"Until today?"

"Yes." She mulled it over as she walked toward him,

145

swinging her hips. "Care to finish what she started?" she asked, opening her robe wide, showing her swollen breasts to him.

He grabbed her and tossed her on the bed. His pants hit the floor and he got into bed beside her.

"I think I can manage that."

He kissed her deeply then moved to give attention to the same breast Rose had.

Lotte rocked against him and enjoyed the moment.

————

### Back to Frank, Lottie, Hen, and Danny

"Yes, but it was to let her know Joseph was who I was with at that time."

"How was the relationship with Rose after you broke up with Joseph?" Frank questioned.

"It went back to normal. On and off," Lottie admitted.

"So, she got what she wanted?" Frank asked.

"No, I wouldn't say that," protested Lottie.

"I would, Lottie. Rose got exactly what she wanted: you, on her terms," Hen said, looking at her.

Frank followed up with, "Was that more her or you who dictated the terms of the relationship?"

"Her," she admitted, trying to see this from their viewpoint. "Hen's right. I can be a bit of a doormat where Rose is concerned."

"What about Joseph's new wife? Can you get me any details on her?"

"I only met her once. I don't remember much."

"When was this?" he asked.

"At their wedding," Lottie muttered turning red.

"He invited you to the wedding?" he asked, wondering about Joseph.

When she didn't answer, he looked over at her. Seeing her guilty expression, he asked, "You weren't invited, were you?" *Was Lottie this passionate about everything in her life?*

"No. I went there to rescue him," she whispered.

"Rescue? From what? A woman who loves him?" he asked incredulously.

"Yes, rescue," she said abruptly. "I thought they'd forced him into that life."

Hen stated, "I'm afraid I encouraged her."

"What's Joseph's last name?" he asked.

"Bancroft," said Lottie.

Frank hesitated and said, "I know that name! That family's well off. What did you think he was getting involved in?"

"Involved in? Evidently, riches and a beautiful wife." Lottie's lips twisted into a facsimile of a smile.

"Was she aware of you?"

"No, I don't think so, and I couldn't imagine he would volunteer that we lived together for a year before their marriage."

"No, I wouldn't think so," he murmured.

"I was a fling," she said. "Just someone he used until he had to face his responsibilities."

Hen moved to sit beside her and took her hand. "We were all taken in by him." She looked at Frank and said, "He worked for Danny in the bookstore and said he was writing a book."

"He seemed sincere," said Danny. "He certainly talked like he was a writer."

*He may have been for a time,* thought Lottie, thinking of their time together, discussing their future.

———

### *Joseph and Lottie's first date*

They wanted to spend a quiet evening together. The village could be noisy, but they located a small café and began talking about books. When Lottie knew every book he referenced, Joseph observed, "You've read a lot."

"I have an aunt who is addicted to adventure books. So, I've always liked to read."

They continued to talk quietly, getting to know each other. On the way home, he put out his hand and she took it. He pulled her in close. "I'd really like that tea tonight," he said.

"So would I," she murmured, looking into his eyes. Since Rose, she hadn't wanted to be with a man, but this one was different. She couldn't resist the gentleness of his touch.

They walked up to her apartment slowly, and Joseph let her hand go as she opened the door for them. As he entered, he turned toward her and lowered his head to give her a slow, lingering kiss. It was a kiss that had her melting into his frame. She helped him take off his jacket and shirt, running her hands over his muscled chest. The jacket and shirt had hidden a compact, muscled body. She enjoyed the contrast between them.

"May I?" he asked as he indicated her shirt buttons.

"Yes," she said.

He unbuttoned her shirt slowly, kissing the exposed flesh as he went down. Once he got to her breasts, he lowered her shift so it provided a frame that held them up. He kissed and sucked each nipple to a hard point.

She reached over and caressed his nipples at the same time.

He pulled back and they finished undressing.

"The bedroom is that way." She pointed and laughed.

He chuckled huskily, lifted her, and set her on him. He took a moment to rub against her. She let out a low moan. He moved them into the bedroom and sat on the edge of the bed with her on his lap, continuing to rub himself against her. She felt herself swelling in response, but instead of consummating immediately, he took her fingers and placed them between her legs, wetting them. He moved them to his member. He curled her hand around it and show her the motion he liked.

When he slid into her, she continued to stroke him and herself, enjoying the sensations. He bent her back to suck hard on her breast while she continued to stroke both of them. Her body quivered and she stroked harder, leading them both to completion. They fell back on the bed, her on top of him.

She hadn't realized she would like to be with a man after Rose. Previous sex with men had been perfunctory, not something she looked forward to. This was different, something special she lost herself in. After the first night, Joseph started spending all of his time with her.

————

### Present day- Frank, Lottie, Hen, and Danny

Frank noticed she was distracted and cleared his throat. "What about Rose's girlfriends? You mentioned there were several."

"Yes, most were short duration," Lottie commented.

"Did anyone stand out?"

She thought for a moment and said, "The one who likes to have sex outside. She stuck for a while."

"Who broke up with whom?" asked Frank.

"Rose broke it off; she normally did. She liked the control," stated Lottie.

"In this case, what was her reason for the breakup?"

"I had come back from Joseph's, and I knew it was finally over. I was available," she said simply.

"She dropped her for you."

"Yes, she would do that to people. You couldn't be sure who she was going to be with next."

Frank wasn't getting a very pleasant picture of Rose. She seemed to use women and discard them on a whim. *Though*, he thought, *there does seem a pattern here with her possessiveness of Lottie.* He would make note of that.

Danny listened to all the questions and observed, "Whatever's happening here involves Rose. From the pictures and notes, she's an integral part of this."

"Yes," commented Lottie, "but has she gotten in over her head thinking it's a game or has she moved the game into higher-level stakes?"

Everyone went silent at that comment.

"Where do we go from here?" Danny asked Frank.

Lottie answered for him. "We wait."

Frank nodded in agreement. "Lottie's right, until we get an actual demand, there isn't a lot we can do. Though, while we wait, I'll start looking into each suspect."

# Chapter Sixteen

Frank and Lottie left together. He looked over at her and asked, "Would you like to walk to Washington Square Park with me?"

"Yes, that would be nice."

It was around 3:00 pm, and the sun was still shining. She looked at him and asked, "Are you working tonight? Shouldn't you get some rest?"

"Not tonight." He didn't say, but last night's stakeout had paid off and a raid was on the schedule for the next week. As they continued to walk, he asked, "Why Joseph?"

She glanced over at him. "Why? I don't know. After all the drama with Rose, Joseph seemed so sweet. He didn't play games. If he said he was going to be somewhere, then that's where he would be."

As they strolled, she thought about that first meeting.

———

## *Joseph*

The bells rang above her head as she opened the door to the bookstore. She looked to the back of the store, expecting to see Danny, and instead saw a handsome man approaching her. *This must be the gentleman Henrietta wants me to meet.* She continued to stare at him, noticing his dark brown hair and green eyes.

He eyed her with the same intense interest. She looked around the bookshop and asked, "Are Danny and Henrietta here?"

"They went to pick up some groceries. Were you looking for a new book to read?"

"I'm always interested in new books, but today I'm just stopping by for a visit. Could you tell them Lottie stopped by?" she asked, delaying her departure.

"Are you Lottie?" he asked with interest. He'd been working there for a few weeks and had heard about her.

"I am."

"Henrietta mentioned you went home for a while," he said, as he walked over to the counter to pick up a stack of books to move to the shelves.

Continuing to watch him, she said, "Yes, a close family friend got married. I helped with the setup."

"Where was that?" he asked over his shoulder.

"Chicago. My family lives there," she explained.

"Hen and Danny mentioned you're a lawyer."

"Yes," she confirmed. "I work for Justice Goff downtown."

He nodded and smiled slowly. "I understand we're having dinner together this evening."

"Are we? Hen asked me to stop by the shop. I would've expected her to be here." Lottie was starting to feel uncomfortable with this stranger. He seemed to know so much about her.

At that moment, the bells sounded and she turned toward the door.

"We're here," said Hen as she pulled Danny in with her. His hands were full of bags of groceries.

"Lottie, you're back! How was everyone?" Hen asked. Before giving her a chance to reply, she took the bags from Danny and handed one to Lottie. She linked her free arm through Lottie's and drew her up the back stairs, leaving the men in the shop.

Lottie leaned in close to Hen's ear and asked, "Did I understand that dinner would be on the agenda this evening?"

"You'll enjoy yourself. Just relax," the other woman said. She turned away from Lottie and opened the door into their living space.

"I don't like setups," Lottie muttered.

"Who said it is a setup?" Hen asked innocently. She got serious abruptly and said, "He's nice. Give him a chance."

"He is very attractive," Lottie admitted.

"Hmm. Someone you could see yourself going out with?"

"Maybe."

"What's your current relationship with Rose?" Hen knew it could be volatile. She understood Rose liked to have many women to satisfy her, but she didn't like the cavalier manner in which she treated Lottie. When she saw Joseph at the bookshop, she thought, *This could be the right person to distract Lottie from Rose.*

"Off again," Lottie muttered.

"Your idea or hers?"

"Hers."

"Hmm. So, you stay and talk to Joseph; enjoy his company."

"Okay, I'll stay," she said, knowing once Hen had made up her mind, there would be no changing it.

"Come into the kitchen," Hen directed.

Lottie followed her in and watched as she unloaded her bags. She also noticed the table was already set up for dinner and drinks. "Hen, this looks nice."

"Thanks, it's all ready. We'll sit down soon."

Danny and Joseph came in the kitchen door talking about how to get more people into the bookstore.

"We'll need more fiction. It sells well," suggested Joseph.

"Maybe we should have a night where we have local authors read from their new works," Danny said, mulling over the different options.

Hen started moving the glasses to the table. Danny noticed and said, "Let me help you." He took them from her. Looking at Joseph and Lottie, he said, "Take a seat."

They sat and watched as Hen put together a platter of roasted chicken and vegetables.

Hen and Danny sat down at the table and blessings were said before they ate.

They ate family-style, passing platters around the table. Lottie ate a few bites. "Yum, tastes like home," she said.

Hen smiled and asked coyly, "As good as Dora's?"

"Well..." She hesitated and then said, "Yes. But don't tell Mama."

Danny looked over at Joseph and said, "Hen and Lottie grew up together."

Lottie put her hand on Hen's. "We've been close ever since."

Hen looked over at her and said, "Joseph went to Harvard."

"You did? What was your major?" she asked him.

"Business, but my true passion is writing. That's why I moved to the village. I was lucky that Danny was looking for a salesman."

"It was my luck that you walked in when you did." Danny smiled as he drank his wine.

"What type of writing are you doing?" Lottie asked.

Joseph shook his head and said self-deprecatingly, "I'm trying a novel." When he saw her look, he acknowledged, "I know, a big challenge right off the bat."

"Why the business degree when you have a love of writing?" asked Hen, curiously.

"That," he said, "was for my family. I was supposed to take over the family business."

"Why are you here and not there?" Lottie asked, wondering about them.

"I just wasn't ready to make that decision," he said simply. "My whole life laid out for me."

He looked over with a heavy frown on his face. "I want to write. I want to be an author and discuss books and politics. This is the life I want. I don't want to be like my father." He shrugged sheepishly. "Sorry, I just get emotional talking about it."

Danny said, "That's why most people have moved to the village, to do something different from their parents."

"How long do you plan to stay?" Lottie asked him.

"I don't have a definite window. I need to work that out. I love it here. It's so freeing."

"Yes, the village is like that. New ideas, new people," said Hen.

Lottie nodded and thought, *The best place in the world.*

They finished the evening, talking about books. Lottie stood and hugged Hen and Danny. "I have to get home."

Joseph rose from his seat. "Can I walk you there?"

"That would be nice," she said.

As they walked, Joseph extended his hand out to Lottie, and after a small hesitation, she placed hers in his. The touch was warm and nice. This felt different. It didn't feel like the other relationships she'd had since arriving. The fast nature, the quick burn and die-out—she had experienced this before, and it was not satisfying. Only Rose had made her feel this deeply.

As they arrived at her home, she asked, "Would you like to come in for some tea?"

He gave her a long look and replied, "How about we go out tomorrow? For dinner."

"I have work until 5:00 pm and then we could go out at 7:00 pm." She suggested.

"That will work," he said and smiled. "I enjoyed meeting you."

"Me too," she said softly

He showed up at the apartment the next day to pick her up. The one date turned into many.

———

### Present day Frank and Lottie

"You were serious about Joseph," Frank commented.

"I tended to be very serious about two relationships: Rose and Joseph. Neither worked out, so I'm not looking for another one."

"Why not?" he asked. He wondered why this amazing person would choose to live alone.

"Maybe it's not the right time of my life or I haven't met the right person. I don't know. What I need right now," she told him, "is a friend. Someone I can trust and talk to."

He considered that and said, "Friends. That works for me also."

"Since you know all about me now, what about you? Are you seeing anyone? Are you married?"

"That's a complicated question for me," he said, not volunteering more information.

She could see the topic bothered him and didn't press for an answer. She let the silence settle around them as they continued to the park. They reached a bench and sat down, enjoying the view.

"Lottie, I don't know you all that well."

"Really?" she teased. "You have heard everything about my romantic life and seen my breasts more than once."

"This is true, and lovely breasts they are," he murmured, watching as her face turned red. "Seriously, though, a woman who can use her breasts as a weapon, holds an important job with the court, and is passionate in her support of friends, how can I reconcile that with the same woman who lets her lovers treat her badly?"

Lottie shook her head. "Frank, you're getting a very narrow view into my life. I chose the relationships with both of them. The end for Rose and myself had been coming for a while."

"Will you take well-meaning advice and cut ties with her?"

"The pictures and the obvious manipulation have made that easy. My concern initially was her safety, but I don't think that is the case now."

"If she turns up..."

"Then she has a lot to explain," Lottie finished for him. *And if she doesn't...* thought Lottie with a slight frown.

# Chapter Seventeen

After their walk, Frank escorted her back to her apartment. He leaned on the door in the hallway and watched her open it.

"I have to ask, what made you keep going back to her?"

She didn't ask who he was talking about. "Love," she said simply. "I love her." *Love or loved?* She asked herself.

"Does she feel the same about you?"

"Sometimes," she admitted.

"Are you willing to settle for that?"

"I took a step away before..."

"With Joseph?"

"Yes."

"And because that didn't work out, you went right back to her."

"I did," she admitted. She looked at him thoughtfully and changed the subject. "So, the list, where will you begin?"

"I'll look into the background of the men."

"Chris, Joseph, and Bob," she supplied.

"And then Rose's assorted female companions."

She nodded, thinking about what help she could provide. She looked over and said, "Thanks for today." With that comment, she started to head inside. Hesitating at the door she turned back to him, and said thoughtfully, "I think Joseph can be removed from the list. He has no interest in me anymore." *But why had she and Jojo seen him by Rose's apartment? He had no reason to be in the area.*

"Okay," he acknowledged but knew he would look into him anyway.

They parted ways at her door. She pushed Franks probing questions out of her head.

As the evening wore down, she fixed herself some dinner and focused her thoughts on what she had learned. Several people could be behind the pictures. Her thoughts shifted to Rose; it was clear that she was involved in whatever this was, at least initially. Those pictures hurt Lottie more than she was willing to admit. They showed her that she was someone to be used and when Rose wanted to move on, she wouldn't give her another thought.

She shook her head, and wiped the tears from her checks, trying not to let it get her down. Moving to the sink, she washed her dishes and set them out to dry. Next, she headed to the bedroom where she picked up the hairbrush and absently pulled it through her hair as she thought about the next day at work. Things would need to be organized, she set down the hairbrush and started pulling together items she would need in the office: notebook, pens, law books, her skirt, and her hair clip. It was still early, but she needed a restful evening; tomorrow would be a long day.

*I hope Chris is right and the case has been delayed. If not, the weekend should have been used to continue preparing.*

The sun had set as she made her way to bed.

# Chapter Eighteen

Lottie woke the next morning thinking of the Becker trial. Thoughts of Rose floated into her head, she pushed them out and focused on getting ready for her day.

She pulled herself together and did a quick review of the floor around the door to check for any notes. The familiar brown envelope was there, just inside the door. *I don't have time for this,* she thought, exasperated. Glaring at it, she moved over and picked it up, bracing herself for another threat. The letter opener was on the side table; she reached for it and opened the end of the envelope slowly. Sliding her hand into it, she pulled out the paper and looked at it. "What is this?" she asked herself. Not understanding what the document was.

Reading it again, she breathed a sigh of relief; It was the letter from Phillipa, detailing the kids from the village needing a place to play. *I'll have to work on this and get it sent over to the committee this week.*

Lottie carried it to the kitchen and laid it on the table. She needed to get organized for her day. *Lunch first,* she thought.

The Justice could change the court's hours at his discretion, and she wanted to be ready. Lunch would be a hard roll, some ham, and some fruit to snack on. Getting the items out, she placed them in a paper bag and ate a quick breakfast.

Moving back to the bedroom, she checked her bag once again. The courtroom could be hot, so she dressed carefully, packing both a light sweater and wearing a lace cotton top. Her pants would be changed for a skirt at the office. Grabbing her bag, she put her lunch inside, pinned her hat in place, pulled on her jacket, and headed downstairs to retrieve her motorcycle.

Lottie unlocked the storage room and rolled the motorcycle out onto the street. Cranking it, she listened for the motor to switch on, when it did she climbed on, revving it a few times. The sun was still coming up, and she thought, *An early start would be nice.* She decided to take the scenic route, enjoying the ride through the village and Manhattan.

Waving at the people who were out as early as she, Lottie continued to her office at the court. The garage was open when she arrived. She pulled in and, after storing her motorcycle, checked her watch. *This time, I've beaten Goff into the office,* she thought with a smile.

She hurried into the building and made her way down the long hall to the Justice's office. She pushed the door open and entered. Chris was already there, he stood quickly and walked over to her desk.

"Hey, don't rush. He won't be in for a while."

She paused and asked, "Why?" The Justice normally kept a very strict schedule.

"We got word that the trial has been delayed until October."

She sat on the edge of the desk and reached up to take off her hat. "We'd expected that."

"Yes, but McIntyre, Becker's defense attorney, still feels he doesn't have enough time. It's only a minor victory.

"What day in October?" She pulled her calendar from her bag and retrieved her pen to add the date.

"October 7," he said, watching her reaction.

Lottie looked up in surprise. "That's a little over three weeks from now. He's right; that isn't enough time."

Chris nodded in agreement. "Another thing..."

"What's that?" she asked as she looked over and grimaced. She'd had enough surprises lately.

"Look a little more forward on your calendar," he said, gesturing to her book with his hand.

She saw what he was referencing. "Goff's vacation? Won't he just cancel it?"

He gave her a look and said, "Goff doesn't bend to the court's will; the court bends to him."

She groaned. "You're right. I've seen that, but why take the case if there isn't time?"

"This one hit Goff's favorite thing to rule on—police corruption. He'd do anything to take them down. He considers it the greatest evil."

"So, he made room in the schedule for a case dealing with corruption, not as its main issue, but existing on the periphery."

Chris moved back to his desk and glanced at the clock. "You might want to change."

She said, looking down, "Oh, yeah." Straightening up, Lottie walked to the small closet to change her clothes and pull her hair back with a clip. Her pants were put into her bag and she headed back into the office.

*Should I mention the threats to Chris?* She wondered, watching him as she moved to her desk.

"Something on your mind?" he asked, noticing her stare.

"No, nothing specific," Lottie said as she looked away. She

put off her questions and walked to the file room. Chris had unlocked it when he came in for the day. The files were located and she walked back slowly to her desk. She looked at Chris again and came to a decision. "Chris," she said in a quiet voice. "Do you see staying here long term?"

He looked over for a long moment, his face darkening. "I'm unsure," he said honestly. "We've both seen things here that give us pause."

"Yes," she said, listening intently for his next statement.

"I'm watching the Becker trial carefully. I see the D.A. coming in here and staying in closed-door meetings with the Justice, and not allowing any of the same to the defendant's lawyers. I feel that, sometimes, we're not on the side of right."

"Can you let me know what direction you're thinking of? If you do plan to leave?" she asked. She knew she wouldn't be happy here without him.

"Of course," he said, sounding sincere.

She looked at him intently and finally nodded. His face was open, and she saw no dishonesty there. The doubt she had about him was erased and she wanted to tell him what was happening. She started, "Chris, I need to talk with you about something..."

At that moment, the door opened, and Justice Goff walked in. She closed her mouth and sat silent as he walked by her desk. He was an average-sized man with white hair and a beard. On the outside, one wouldn't see him as the sometimes-callous man he could be. *Though,* she thought, *the people in his court know this callousness as fact.*

"Morning, sir," Chris said as he went by them. He never acknowledged them until he needed something. Stopping at his door, just before entering, he turned to Chris. "I will need our revised calendar." He didn't wait for a response and continued into his office.

Lottie rolled her eyes at Chris. His eyes twinkled as he pulled out his calendar to take into the Justice's office.

She took the opportunity to write a formal letter to the Washington Square Association, detailing the children's need for a playground within the park until one could be developed in the village. Her letter would suggest that their committee meet with the association to find an equitable solution. Typing it up, she addressed the envelope and placed it in her bag to be mailed on her way home.

About an hour later, Chris emerged from Goff's office.

"Lottie, I need you to research some case law, to be ready in case they come up." He handed her a list, and she took it to review.

The books were on the far wall of the office. She walked over and began pulling those required. She was glad for the delay. It appeared that both sides had challenges that needed to be addressed before going to court.

She knew the case research was important to Chris. As the senior law clerk, he influenced the Justice's decisions. He and Lottie would compile the necessary research, relevant legal materials, and other information that they would present to the Justice at key times during the trial. The expectation was for them to speak about each item before the court and clarify as needed.

Chris was careful when to apply his influence. The Justice could be hard to sway from his course if he had made up his mind.

She worked into the evening, preparing the cases. Getting ready to head home, she helped Chris compile the files and placed them in the file room to be locked up. She slipped several books into her bag for her evening reading.

# Chapter Nineteen

As Lottie rode home that evening, not quite out of Manhattan, her thoughts shifted unexpectantly back to Rose. Now that the Becker case wasn't the main thing on her mind, the memories threatened to overwhelm her.

She pulled over to the side of the road, shaking so hard, that she had to lay her head on her handlebars. When she was calmer, she slowly climbed off the motorcycle and stepped up on the sidewalk. Slumping down on the curb, she pulled her knees to her chest and rocked back and forth. The trial preparation had allowed her to focus on everything but the fact Rose had not come home.

People were walking by looking at her oddly, but she ignored them as she continued to sit. *I've been burying my feelings, acting like not hearing from Rose is okay,* she thought. The facts and her feeling were getting entangled.

*Facts,* she thought. *Think it through.* Feeling steadier, she took several deep breaths, straightened, and pushed herself up to her feet. She swung her leg over the and revved the engine, forcing herself to think of the facts as she headed home again.

First the pictures, then the Becker Trial. It was something that could not be ignored.

The suspect list was more important now. They needed to find the connection between her and the Becker trial. *Who was it and what did they want from her? Would Rose come home once the trial was over?*

*If the police were involved, they could find a reason to arrest me or Hen; rather than kidnapping Rose, they could have just set her up and arrested her.*

*Was it gangsters?* Kidnapping was part of their regular activities, but she didn't normally have many day-to-day crossovers with them. They frequented the Village's many bars, including the ones Frank was investigating for illegal activities. Lottie had tried a few of these when she first moved to the area but realized the danger there. Since then, she had avoided most of the bars and spent her time at the tea room.

Her evaluation helped to steady her as she pulled into her building storage area. That feeling stayed with her as she opened her apartment door. She looked around the floor, a new habit she didn't like. That was when she spotted the envelope. She didn't pick it up right away. Instead, she took her bag and moved it to the bedroom. Deliberately taking her time there, she removed her hat slowly, placing it on her dresser. Finally, she made her way back to the door and bent down to pick up the envelope off the floor.

Tapping it on her hand, again delaying opening it, she went to her chair in the main room and sat down. Picking up her letter opener, she slid it inside the fold and opened it. No pictures. She pulled out a single piece of paper.

It was the note she was expecting. She read through it; there wasn't much there. *You will be notified once the trial is underway, after October 7$^{th}$. More instructions to follow.*

She turned it over but didn't see any other writing. There

were none to be found on the paper, but this did connect the trial to the threats. She tapped it and thought, *This doesn't change our original list of suspects. Though it did confirm her suspicions, the trial was the main factor in the blackmail.*

She took the letter and envelope to where she kept the other photos. She glanced at the clock and thought, *I have enough time to get to Rose's.* On her last visit, she had set traps at the window and door. These involved strings laid strategically so that, if someone came into the room, they would be disturbed.

She made her way there quickly and entered Rose's apartment, being careful not to shift anything. Each trap was checked carefully. *Still nothing,* she thought. Heading home, she rubbed her arms, noticing the evening was starting to cool off. Her evening plans involved a review of the books of case law she had brought home.

She took a break for dinner, and then pulled out her law books, thinking about how the trial would progress. *Voir dire would be first,* she thought. *What kind of people would they want on the jury?* She had experience watching voir dire early in her life. She'd accompanied her Aunt Emma to court a few times. Emma worked as a trial expert, she could read the jury pool and make recommendations on who would have their client's best interest at heart.

Aunt Emma's advice was, "If you're sloppy at this stage, you could inadvertently put someone on the jury who may not be able to identify with your client." So, for this case, she thought, *Becker is a large Irishman, married and, according to the papers, with a baby on the way. That's who he'll want, people like him, hardworking men with families. His imposing stature will also be a factor. He is over 6 feet in height, so bigger men would be preferable to smaller ones.*

The concern would be timing. To select the jury correctly,

you needed to ask the right questions. Justice Goff would push them to be quick. Becker's attorney would have to push back and use that time appropriately.

She would be there to see if any of the people she thought should be picked, would be. It would be a front-row seat, which was probably why she was targeted by the blackmailers.

Sitting back in her chair, she considered the upcoming trial while absently picking up the newspapers and opening them. No surprise, Becker was in all of the headlines. The idea that a police officer could be charged with murder was unheard of. They were already calling it the trial of the century. *Goff would love that headline*, she thought.

# Chapter Twenty

L ater that evening a knock rang out at the door, startling her. Laying her pencil down slowly on the kitchen table, Lottie made her way to the door. She leaned into it and called, "Who is it?" *Were there threats coming in person now?*

"It's Frank."

Relief washed through her as she opened the door and looked at the man with a frown on her face. "Were we supposed to meet tonight?"

"No, but I thought you might want dinner." He held up the basket he was carrying.

She had already had dinner, but she smiled at him. "Dinner? That would be lovely. Come in."

When he started toward the kitchen she said, "I have work stuff in there. Why don't we set up in here, eat more casual?" She grabbed a large scarf from the back of the couch and covered her low living room table with it.

He followed her direction, opened the basket, and started

unpacking it. She watched for a moment and said, "I'll get the drinks. Beer okay?"

"Perfect," Frank said as he continued to set up.

She got the bottles and called, "Bottles okay?"

"Yes."

"Do we need silverware or plates?"

"No, I have everything."

She walked back in with the beers and saw he had finished arranging the food. There was steak, seafood, salads, and sides.

"Oh, how wonderful. What made you think of it?" she asked as she handed him his bottle and started to sit beside him. Hesitating she said, "Wait, I have something that will help us be more comfortable." She reached over and took the decorative pillows from the couch; handing him one. He took it and put it under him; she did the same as she sat beside him.

They moved the food to the plates and started eating. "Yum," she said sincerely. "So, why the visit?"

"Besides a nice meal with a nice lady?"

She sent him a sideways look, and his mouth twisted briefly in amusement. "I wanted to find out if there was any change on the date of the trial. You mentioned it might be moved."

"Well, I'm glad you brought that up," she said as she stood and headed to the kitchen.

He watched her leave. When she returned, she was carrying an envelope.

She sat down silently and pulled out a piece of paper and handed it to him.

He took it from her. "At least it's not more pictures." He unfolded the note and read it. "This confirms it, the threats and pictures are related to the trial."

"It appears that way," Lottie commented. She picked up her beer to take a drink.

"At least we're on the right path."

"That note also tells me it's someone close to the case."

"What makes you say that?"

She inclined her head toward the note in his hand. "It seems they know about the trial postponement."

He looked down and noticed the date in the note, "Postponement?" he asked.

"Yes, we got word this morning. It's set to begin on October 7th. Though it seems like the blackmailers got the same information."

"You mentioned that you expected a move, but isn't that still soon?"

"Yes, but the Justice has his reasons," she said quietly.

He frowned over at her, wondering what the reasons were. When she wasn't forthcoming, he said, "I'd expect more time than that."

"Yes, there was no compromise. There'll be more meetings about it and about the amount of time the defense has to prepare. We should know the schedule closer to the trial."

They finished dinner and sat quietly.

"Do you mind going over the suspect list with me again?" Frank reached into his pocket and pulled it out.

"Of course," she said as she straightened a bit on her pillow.

"I'd like to start with Henrietta and Danny. We didn't discuss them at our last meeting."

"Danny and Hen?" She laughed. "No, I don't think they're involved."

"You mentioned Henrietta has a background in civil disobedience," he said, taking notes.

"She does," she confirmed hesitantly, not wanting to involve her friends.

"Would it be a stretch to say that Henrietta would break some laws if she thought something good could come out of it?"

Lottie let out a long sigh, thinking of the circumstances that

171

had led Hen to Lottie's family. Hen had taken the law into her own hands. She blamed a local factory for her brother's death and started sabotaging the equipment there to get even. No one knew about Hen's involvement and Lottie didn't plan to tell anyone now. "I disagree with her and Danny being on the list, but I see your point. What are your questions?"

Frank was thinking and looking at his notes. "Let's start with Danny. How long have you known him?"

"Danny?" she asked. She thought of the earnest man she had grown to love like a brother. When he nodded, she continued. "Since I moved to Greenwich Village two years ago. You could say he's the reason I live here now."

"Why's that?"

"Henrietta met him at a suffragette demonstration here in New York."

He looked up, surprised, and asked, "Aren't those mostly women's demonstrations?"

"Yes," she explained, "but there are a few men committed to the cause. They met at that first event and were engaged by that evening. Hen has always known what she wanted, and she wanted Danny."

"How is he with you?"

"He's always treated me like family."

"Does he ever react badly to any of Hen's, shall we say, shenanigans?" he asked, treading carefully.

"I still feel she isn't involved, but I'll answer your question. He's supportive, but I think his patience is running low," she said honestly.

"If he thought she was involved in something like this, what would he do?"

"I really don't know. I don't think that would go well, especially now."

"You mean with the baby on the way."

"Yes. It's not just Hen that he feels he has responsibility for now. I think he'd stop her."

"We'll keep both on the list." When she frowned at that, he quickly amended, "Low down."

They talked until late in the evening. "We're probably not going to be able to find Rose before the trial begins. How are you holding up?" Frank asked.

Lottie stood up. "I'm having trouble with not knowing where she is," she admitted. "I want to know she's okay. I'm afraid that we won't be able to find her until the trial is over."

"Her involvement will make it harder," he allowed. He was thinking this was bigger than just one missing woman.

She stood up and started pacing. "I've been thinking, wherever she is, she'll want women brought to her." She looked over at Frank. "She could never go more than one night without sex."

"Who was she involved with?"

Lottie laughed, but it didn't sound pleasant. "There were many, many women."

"How about now? Is there a current person?"

"Yes, that would be Lily."

"And yourself," he commented laconically.

"Yes," she said in a deprecating tone. "I let her use me and I used her. I can see if Lily's still around."

"This week?"

"She's normally at the tearoom on Thursdays. I can check in with her then."

She started picking the trash up. "That isn't necessary," he protested.

"You don't want to carry food or dirty plates with you. Come into the kitchen; this won't take long."

He shrugged and picked up the dishes and followed her

into the kitchen. As they started washing, she looked over and saw he looked uncomfortable.

"Is everything ok?" she asked.

"Yes. I was hoping, as a friend, that you could go to the Carmine Theatre, over on 6th. With me. On Saturday," he said in a rush.

"The small theatre?"

"Yes."

"I'd love to. The distraction would be nice."

"You would?" He smiled broadly. "It's a cowboy movie."

She grasped his hand and said, "Just friends, right?"

"Right," he answered, knowing he wanted there to be more.

"I'm glad. I'm enjoying our time together."

"Me too."

They took the clean dishes back to the living room. He packed them up and closed the basket.

She looked at him regretfully. "I'm sorry to have to ask you to leave, but I have a pile of case notes to get through tonight."

"Is that what a law clerk does?" he asked. He was curious about her job.

She nodded. "We research precedent and cases that may be similar to ours. The prosecution and defense will be using these to support their side. Justice Goff must be aware of any that might be brought up in court. We do the research and summarize."

"I understand Goff's not the most studious Justice," Frank commented as he walked with her to the door.

She laughed. "No." Goff's lack of judicial knowledge was not a secret. "Chris says he needs clerks who can think on their feet and fill in the gaps he can't."

He thought about where he was going and looked at the basket. "Can I pick this up when I see you on Saturday?"

"Of course." She took it from him and set it by her chair. "Are you working tonight?" she asked.

"Yes," he said noncommittally.

She understood confidentiality but couldn't resist asking a question. "If you're in the village and you seem to be able to leave here and go to where this event is happening, it must be nearby." She looked at him consideringly and guessed, "The Golden Swan?"

He lowered his eyes to hers and said, "I'm not confirming anything, but don't mention this to anyone."

She immediately thought of the tearoom ladies. There were several who liked to go there to dance. Should she...

He read the look and warned softly, "You can't tell anyone. If you choose to, I could lose my job."

She looked over and thought about the tall silent man waiting for her promise. She didn't make him wait long. "Yes, I'll keep the secret."

"Thank you," he said. He knew he could trust her to keep her word. He picked up his hat. "Saturday?"

"Yes, I will be here," Lottie said slowly.

"Will you have to work that day?" Frank asked.

"I'll have to organize and review the information, but we're still a few weeks off."

"Dinner out, before the movie?" he asked.

"I would like that," she said softly.

As he headed out, she stood in her doorway and watched him start down the stairs. She ran over to the banister and called down, "Frank, be careful!" She knew these raids could be violent.

"I will," he said, looking up at her searchingly. He watched as she nodded and went back in. She seemed to care for him, but as a friend -could it be more?

She returned to her apartment, closed the door, and leaned

back against it for a moment before moving back to her kitchen table and her books. The case law was required reading and she continued late into the evening. When the words started to blur, she stood and turned off the light, and made her way to bed.

# Chapter Twenty-One

The next day was standard for trial preparation, with more paperwork and motions from opposing lawyers. Motions presented could determine what evidence would be used at the trial. There would be many more motions to review before it started.

After a long day at the office, Lottie ate a quiet dinner while making notes in her journal. She noticed the time and went to bed. Loud noises, sounding like gunshots woke her. It was a still night and sound traveled. She turned over and went back to sleep.

A short while later, banging at the door woke her up. "Yes," she called as she pulled on her robe and walked to the door.

"Phone, Lottie," called Leigh. She had an apartment down the hall.

She pulled her robe tight, pushed her hair out of her face, and opened the door. "Thanks."

Leigh grunted and headed back to her apartment and back to bed. She turned around just before she entered, "Did you hear the noise earlier?"

"Yes, and I'm guessing this call is related to that."

Leigh nodded as she watched Lottie walk over and pick up the dangling receiver. "Hello, this is Lottie Flannigan."

"Lottie! You must come!" She looked around and saw Leigh was still listening. She mouthed "Private" to her and watched as the woman went back into her apartment before putting the receiver back to her ear.

"Lottie!" called the impatient voice.

"I'm here. Now, who is this?" Lottie asked, frowning. The voice was familiar, but she couldn't recall the name.

"Lottie, it's Daisy."

She knew who it was immediately. "Daisy? Why are you calling?" She looked at her watch and said, "And at this hour?"

"I need you to come to the 6th precinct. I've been arrested."

Lottie was instantly all business. "Daisy, you must stay calm. What are the charges?" Knowing Daisy, they could be anything.

"I didn't do anything," she said defensively.

"What didn't you do?" Lottie asked, rubbing her forehead.

"I got caught up in the raid at the Golden Swan."

*So, that was tonight,* Lottie thought "Were you gambling? Or drinking?" she asked.

"No!" she said forcefully.

Lottie had to ask. "Daisy, was it sex in public?"

There was a long silence before she admitted, "Yes."

She sighed, careful not to let her hear. "Okay, I'll be there in about 20 minutes. Have they mentioned bail?"

"Yes. It's crowded here." Daisy waited a moment and requested nervously, "Please come quickly."

"I will," Lottie promised. "Tell them I'm your lawyer and I'm on the way."

"I will."

They hung up. Lottie went quickly to her room and dressed

in pants and a loose blouse. She grabbed her short jacket, pulled on her boots, and went downstairs to get her motorcycle. Rolling it out, she cranked the motor, hopped on, and headed to the precinct. It was early morning and no one was on the road, she was able to get there quickly. As she pulled up, she rolled the bike to the underground garage.

"Would you mind watching it for me?" she asked the attendant.

"For a price," he said as he looked at the motorcycle with interest.

She turned it off. "I'll give you five now and five when I'm done."

"I think we can work that out. Roll it over here."

She followed him, parked it beside his desk, and handed him the five dollars. She headed out and up the stoop to the station.

# Chapter Twenty-Two

Lottie stepped in and thought, *Yes, they hauled in everyone from the Golden Swan.* The place had the nickname Hell Hole and the Bucket o' Blood. She'd only once gone to see the place famous for Djuna Barnes, Dorothy Day, Charles Demuth, and Eugene O'Neill.

She looked around and recognized various artists and writers. There were others there she didn't recognize. The bar was an eclectic mix of artists, writers, gangsters, and other assorted lowlifes.

She looked over at the window where the prisoners were being processed and grimaced inwardly. *This is going to cost me.* She took a deep breath and forced herself to walk up to the window.

"Hello, Bob."

"Lottie Flannigan, fancy seeing you here," King said with a smirk.

She let him have his joke and said quietly, "I need to have Daisy Wilkins brought up."

He let out a long whistle and shook his head. "I don't know,

Lottie; this one was caught in the act, as it were." He started to laugh long and hard at his joke.

"Bob, what can we work out?" she asked, trying to reason with him.

"It's going to be extra this time," he said maliciously, leaning toward her.

"How much, Bob?" Lottie was quickly losing her patience.

He opened his mouth to tell her the fine, but then he leaned back and said, with no expression, "That will be 40 dollars."

"What?" asked Lottie. She didn't understand. King hadn't added the graft that normally accompanied his price.

"Forty," he muttered, looking down. His whole demeanor changed.

"Okay." She pulled out the money and handed it to him. "Will you bring her down?"

He didn't answer instead calling over his shoulder, "Jeff, go get Daisy Wilkins."

Lottie looked at him and wondered why the man was acting so odd. She got her answer when she turned around and nearly ran into Frank.

He narrowed his eyes in a warning so she wouldn't 'know' him. She got the message.

"Excuse me, please."

He moved out of her way; she headed to the corner to wait for Daisy to be brought down. She noticed he stayed in the area until Daisy was present.

Daisy spotted Lottie and ran to her. "Thank you so much!"

"Lottie!" called Bob. "Her court date will be tomorrow afternoon with Judge Patterson."

She looked over and said, "Thanks, Bob." She turned back to Daisy and said, "Let's go."

Daisy did as she was told and followed her quietly out.

Lottie hailed a cab. As it pulled up, she turned to Daisy and requested, "Go home and get some rest. We have our court date tomorrow, be there at 1:00 pm. Be there and wear conservative clothes."

"I will. Will this go like last time?"

"I am really not sure what happened last time; you should have at least paid a fine. Be prepared to have that fine applied this time," she warned.

"I understand. Will you have time to see me this weekend? I'd like to talk to you about something."

She looked at her searchingly and finally said, "Come by on Saturday morning. Do you know where my apartment is located?"

"I do. I'll be there. Thanks again, Lottie," Daisy said gratefully.

She watched her get into the cab and headed to retrieve her motorcycle.

"You back?' the attendant watching her bike asked.

"I am."

"You really a girl lawyer?"

"Yeah," she commented quietly as she got the cycle and rolled it out.

"My money?" he asked.

"Yeah, sure," she said and handed it to him.

"Nice cycle," he commented while he counted his money.

"Thanks." She kneeled, cranked the bike, stood up, and got on, this time revving it a bit.

"Oh, and it's woman lawyer," she said over her shoulder as she headed home to get some sleep.

# Chapter Twenty-Three

*ourt day with Daisy—Wednesday*
"Chris," she called softly from her desk and
tapped her watch.

He glanced over, nodded, and said loudly, "Lottie, I need you to take these over to the court. They're waiting for them."

She hurried over and took the files. Glancing at them quickly, she saw they were empty. "I'll be on my way now."

He waved her on. "Thanks," she mouthed to him.

She grabbed her bag, slid the files inside, and made her way to the courthouse. Daisy was waiting outside her assigned court. Lottie was happy to see that she had followed her directions on what to wear. Her dress was a light blue, one that was long enough to cover the tops of her boots; it had a high collar and long sleeves. Her hair was pulled back and makeup was kept to a minimum.

"You look exactly right," Lottie said as she joined her.

The other woman grimaced and pulled at the collar. "I don't feel like myself in this get-up. Lottie, will this work?" she asked worriedly.

"I know this judge," she assured her. "It'll work."

Lottie took Daisy's elbow and, as they started to enter, she thought of something and pulled Daisy close to whisper, "Let me do the talking. If the judge says anything directly to you, answer with a yes sir or no sir. The reason for your arrest might get brought up in court. If it does, please be calm."

Daisy nodded. She understood the reasons for the instructions.

As they entered the court, it was quite busy. Lottie guided Daisy to stand in the back. The clerks were processing the large group quickly.

"We'll wait here until we're called," Lottie commented softly. She reached into her bag for her writing tablet and heard Daisy's name called.

"That's us," she said and looked over at her. She saw that Daisy had lost most of her color and looked anxious. "Are you ok?"

She took a deep breath to steady herself. "Yes, let's get this over with."

Lottie took her arm and stood with her. "Here we go."

They made their way together to the judge's bench and stood in front of him.

Judge Patterson pulled his glasses down the bridge of his nose and addressed Lottie.

"Miss Flannigan, I've gotten to see quite a bit of you lately."

"Yes, Your Honor," she said in a loud, clear voice.

"How is Miss Lawson? I understand she found a job to keep her busy." Lottie had taken the papers to the court clerk on Monday to be processed.

"Yes, sir. She took your recommendation to heart. Thank you for that solution," she commented sincerely.

"Yes. Now, who do we have here? Miss Sinclair?"

Daisy nodded and said, "Yes, sir."

He glanced at the charges and then at Daisy. He was a compassionate man and it showed when he began to question her.

"Miss Flannigan, will you wave a reading of the charges?"

She felt Daisy tense up until she replied, "Yes, sir, and thank you."

Daisy leaned into Lottie, grateful for the private manner in which he was handling the trial.

"Why don't you start," Judge Patterson suggested.

Lottie said, "Judge, Miss Sinclair made some poor decisions when in the company of friends. We would like to ask for a fine."

Judge Patterson looked closely at Daisy. "Is that about right, Miss Sinclair?"

"Yes, sir." She tried to keep her voice even.

"You've never been in my court before, and I think this looks like a foolish prank. Therefore, I think a fine of 100 dollars is in order. Would that suit you?"

Lottie and Daisy responded at the same time, "Yes, sir."

"Dismissed. See my clerk," the Judge said and waved them on.

As they turned to go, he spoke again. "One moment," he said sternly. "Miss Sinclair, if I see you in my court for this activity again, you will serve jail time. Is that understood?"

Daisy nodded quickly.

Lottie took her arm and walked her over to the clerk. Daisy took 100 dollars out of her purse to give to him.

"Wait for the receipt," cautioned Lottie when she saw Daisy ready to bolt out after she paid.

"Oh, of course," she murmured. Daisy stopped and tried to wait patiently. The woman was in a hurry to get out of there.

They obtained the receipt and made their way out of the

court. As they retreated into the hall, Daisy grabbed Lottie in a big hug.

"Thank you so much for this. I'll get you the 40 dollars back on Saturday, if that's ok?"

"It is," Lottie commented. The color was back in Daisy's face, and she was smiling broadly. Lottie hated to dampen her mood, but she had to warn her. "Daisy, you got out with a fine, but try to limit the public exposure, okay?"

"I'll try," she teased. She was feeling so much better about the day.

Lottie grimaced. She saw she wasn't getting through to her. "Do more than try. I don't think you'd like jail."

"I understand, Lottie," Daisy said sincerely.

Lottie glanced at her watch, trying to not look impatient. She needed to get back to the office. "I have to go now."

"I will come by on Saturday," the other woman said.

"Morning is best," she confirmed.

"See you then."

They separated and Lottie headed back to work.

# Chapter Twenty-Four

Lottie woke later than usual. She lay there, smiling to herself, thinking, *It's Saturday!* Saturdays were lazy days. There were a few more weeks to go until the trial. She and Chris would continue to work longer hours getting the casework organized and filed for all of the motions. It was a relief to be out of the office. She was looking forward to seeing Frank at the show tonight. Between her schedule and his, she had not seen him since the raid at the Golden Swan.

Later that morning, she heard a knock on her door. She put down the novel she was reading and went to answer it.

"Who is it?" she called.

"Daisy," answered the voice through the door.

Lottie unlocked it and saw her standing there. She looked more like the Daisy she knew. Her dress was loose, showing her curves, and her hair was mussed. She was a lovely woman, just not someone Lottie was attracted to.

She noticed Daisy seemed nervous. "Would you like to come in?" Lottie asked.

Daisy stayed where she was and said, "I wanted to thank you again."

"It isn't necessary. Please, come in."

She finally entered. "It is necessary," she said simply. She reached into her pocket and pulled out some money. Handing it to Lottie, she said, "Here's your 40 dollars. Thanks for giving me a few days."

"That's all right. I didn't mind."

Daisy stood in an agitated manner and walked to look at the small corner table with pictures. She picked them up, gazing at the people in them.

"Nice looking group," she said.

"My family," commented Lottie as she walked up behind her.

"Photos," Daisy commented again.

"Yes," said Lottie, wondering where this was going.

"That's what I want to talk about."

"I'm afraid I don't understand. Why don't we sit down?"

Daisy nodded and followed her to the couch. She sat down next to her.

"You mentioned pictures?" Lottie prompted.

"Yes. There're probably some of you as well," she said without explaining.

Lottie perked up. Daisy noticed and sat back. She said, "Oh, so you've received your envelopes also."

"I have." Lottie didn't say much more. She was unsure of how much to share.

Looking directly into her eyes, Daisy said, "I'd like my pictures back and the negatives. I don't want anyone else to have them."

Lottie started to mention Jacko might have them but was interrupted.

"I know where Rose keeps them."

"You do?" Lottie was surprised at this information.

The other woman nodded.

"Can you show me?

"Maybe. Do you have a way to get into Rose's apartment?"

Lottie looked at her consideringly and said, "I do."

Daisy stood up, held out her hand, and said, "Do you want to go now?"

She hesitated only briefly before taking the offered hand and stood. "Yes."

Daisy gave her a slow smile, keeping Lottie's hand in hers.

"Sugar, would you like to get to know one another better before we go look for the pictures?" she asked, using her thumb to caress Lottie's palm.

Though Lottie reacted to Daisy's raw sensuality, she smiled. "Maybe some other time."

Daisy slowly let her hand drop and said, "Maybe I'll ask again."

Lottie smirked as she started to gather up her things. "Ready?"

"I am."

"When did you get your envelope?" Lottie asked as she continued to get ready. She was curious about the timing.

"It's been a few months now."

Lottie pulled on her shoes and tied them. She grabbed her hat and held the door for Daisy, locking it behind them. They walked together the few blocks toward Rose's apartment.

Once they arrived, Lottie pulled out the key and opened the door. "Wait just a moment," she said. She wanted to check the traps before bringing the other woman into the apartment. She looked quickly and didn't find any of them disturbed. She would reset any that they disturbed before they left.

She waved her hand to Daisy to come in. Without hesitation, she sauntered over to the fireplace.

"They're hidden there?" asked Lottie.

"Yes, Sugar," she said over her shoulder. "Could you come and help me with this?" she asked, indicating the stone. Lottie joined her. "Place your hand like this," Daisy said as she demonstrated what she wanted her to do. Lottie followed her directions and put her hands in the crevices to remove the large stone. Daisy continued, "Once I get it moving, be careful. It's heavy."

Lottie nodded and watched. Once it was loose, she placed her hands on the opposite side of the brick and they slowly slid it out. Lottie saw why her help was needed; it was heavy. "Let's take it slowly," Daisy directed. "I don't want to lose a foot over this." They lowered it carefully down to the wood floor.

Daisy straightened and went back to the hole where the brick had been and reached her hand in. She pulled out stacks of envelopes.

"All of those?" Lottie asked in amazement.

"Yes," she said. "Our Rose liked to review her conquests after the fact."

"How did you know they were there?" Lottie asked curiously.

"I got Rose drunk and she told me," she said simply.

"You haven't tried to get them yourself?"

"I didn't have a way in, and I didn't want to anger Rose. She could have reacted badly."

"Yes," Lottie agreed quietly.

Daisy sat down on the floor by the stone, quickly flipping through the envelopes, opening them until she found hers. She looked at them briefly before sliding them back into the envelope. "I'll keep these if you don't mind."

"I don't," Lottie said as she took the discarded pile of envelopes to the sofa. She began opening them. She was shocked as she realized she recognized the different girls. She came to the last envelope and slid out the pictures.

She tapped the picture. "Where do I know this girl from?"

Daisy stood and kept her envelope close to her as she walked over. She sat next to Lottie. "Let me look. I may know her." She eyed the pictures carefully. "That one, I would've remembered. Lovely girl, long legs, and she's kept her hair long."

Lottie looked again, frowning. "I know this girl. I just can't place her. I'll take these with me."

Daisy frowned and said, "Sugar, those are private and could hurt the people in them if they got out."

"I'll keep them hidden. With mine," she said quietly.

Daisy frowned and asked, "Did you have an envelope in the pile?"

"No. but I did receive a set at my home." She looked over at Daisy and said, "Can I ask you a question?"

"Yes, Sugar, go ahead."

"In your pictures, how did Rose look?"

"What do you mean?" she asked, bewildered.

Lottie thought it best to share. "She appeared to be dead in my pictures."

Daisy looked shocked. "Dead, no!" She opened her bag and pulled the envelope out, handing them to her. Lottie saw that Daisy and Rose were in various positions.

"You weren't asleep?" Lottie asked, mentally reviewing her pictures.

"No, we were awake in them."

She asked the hard question. "Were you aware the photographer was there?"

"No, I wasn't," Daisy muttered, gathering up her pictures. She didn't like the implication that she had allowed someone to do this to her.

Lottie had to ask, "Daisy, you're pretty free with your body in public. Why do these bother you so much?"

"That was my decision; this was not."

*How are these pictures related to mine?* "Daisy, can you help me identify the women in the other envelopes?"

"Let me try."

Lottie handed her each packet; there were 6 different ladies. She opened the first one. "You should recognize this one; she's at the tearoom nightly."

"Annie?"

"Yes, that's her." Daisy opened the next one. "This one was before your time; I think it was Molly."

"What happened to her?"

"She went home. Some people come here to experiment with the life. They get their thrills and head back home. "

Lottie had also seen both sexes do that; Joseph did it to her. She shook herself and pulled out the third envelope, sliding out the pictures. "This one?"

"Bernice. She's with Patrice now."

"That's right."

The last three, Lottie didn't recognize. Daisy reviewed them and confirmed their names and that they had moved back home.

"What did Rose plan to do with these?" Lottie asked, bewildered.

"She didn't just plan; she put that plan in motion."

"But why? What was the reason?"

"Money, Sugar," said Daisy.

"How do you know?" Lottie still didn't want to believe Rose was involved.

She looked around at the luxurious room and asked, "How do you think she keeps this place?"

"She inherited the money," Lottie said weakly. She realized that she didn't know Rose at all.

"That was gone a long time ago. She has expensive tastes," Daisy said, fingering the clothes laying on the table. "And I paid monthly for this to be kept quiet." She sat back and said, "You know you're special to her."

"Rose?" Lottie asked, bitterly looking at the envelopes again. "No more so than any of these women or you."

"Sugar," she said. "You're wrong. She cared about you."

"Maybe in her limited way." For her, it always came back to the first time she had caught Rose in bed with another woman. "It looks like I'm just another one of the women she's taken advantage of."

Daisy asked, "How long after your relationship started, did she send you the pictures and notes?"

"I got mine just before she disappeared, last week," she admitted. "When did you receive yours?"

"It was a few months after we were together. She just now sent these to you? You were together off and on for two years."

"Yes."

"As I said, special."

Lottie wanted to believe her, but the pictures had been sent and threats had been made. "Daisy, was it always about the money? Did she ever ask for anything else?"

She frowned. "Other than money, no."

"Are these threats active? Is she still sending notes?"

"Prior to her being gone? I believe so. I was still getting them. We can ask Bernice and Annie."

"Yes. We'll have to be discreet," she commented. "Were you still paying?"

"Oh, yes," the other woman said quietly. She was thinking of how she would dispose of the pictures and negatives. "But not anymore."

"Rose is so complicated. There were times I felt I knew her better than anyone else in my life, and now I feel like I didn't know her at all." Lottie felt lost.

Daisy watched the emotions cross her face. So, trusting. Changing the topic, she commented, "She's been gone longer than usual this time."

"Have you heard from her?" asked Lottie, hoping she had.

"No, but I expect to. The payment will be required soon. She's always right on time with her demands."

Lottie looked thoughtful and asked, "How do you normally give her the money?"

"She has a post office box. The demand would come, then I was expected to put it in the mail."

Lottie was curious. "Daisy, how did you connect Rose to the money demands?"

"I just knew. I could tell from the pictures that the person was there with us. We only ever used her room. It was obvious when I confronted her."

"How did she respond?"

"She laughed at me," she said, looking down. "She said I was playing at this life."

"Yes, that is one of her favorite lines," Lottie muttered. "How did you take that?"

"Not well. She could read me," Daisy admitted. "That's why she was so good at getting the blackmail set up."

"Do you think someone else is part of the blackmail scheme?"

Daisy sighed. "It has always been just her. The notes were pretty clear, money or exposure. I paid to keep them from getting out."

"Why these girls? Why you?" *And why me?* she thought silently.

"Me? I shared too much about where I'm from."

"What do you mean?"

"Money," she said simply. "My family still supports me."

She let that go and asked, "The other girls?"

"Yes, she targeted the young ones. She could tell from the cut of their clothes or where they lived if they had money. They also, like me, shared too much with her. It made them vulnerable."

"Those girls who went home?"

"She knew they wouldn't stay. She went after girls with families who wouldn't want to know their precious daughters were straying off the path."

"That would explain why it seemed she would approach every new girl in town."

"One of the reasons anyway," said Daisy sarcastically. She looked over at the envelopes Lottie still held. "What will you do now?" She was concerned about those pictures and who they could hurt.

"I'm not sure, but I will protect these. Once we find Rose, I'll destroy these and send letters to each girl, letting them know it's over," Lottie promised.

"Good," Daisy said, feeling suddenly tired. "I'm going to head home now unless you would like to lay about?"

Lottie smiled, flattered by the question. "Maybe next time. I'll walk out with you."

Daisy looked at the brick and said, "We should probably put that back. Can you help me lift it? I'd rather no one knew we found these."

"Yes, of course." Lottie laid down her envelopes and went to help lift the brick into place. After they finished, she said, "I'll meet you in the hallway."

Daisy headed out and Lottie reset the traps. She exited the apartment and took Daisy's arm as they descended.

# Chapter Twenty-Five

Lottie let herself into her apartment and locked the door behind her. She pulled the envelopes out of her shoulder bag and looked at them, thinking about what she could do next. Moving into the living room, she sat on the floor in front of the low table and opened each one, placing them in stacks on the table. She studied them over and over, looking for any similarities.

Oddly, she was the only one who had been asleep in her pictures. The other girls had looked to be actively involved in coitus when theirs were taken. Jacko must have had plenty of room to move around. Lottie couldn't imagine any of these girls would have done this with someone looking on.

*Jacko. He knows more than he's saying*, she thought again, glancing at the time. Frank was due to come by for their date that evening. She would have to wait and see.

A few hours later, she sat dressed and ready, waiting for him. There was a knock at the door. Lottie opened it without asking who it was. She was relieved to see him and said, "Frank."

"Good evening, Lottie," he said, removing his hat. "You look lovely this evening."

"Thank you, come in. I haven't seen you much this week."

He nodded and said, "Lots of people to process."

He didn't mention it, but a group of men who had been taken in was charged with alcohol distribution without a license and facilitation of prostitution. He hoped to clean it up, but he knew that, for every man he took down, there was another in line to take his place. It was unfortunate that they couldn't shut down all of the illegal businesses in the area. The silence lingered in the room and his eyes sought her out. She wasn't smiling.

"Lottie, what happened? What's wrong?"

Rather than answering, she picked up the envelopes and moved them to their hiding place in the kitchen.

When she came back, he raised his eyebrow at her and waited.

"For now, how about we go out and have a good time?" she asked.

"I could use that also." He was grateful they were going to have their night out.

"Ready for a nice evening?"

"I can provide that," Frank said, offering her his elbow.

They walked toward the village's Italian quarter near Bleecker Street and Our Lady of Pompeii Church. He looked over at her and said, "Would you like to stop for dinner on the way?"

"Do we have time?"

"Yes, we don't have to be there until 8:00 pm."

They passed several casual cafes, stopping to peer in the windows until they found one they liked. "This one?" he asked, indicating the small Italian café.

"Yes, please," she said, suddenly feeling hungry. *Maybe this is what I need, a break from all of the drama.*

They entered and found a table in a quiet corner. The menus were brought over and they ordered quickly.

"How's work going?" he asked.

"Oh, it's busy and something else is taking up all of my spare time," she said, looking at him pointedly, thinking of Daisy.

He knew what she was referencing. "Yes, sorry about that. I couldn't let anyone know."

"I understand."

"The person who got swept up..."

"Daisy?"

"Did the judge treat her all right?"

"Yes, and thanks for the help with Bob. I don't have a lot of spare money right now."

"I'm keeping my eye on him," he said. "Will the trial start soon?"

"Yes, it is still on schedule -three more weeks."

Conversation stopped when the waiter walked up with their food. "Still fast," he commented, enjoying his dinner.

"Yes, and it will be long days once we start." She looked at her watch and said, "The movie will be starting soon."

Frank nodded, waving to the waiter to pay the check.

They headed down to the theatre. The featured film was a melodrama about a cowboy who became a thief to provide for his dying wife. After the film ended, as they walked to her apartment, she looked at him and said, "You didn't seem that involved in the film."

"I was watching the little girl across the aisle from us," he said with a slight smile.

"What was she doing? Laughing like the other children?" The audience had been in high spirits.

"No, she seemed spellbound. She stared so intently at the screen."

"It does seem like magic, moving pictures."

"Yes," he said.

When he didn't say more she looked over at him and asked, "Frank, you mentioned you were seeing someone."

His face flushed and he said, "Not exactly. I said there was someone."

"Someone?"

"She died," he said simply.

"Oh, Frank, I'm so sorry." She remembered the theme of the movie and asked, "The movie, did it bother you?"

"It didn't help," he admitted.

"What happened to her?"

"That bar, the one we raided this week."

"The Golden Swan?" she supplied.

"Yes. It's all wrapped up with that place. Carrie, that was her name. She got sick, just a cold. I had some cough syrup from when I was sick. I didn't think it would be bad for her. She started taking it and, before I knew it, she drank multiple bottles. When I realized there might be a problem, I stopped the pharmacy from giving it to her. When she couldn't get it there, she started hanging out at that bar."

"What could she get there?" she asked, confused.

"Opium," he said simply. He went on to explain, "Opium isn't illegal yet. President Roosevelt is taking the first steps to limit it, but more on the international level."

"That sounds like a positive start," she said.

"Trouble is," he said bitterly, "it doesn't do anything for the opium being distributed around here."

"If you can't get them for drug distribution, what do you charge them with?"

"Prostitution, illegal gambling, alcohol distribution."

"Items that are illegal," she murmured.

"Yes, until the opium is stopped."

"What happened to her?" she asked quietly.

"I was working late. When I got home, I found her on the floor."

"Dead?"

"Yes, she overdosed on the opium," he said, not wanting to relive that horrible day.

"Frank, I'm sorry," she said again.

"Thank you."

"How long has it been?"

"Over a year," he admitted.

"And you had no one else in your life since then?"

"No," he said, giving her a sideways look.

She ignored it and they continued walking slowly to her apartment. When they reached her stoop, she looked over at him and made a decision.

"Frank," she said softly, "would you like to come upstairs?"

"To talk about what you were concerned about earlier?"

"No," she said in the same soft tone.

"No?" he asked, looking confused.

She smiled. "No, I'd like you to come up and spend some time with me. "

"Time?" he asked confused. Then he realized the meaning behind her words "Oh! I'm an idiot. Yes. I would love to come upstairs with you."

She held out her hand and he took it. They made their way up the stairs together. Her hand remained in his, even as she opened her door. They made their way to the bedroom.

When they entered, she turned to him and pushed his suit jacket off his shoulders. He removed her hat and threw it onto the side chair. She smiled and started to reach for her buttons, but he brushed her hands away.

"I want to do that," he murmured in her ear, kissing her neck. "I've wanted to do that since you used them as a weapon."

She let out a low laugh. "I will admit, I had a thought or two of that."

He chuckled low and abruptly picked her up, tossed her on the bed, meeting her there before the second bounce.

He stripped his shirt; the rest of their clothes were tossed to the side of the bed. Pulling her onto his lap, her legs straddling him as he rubbed against her. She ran her hands over his shoulders, enjoying the heavy muscles. He arched her back and caressed her breasts, his lips following his hands. He squeezed them together, licking in between.

Losing herself in the sensation, she reached down to take him in her hand, sliding up and down. She moved the tip to where she needed it most, rubbing it all around the opening but not inside. She moved closer, opening her legs as the blood swelled. He penetrated swiftly and she let out a small scream and rolled against him. He pulled her back on the bed, enjoying the view with her on top.

The friction between them continued until she felt explosions throughout her body. He finished and they lay together quietly.

"That was nice," she said, laying her head on his chest.

"Yes," he said, absently rubbing her back. He would like to ask if this were a one-time thing or if they could do this again. *Probably best to not ask*, he thought.

"Do you want a dessert and some milk?" she asked, rolling away from him.

*Milk?* he thought and smiled. "Yes, that would be nice."

"I'll head to the bathroom first."

"Ok," he said, slowly sitting back, watching her get up and put a robe on. He admired her walk and turned his gaze to the ceiling as he waited for her to come out. He heard the water running and, a few moments later, she reappeared, looking refreshed.

"It's all yours now. Meet me in the kitchen when you're done?"

"I will." After she left, he made his way to the bathroom to wash up. As he was dressing, she called, "I have it ready in the kitchen."

He finished getting dressed and made his way there. The cake and glass of milk were waiting for him at the table. The site of the chocolate cake made his mouth water. He grabbed a fork and took a large bite before sitting. With his mouth full, he looked at her and, swallowing quickly, asked, "Did you make this?"

"I did," she confirmed.

"It's good. How did you learn?" he said, gobbling up his cake.

"Would you like another piece?" He nodded quickly and she laughed as she cut him another slice. "My mama is an amazing cook, and my family are bakers by trade."

"And you went into law? That's a crime! If you can cook as well as you bake, I may never leave," he teased.

"Well, I can save you there. I'm not a great cook." She eased back in her chair as they talked, neither of them taking their conversation seriously.

After a few minutes, Frank asked, "Are you ready to tell me what was bothering you a while ago?"

"Yes, I think so." She walked to the refrigerator and reached behind it to pull out the envelopes. "This is what's wrong."

"What are those?" he asked, curious.

"More pictures, not of me," she quantified.

"Who then?"

"Other women Rose was blackmailing," she said her tone turning bitter.

When he started to reach for then, she stopped him. "I'd rather you didn't."

He looked at her questioningly. "Why not?"

"Those are private. No one should see them."

"You've looked at them?"

"I have," she confirmed.

"These are pictures like yours?"

"Similar, but there are definite differences."

"Can you explain the similarities and differences to me?"

When he didn't ask for the pictures again, she relaxed. "Yes. They're similar in the fact that Rose was in sexual situations with different women."

"Was that the only similarity?"

"The differences were what struck me. The more obvious one was that they were all taken at Rose's apartment and never in the girl's apartment."

"What else?"

"They were usually in the middle of a sex act."

"Not sleeping?"

"No."

"Were they aware Jacko was in the room?"

"No."

"How can you be sure?"

"I spoke to one of the ladies personally."

"What? You went looking for the ladies in these photos?" He stood, agitated that she may have put herself in harm's way.

"No, no. In fact, this lady came to me."

He paced the small room and turned to her stating, "We need to go to Rose's and review the angles these pictures were taken."

"What we need is Jacko in that room with us," she stated firmly.

Frank checked his watch and said, "I can arrange that tomorrow."

She frowned, she wanted to go over there TONIGHT and figure this out now. But she understood it would have to wait. "Will you and Jacko meet me here in the morning?"

"Early?" he asked, thinking of his calendar.

"Yes, that works."

He looked over at her. "Come here."

She walked up about a foot from him. "Here?"

"No," he said, pulling her to him. "Here." Frank lowered his head to her, kissing her deeply. When he lifted his head, he said, "I'd like to do this again sometime."

"So would I," she said, leaning into his embrace.

He pulled back and asked, "Was this because of my wife..."

She hesitated and said, "Honestly, that was part of it." When he stiffened, she said, "It was for me also. I think we both needed this time, this closeness with another human being."

He smiled slowly. "I enjoyed our 'closeness.'"

"Me too." She walked him to the door. "Now, go on home. I will see you in the morning."

# Chapter Twenty-Six

L ottie heard a knock and looked at the clock. *I know I said early, but 8 am on a Sunday?* She sighed and climbed out of bed, grabbing her robe.

She pulled it on and staggered to the door. Leaning on it she asked with a yawn, "Who is it?"

"Frank," the voice answered.

She opened the door and saw Frank there, holding Jacko by the collar. She stepped back, letting them in.

"Your early," she commented.

"Yeah, sorry about that, it was necessary," he said giving Jacko a shake. Jacko had tried to run off several times that morning.

"So, he came willingly?" she asked dryly.

Frank gave him another small shake and let him go. "You stay where you are," he warned. He looked over at her and said, "Yeah, willingly."

She looked at both of them and said, "I have pastry and fruit in the kitchen if you want some. I need to get dressed."

"We'll be in the kitchen," Frank said. He motioned to Jacko, who followed quickly.

She took a quick bath, added her makeup, and brushed her hair. After slipping on some pants and a loose shirt, she sat on the bed, pulling on her socks and mannish shoes. She stood, grabbed her things, and moved to the kitchen. Entering, she found Jacko and Frank at the table.

"Breakfast okay?" Lottie asked.

"It's good," said Jacko, moving away from her. He was still afraid of her.

"It is," Frank agreed. "I made some coffee if you'd like some."

She nodded gratefully and poured a cup. Before sitting she took a long sip.

They finished their breakfast and headed out.

At the door, Frank stopped Jacko. "I'd like to walk over civilly. Will you behave?"

"Yeah," Jacko muttered.

Frank looked at him suspiciously and reminded him, "Just remember I'm faster than you."

The three walked to Rose's apartment. Before they entered, Lottie held up a hand. "Wait here, I want to check a few things."

They nodded and waited. Frank kept an eye on Jacko.

She went in and found the traps tripped. She glanced around to see if anything had been moved. When she saw nothing out of place, she went to Rose's closet. Dresses that had been there before were now missing. *Rose, you were here.* She would keep that to herself for now.

Lottie quickly walked over to the door. "You can come in."

Frank looked around the apartment. "Anything out of the ordinary?" he asked.

She looked away. "No, I don't think so."

He gave her a considering look and thought, *I'll have to look into that.* "Where do we start?" he asked. Jacko was silent and offered no help to their investigation.

"Bedroom, I think," Lottie said.

They followed her in and watched as she looked around. She went to the bed and looked in the direction the camera would have been placed. "That wall. There's something odd about it." She stepped out the distance from the wall to the bed. She had never noticed it before, but it was much wider than it should have been. She tapped the wall and walked to the wall opposite, it sounded different from the other ones. She looked at the two men triumphantly. "It's a false wall."

"Jacko, your turn. Show me how this works," Frank said and pushed him forward.

He looked at Frank and whined, "Do I have to?"

"You do," he said firmly.

"How much did she pay you?" asked Lottie, watching him head toward the wall.

"She didn't," he mumbled, dragging his feet.

"What? Why?" she asked.

Frank sent him a disgusted look and moved his gaze to Lottie, saying, "She didn't have to."

"Why? Oh—sexual gratification." *And yuck.*

"Jacko don't make me come over there. Show us how you got in," stated Frank. His patience with his brother had waned.

Jacko shrugged and went to the wall, moving a picture and pulling a lever. A small door opened. Lottie started to go in, and Frank cautioned, "I wouldn't."

She got the message and stepped back. "Clever. Did Rose have this built?"

"No, it was already in place when she moved in," Jacko admitted.

"Another pervert must have lived here," said Frank.

Jacko continued. "Rose found it and contacted me with a proposition, a trade."

"How did you know each other?" his brother asked.

"She came into my shop and said she wanted to have some intimate pictures taken of herself. She liked my work."

"For Rose, this was about money," Lottie said. *This scheme had gone on for a long while. Why the change and how was this tied to the Becker trial?*

She stared at the bed. The pictures from yesterday were on her mind. That last blonde. She wasn't one of their group. *The hair—I know I've seen that hair before.* She walked around the room, thinking.

"Do you see anything else?" asked Frank, watching her closely.

"No," she said absently. "I'm good. I do need to get back to my apartment and work on my trial notes." She looked at Frank. "Do you have any plans?"

He looked at Jacko and said in a low, menacing voice, "Yes. Yes, I do."

They split up downstairs.

# Chapter Twenty-Seven

Lottie wrote the letters and put them in envelopes before she fixed lunch. The addresses had been included with the pictures, except for the blond, hers wasn't there. A sudden thought came to her. *Joseph! That was where I saw her; the blonde in the pictures is married to him!*

She laughed suddenly, thinking, *He just can't get away from women who like women.* She pulled out those pictures and looked at the blonde and Rose again. *And it seemed she really liked women.*

*If Rose was... no, Rose was blackmailing her. She must have felt certain that she hit the money,* she thought, remembering that house. *How much would she have asked for and is Joseph aware of the relationship? I need to go back to Rose's apartment.*

She looked down at her pants and thought, *These should be fine.* She picked up her hat and pinned it in place. Locking the door behind her, she took the stairs two at a time to the sidewalk. The first stop would be the post office to drop off the envelopes, with the blackmail inquiries. After dropping in the final one, she headed directly to Rose's apartment. It was quiet when she opened the door to enter. The traps were checked, and nothing was found out of place.

*The money, how much money would have been demanded? And where would she have put it?* She looked around the brick fireplace. The only block with missing mortar was the one they removed to access the pictures. She wandered around and tapped the floorboards with her feet. Failing to hear the hollow sound she was looking for, she headed toward the kitchen. Rose didn't cook.

The room was mostly empty, it wasn't used often. Her eyes kept returning to the stove. *That has to be it,* she thought.

Lottie reached over and pulled on the heavy black handle to open it. Slowly moving the door to the side, she looked in. The inside was black and hard to see into; she reached in and felt fabric. She pulled it out and saw it was a long, full black skirt. Looking further into the stove, she found what the skirt was hiding.

A package, she pulled it out and took it to the kitchen table to open it. Newspaper was used as wrapping paper and it crinkled as it was opened; revealing the money. *There must be thousands.* She looked at it, realizing how much the women were paying for the pleasure of sleeping with Rose.

*What do I do with it? I can't leave it here in the oven.* If Rose was still behind this, which appeared to be so, then she'd think the money was still safe. Lottie would take it home with her. *There must be a way to get this back to its rightful owners. I need to talk to Frank.*

# Chapter Twenty-Eight

Lottie carefully wrapped the money back up and stepped into the hallway to call Frank's apartment. He had given her his number in case she needed it.

When a voice answered, she asked, "Could you tell Frank Griffin he has a call?"

"Sure, just a sec." She could hear the man calling, "Frank! Phone!"

She just had to wait a moment for him to answer.

"Hello," he said.

"Frank, this is Lottie."

"Lottie," he said, drawing her name out.

She sighed before pulling herself back together. "Frank, I have something I need to share with you."

"Hmm," he murmured. "I can be over in about an hour. Would that do?"

"Yes," she said, grateful he could make the time for her. "I'll be at my apartment."

"I'll be there soon," he promised.

She headed there and kept herself busy going over case

notes and summing up her upcoming work week. As Lottie was closing her books, there was a knock on the door.

"Frank?" she called as she got close to it.

"Yes."

She opened it quickly and waved him in. "Would you like to sit down?"

"Please." He followed her in and took a seat on the couch.

She sat across from him.

"Is this about what you saw in the apartment this morning?" he asked.

She smiled, and sat back in the chair. "Saw that, did you?"

"I did," he acknowledged.

"Why not confront me then?" she asked curiously.

"You looked like you needed time to process whatever it was you saw."

"Thanks for that."

She explained about the clothes she had noticed missing from Rose's closet. Lastly, she covered the blackmail money and the letters she had sent to find out if the money was still being collected.

"Do we know Rose's background? You mentioned she came from money."

Lottie looked down and reluctantly raised her eyes to his. "We talked very little about her family."

Frank looked at her, thinking of all the conversations they'd had in the short time they had known each other. They talked extensively about their families.

She didn't mention the physical part of their relationship was what they did instead of talking. She looked over at him consideringly. "How would we look into her background?" she asked

"Do we know where she's from?"

"That, I do know. She's from New York. I'm just not sure which part."

"I can trace her birth certificate and census records."

She frowned. "That may be harder than expected. I'm not sure the last name I know her by is a real one."

"What makes you say that?" he asked, surprised.

"Just a feeling. So much of what we're finding about her has been a lie."

"I can check arrest records; you mentioned she has been arrested."

"Yes, it's funny, though. Before that event, Rose went out of her way to not be arrested. She seemed to know when she should clear out of certain establishments."

"But an arrest happened," Frank stated.

"Yes, but I don't think she wanted me involved."

"Isn't that unusual?" he asked. Frank knew the ladies called her when they got into trouble.

"Yes," she admitted. "I should have realized something was off when I wasn't called to help. It was especially odd because we were together at that time."

"Can you give me the date?" he asked. She nodded and quickly wrote it down, handing it to him.

"I should be able to pull the record. I doubt she would have lied then."

"Could you let me know?" It would be nice to know who she was involved with.

"I can," he promised. "It may be a few days; I don't have direct access to the records room unless it's a case I'm working on. I'll take this and, when I can, I'll check it out."

She hadn't mentioned the money she had taken from Rose's apartment. It was hidden, safely inside a small false compartment that Patrick and Papa insisted she have for her valuables. No one would know to look there.

"I was wondering," Frank started.

"Yes?" she asked, thinking he wanted to discuss the topic further.

"Would you like to take a walk with me?" he asked in a rush.

"How about a ride on my bike and a walk-through Central Park?" she countered.

"That would be nice," he said. He looked at her pants and commented, "I'm not sure those will be okay in Manhattan."

She looked down and said, "Agreed, but I do have something that will work." She walked to the bedroom and, as she was changing, she called out, "What have you been doing today?"

"Nothing much, just resting," he said, thinking about the Becker trial. It would start in a few weeks. It didn't just affect the people directly involved in the trial; it affected the entire police staff. They were working extra hours, closing down as much graft as they could. The department was rife with it, and it was taking time to follow the money.

"What will your weeks be like when the trial starts?" he asked.

"We got word from Justice Goff that we'll be working a very different schedule during the trial."

"How so?" He knew the judges normally set up hours from eight to five.

"We're working 8 to 11," Lottie said as she entered the room, tucking her shirt into what appeared to be a skirt.

He frowned. "11:00 am? That's a very narrow schedule."

"No. 11:00 pm," she said, looking at him through the reflection in the mirror as she pinned on her hat.

He reacted as she had expected. "What? That is ridiculous."

"That's Goff," she explained simply. "He'll wear everyone

214

down to get the result he wants. I haven't told you the other part. He wants this trial to go seven days a week and to finish in just two weeks."

He was astounded. "Two weeks! How can he do that and why would he want to?"

"He has a vacation coming up and he refuses to miss it," Lottie said, trying to keep the emotion out of her voice. She already felt they were going into the trial with a guilty verdict.

Frank shook his head. "Becker, what a mess he created. The graft alone is going to make this hard for all of us, much less the murder charge. My question is, had he been an honest man, would he have even been considered a suspect?"

"I can't talk to that. We have to stay neutral on both sides."

"Yes, but in your opinion?"

"My opinion? It's going to cost him and that pretty wife of his plenty."

"Hmm. I just hope he doesn't take down the police force with him."

She looked at him curiously. "Frank, have you ever taken graft?

He considered her question carefully before he replied, "I'm not perfect. Early in my career, I was included on the allotment of it."

"Do you take it now?" she asked quietly.

"No, I don't," he said simply. He didn't mention the task force he was assigned to was looking into this issue. That's why he moved between departments. Internal affairs wasn't a comfortable place to be. He was the cop's cop.

"I'm glad," she said. "And thank you for helping with Bob. I brought the money with me, but 100 dollars would have hurt."

"I'm glad I was there to help."

"Bob looked scared of you," she observed.

He chose not to comment, saying instead, "Are you ready?"

"I am." She let the topic go and smiled brightly at him. She was glad for the break in her day.

They headed downstairs to get her bike.

"Have you ever ridden one of these?" she asked, rolling it out.

"No, can't say I have," he commented. Frank walked around the motorcycle and wondered if this thing could hold him.

"The seat is small, and it's about balance," she explained. "Do you mind sharing while I drive?"

"Lottie, I think we should take my auto, that seat will not hold me and you."

She looked at him and agreed, "I guess you're right, let me put this back in storage." When she started to move it back, she heard Jojo's voice call her name. "Lottie!"

She turned and watched him run up, with Annabeth walking at a slower pace behind him. Lottie hugged Jojo and called out a greeting to Annabeth.

Lottie introduced them. "Jojo, Annabeth, this is Frank Malone, he is a police officer."

"It is nice to meet you," said Annabeth, holding out her hand.

Frank took it and looked at her for a long moment. "It is nice to meet you," he said.

"Yes," she murmured, removing her hand.

"Lottie," said Jojo. He was pulling on her arm.

"What's up?" she asked, looking down at him.

"He has been around again," said Jojo.

"Who? Joseph?" she asked.

"Yes," he said. "Over by Rose's apartment."

"Did he see you?" Lottie asked, concerned.

"No, I stayed hidden," he reassured her.

"Jojo has seen Joseph a few times," she explained to Frank.

216

Frank asked Annabeth, "Would you mind if he lets me know about any other sightings?"

"Yes," she said. She looked at Jojo and said in a stern voice, "But only if you come and tell me first. You don't try to talk to him on your own," she cautioned him.

"I can do that," Jojo said. "I will be on the lookout."

"Thanks, here's my number," said Frank, handing it to him.

Jojo took it and slipped it into his pocket.

"We need to be going. Jojo and I are headed to the market," said Annabeth.

They watched them walk away, and she noticed the way Frank's gaze lingered on Annabeth's form. "She is very attractive, isn't she?"

"Is she?" he asked, continuing to watch them walk away.

She smiled slightly and moved the bike back into the room and locked it. "Are you ready?" she asked.

He smiled slowly and said, "Yes, I am." He took her hand and walked her to his auto.

They started off and they headed to the park. The sun was shining and there was just enough cool air to make it a very pleasant ride. He deliberately took a longer path, enjoying her company. He didn't stop at the beginning of the park but took her to the reservoir to start their walk.

"I'll miss this time with you," she said as they stood by the water.

He put a hand on her shoulder and turned her. "The trial doesn't start for a few more weeks. Can I see you during that time?"

"No, it just isn't possible. We'll start putting in long days, nights, and weekends to get ready."

"I'll miss you."

"That's nice to know."

"Lottie, do you think we could ever be more than friends?"

She tilted her head and considered his question. "I make bad decisions in relationships."

"It could be you just picked the wrong people," he reasoned.

"Yes, that might be true. I also start expecting things like commitment and monogamy."

"That's how I feel."

She looked at him. "Why not talk about this after the trial?"

"Can I count that as a maybe?"

She smiled. "Yes."

He grinned. "Then I can wait until after the trial."

They continued their walk. He held his hand out and she took it in hers.

# Chapter Twenty-Nine

Sunday evening rolled around, it had been a nice day and most of it was spent with Frank. Lottie was looking forward to the evening, she hadn't been to the tearoom since her last interaction with Lily. *No drinking*, she promised herself. She also hoped to see Henrietta. Since this Rose-stuff started, she hadn't seen her friend and missed her.

The establishment was busy and full of people when she entered. Immediately, Henrietta spotted her and walked over. She was glowing and looked happy.

"Hen, you look beautiful," Lottie said, hugging her.

She fairly beamed at the compliment. "Thank you. It's the baby; it just makes me so happy."

"I'd love to spend some time with you this evening. Are you committed to any one group?"

"Not tonight," Hen assured her. "I'm just stopping by to check in. I'm keeping my promise to Danny to limit my time with the more active groups."

Lottie leaned in, speaking in a low voice. "Has Lily been around?"

"Trudie would know. Trudie!" Hen called out.

A tall, thin woman looked up when she heard her name. She walked over to the two.

"Lottie, hello. We haven't seen you in a while," Trudie said.

Hen got to her question. "Trudie, have you seen Lily lately?"

The woman frowned. "Oh yes, Lily mentioned that she'd be out of town for a few weeks. I believe to visit her family." She looked over at her group. "I should get back. Do you need anything else?"

"We're good," Hen assured her, and they watched her go.

*Lily's disappearance is certainly convenient*, thought Lottie. She was probably with Rose, feeding her sexual appetite.

Hen looked at her. "I'm not finding anything holding my interest tonight. Would you like to accompany me home?"

Lottie looked around and thought her friend was right; she'd much rather spend time with Hen and Danny. She nodded. "That would be nice."

Hen took her by the elbow, and they exited the tearoom together. Lottie leaned her head on Hen's shoulder and said, "I've missed you."

"Us too," she said, pulling Lottie closer. "Is your new trial taking up your time?"

"That's part of it," she admitted. "Rose is the other part."

Henrietta grumbled when she heard that name.

Lottie said, "I know you would like me just to ignore the fact she disappeared."

Hen interrupted. "She didn't disappear."

Lottie looked contemplative and said, "I'm starting to believe you are right."

"You shouldn't keep..." She stopped when she realized Lottie had agreed with her.

"What have you found out?" She knew Lottie would listen to facts; it was the only thing that could change her mind.

"It's a number of things. The pictures and the fact we've proven she is behind them."

"But, Lottie, you knew about that already and you were still thinking Rose the victim. What else have you found out?"

"Today, I noticed certain dresses of hers are gone."

"Gone?"

"Yes, her favorites from her closet."

"Hmm... what else?" asked Hen contemplatively.

"Lily," she said simply. "I believe she's with Rose. And I found out something else this weekend."

"What would that be?"

"Rose has been using pictures of the women she sleeps with to blackmail them."

Hen stopped. "Let's continue this discussion inside."

They had reached the bookstore. Hen leaned forward and peered through a window; she tapped on the glass when she saw Danny. He glanced their way and put down the stack of books he was carrying. Making his way to the door, he opened it for them.

"Lottie, it's good to see you. Hen," he said as he lowered his head to kiss her. He lifted his head. "Are you ladies heading upstairs?" he asked.

"We are," Hen confirmed. "Danny, could you come up? Lottie has more information on Rose to share."

He looked surprised and said holding up the books in his hands, "Let me finish with these."

"I'll put the tea on while you do that," said Hen.

Lottie followed Hen up to their apartment. They went to the kitchen and started putting the tea and cookies together.

Shoes sounded on the stairs and the door to the kitchen

swung open. Danny shrugged out of his jacket, laying it on a chair. "Let me move that to the living room for you," he said.

Hen smiled. She was enjoying Danny taking care of her. He picked up the platter, and they followed him into the sitting room. Sitting down, Danny looked at Lottie and said, "Now, what's this about Rose?"

"I located some more envelopes of other women who have been involved with Rose," said Lottie.

"More pictures?" asked Danny. "Of whom?"

"I can't say," said Lottie. "But one of the women was relieved Rose is gone. She was tired of paying her. I thought I would find out if the payments are still required. I sent letters to each person still here in town."

"What do you expect to find out?" asked Hen.

"That the blackmail is still ongoing; it will be additional proof that Rose is not being held against her will," explained Lottie.

Hen sat back with her cup and said, "You don't look upset."

"No," her friend admitted. "I don't think I am. There's too much evidence to deny her involvement."

"But there is something else," Hen guessed.

Lottie flushed. "No, not really. It's more that I've been outside of her influence."

"You're seeing things clearer?" asked Hen.

"Yes."

"What next?" asked Danny, moving them forward.

"The trial and any further threats that come from that." Lottie laughed suddenly and said, "Enough of that. Hen, I haven't heard about your new job. Do you like it?"

Hen glanced at Danny and said, "I didn't expect to, but yes, it's wonderful."

"What are you doing?" Lottie asked curiously.

"I'm working as an assistant teacher," stated Hen.

"They say she's doing so well, she'll have her own class next year," Danny said proudly.

"Oh, Hen, that's wonderful!" exclaimed Lottie, tears threatening to fall from her eyes at the news.

"I think so," she said, turning bright red. "The kids are delightful, and it makes me want this one even more." She rubbed her stomach lovingly.

"Will they let you stay after the baby is born?"

"Yes," she commented. "Danny will help out, and we can hire a cleaner to deal with the apartment."

"What about the protests and community service?" Lottie knew these were Hen's passions.

Henrietta looked at Danny and he nodded. "I've agreed I would be involved in the management but not the actual demonstrations. I need to keep me and this little one safe."

Lottie put her hand on Hen's belly. "I'm glad."

They stayed together and enjoyed the quiet evening.

The clock chimed and reminded Lottie of the time. She said regretfully, "I need to head home."

They hugged and she headed out. On her walk there she considered her week. She had gotten herself disconnected from Rose and had formed a small connection with Frank. He wasn't her knight in shining armor, but he was a man she liked and hoped to continue to see. The relationship didn't have the same intensity as that of Rose or Joseph. It didn't need to. She didn't want to be pulled into that kind of overwhelming relationship again.

The expectation was that the trial start and the blackmail would go full circle and put her in front of Rose. This time, that meeting would be on her terms; until then, she would work and live her life. It would be her new beginning.

# Chapter Thirty

T he next weeks were a blur. She and Chris barely left the office during that time. She did receive letters back from all of the women who were being black-mailed. The request for money had not abated. She assured them that she had custody of their pictures and requested that each stop paying. Her final message to them was that she would be in contact soon. The confirmation that Rose was still involved allowed her to move forward and concentrate on her job.

The day before the trial was to start, Lottie picked up an assortment of newspapers, including The World. All of them were full of conjectures about the methods the defense and the prosecutors would employ. They all implied the same thing: Charles Becker was guilty. The actual outcome was more spec-ulative. Police officers, even if found guilty, were not expected to go to jail. Even Becker.

She was reading one of them as she entered the office. Chris was at his desk and she commented, "I just don't under-stand how the papers can know the methods of defense. *The*

*World* talks like they've already been in the courtroom, witnessing testimony."

He didn't spare her a glance but continued to look through the book in front of him. "They're just guessing," he replied gruffly.

She wouldn't let it go. "Are they, though? The details listed here are suspicious. Could someone be talking? A leak in one or both of the legal offices?"

"I'm sure you are wrong," he said not looking up at her.

# Chapter Thirty-One

## Trial Day, Early Morning

L ottie was in the office earlier than usual; she wanted to get the files ready to take to court and read through her notes. The door opened from the hallway and Chris stood there. She teased, "You are running late this morning."

He looked distracted. His hair was mussed, and he carried a newspaper.

"Chris, what's wrong?"

He looked over at her and said in a dazed tone, "Zelig was murdered last night." Jack Zelig was a trial witness, he would testify that he took the money and arranged for the gunman accused in the Rosenthal murder. He had testified in front of the grand jury, but the information he shared had not been leaked.

"Murdered? Does it have something to do with our trial?" she asked, giving him her full attention.

"I think so, though I don't know which side will care more. He was on both lists as a witness."

"Did one side or the other think his evidence would be damaging? Enough to kill him?"

"He would either be testifying and corroborating Baldy Jack's testimony—helping the prosecution or he could testify that Baldy Jack acted alone, helping the defense. Now, we will never know."

They heard a noise in the hallway; Goff and Whitman entered together. Whitman was saying, "My God, what next?"

"Let's talk in my office," Goff said, pushing him along.

Whitman continued to mutter as he went in, "Jack Rose said Zelig wouldn't make it to trial."

The door closed and Chris and Lottie looked at one another and shrugged.

# Chapter Thirty-Two

**T**rial day—afternoon of October 7
The office had settled down after learning about Zelig. Whitman appeared to be calmer when he left Goff's office. He didn't acknowledge them as he went by.

After lunch, Chris and Lottie made their way over to the courtroom. They needed to organize the files for the start of the trial. When they got there, the courtroom was stifling hot. *We must have the worst court in the building*, she thought, looking around.

There were rumors that the entire criminal court building would be condemned at some point in the future. Long ago, the building had been a stylish location with a huge central rotunda rimmed with mezzanines and corridors with a glass roof. Now, that glass roof was encrusted with soot and the air rancid with garlic, stale cigar smoke, and sweat.

*That heat*, she thought, trying to breathe in the sticky air. The only air movement was coming from the fans mounted on the walls and opened windows. These brought little relief and a lot of noise. *It'll be a wonder if we're able to get through this without passing out.*

Their table was situated to the side of the Justice's bench. She looked over at Chris and saw he was already straining against his collar. Leaning toward him, she said in a low voice, "He's not here yet. He won't notice if you loosen it."

"Oh, he'll notice," Chris said, sending a disgusted look toward the Justice's bench. The man never seemed affected by the heat. "I don't know how he does it," muttered Chris.

She thought about all the times they were in court and the Justice always looked pristine, nary a hair out of place.

She and Chris sat waiting for the trial to begin. After this, she would be working the majority of the time in the court while Chris managed the office. It was required to be kept open as long as the trial was in session. Goff would expect them to be available at the end of each day to do a final review and update the calendar in preparation for the next day.

From their table, she watched as Becker was escorted into court with his lawyers and his wife. Lottie studied him closely, noting how solicitous he was, putting her in a chair located just behind him. *Demure and more than a little pregnant,* Lottie thought as the wife slipped off her jacket. *That will play well with the jury.*

The closer Becker walked toward Lottie, she noticed how imposing he was. He also didn't have eyes for anyone but his lawyer and his wife.

Watching the man, she could picture him in his uniform. He would make a formidable figure. *How did he get himself into this mess?* she wondered. *Was it, like Frank, small graft little by little until he just didn't think it was a bad idea to take the money?*

She looked down at the large reams of paper in front of her. They contained notes and references that may be needed for trial. Her job was to second guess every piece of evidence and motion, looking for prior trials that may offer precedent. She and Chris knew as much or more about the case than the lawyers and Justice assigned to the court. As the trial progressed, notes would be sent to Chris to provide additional research, as needed.

There were two things Becker would have to overcome: Jack Rose, a known gambler and lead witness, and then Becker's own integrity.

She looked at him, trying to see any villainy in the man. *Did he do it?* She shook her head; she was letting the graft influence her in the case. Unfortunately, this was also how the jury would see it. There was so little actual evidence other than graft. But this wasn't about that or the man's integrity, the charge was conspiracy to kill a witness, Herman Rosenthal. It would be up to Becker's lawyer to communicate that to the jury.

Herman Rosenthal was a special witness. He was giving evidence to the grand jury on police corruption, and worse, he named the Special Squad as the frontline men. Becker's entire career could be damaged based on that testimony.

The Special Squad that Becker led was responsible for raiding gambling clubs, which made him an invaluable asset to Commissioner Waldo, the city's young, reform-minded police commissioner. The clubs were in the Tenderloin, an amorphous district on the West Side, extending from 23rd Street to 42nd Street and northward. It was named "Satan's Circus" by clergymen, looking to close down the haven for prostitutes, con men, gamblers, and thieves.

Becker was leading a divided life that had finally caught up with him. She knew something about divided lives and could understand that part, but she knew what was right and what wasn't.

She watched Becker closely and thought, *He should admit to the graft. It would've been a better case if he'd admitted to it. Instead, he is still claiming he's innocent.* She understood that admitting to anything would be hard and would require jail time. *But, if convicted in this case,* she considered, looking at the Justice's bench and back at Becker, *he could be facing the electric chair.* A police officer had never been sentenced to death in New York before this, and he may not expect it to reach that level. She frowned heavily at him. *He's in trouble.*

Justice Goff walked into the court and paused as the bailiff instructed everyone to stand. He didn't look up as he took his seat and waited for the bailiff to announce court was in session.

As they sat back down, Chris nudged her and nodded at the Justice. "Thanks," she mouthed. She walked up to Goff and quickly explained the files in front of him. He had to be prepped before his appearance in court. She laid out the witness list and the files for each person.

She went back to her seat and watched as the jury selection began. She pulled out her notebook to take notes on the members selected. The jury pool to be questioned filed into the room, one man after another. When they finally were all in one place, she realized there were over 250 people empaneled for the voir dire. Her eyes were wide as she looked over at Chris; he shrugged.

The next two days went by in a haze of questions. It became obvious that Becker had requested a certain type of juror. His lawyer dismissed most of the single ones, having a strong preference for married men. *That's logical,* she thought, glancing over at Becker's wife.

She also noticed that the shorter men were being removed. Also, logical. Becker was easily over six feet and wouldn't want his size to intimidate them.

It wasn't until the fourth day that they seated the 12th

juror. Justice Goff's mood worsened as the voir dire drug on. Chris had returned to the office as the trial was scheduled to begin, leaving Lottie to manage the Justice.

Justice Goff stated to the court, "This trial will begin immediately." He then confirmed with the court what she already knew. "We will be through with the trial in just two weeks."

The defendant and his council looked astounded. D.A. Whitman's side of the table looked satisfied. This was what they had wanted all along.

The Justice continued. "We will do this as fast as possible and get it over with. It has been in the public eye long enough. The two weeks will include the time we spent on voir dire."

John McIntyre, Becker's attorney, stood up to object. "But that isn't possible..."

Goff interrupted him with a look. "Overruled. In this court, we do things my way. The hours will be 8 am to 11 pm, and we will go through the weekends."

There were groans from everyone in the court once the announcements had been made. Even Whitman looked shocked. He hadn't realized the hours that would be required. His co-council whispered furiously in his ear. He nodded and seemed to say something that mollified the other man.

The first day included opening statements that led straight to witness testimony. The temperature inside the room continued to rise, and the atmosphere became increasingly muggy. Fans pulled in the small amount of air from the opened windows. Lottie raised her paper to fan herself and got a hard glare from the Justice. She carefully put it back down.

Though the case had plenty of drama, the beginning was a slow start. The first witnesses were Patrolman Brady and Detective File, a police surgeon, and a doctor detailing the wounds. They gave standard testimony that didn't require much review.

Whitman was up first to question and had to stop when there was a disturbance in the jury box. The Justice looked over and asked forcibly, "What is the problem?"

The juror in the first seat closest to him said, "Your Honor, we can't hear over the fans."

"Turn them off," Goff directed the bailiff.

As the fans were shut off, the small amount of air movement settled, and it got hotter in the room. The testimony started again and there was more rumbling in the jury box.

"What now?" Goff asked. He was becoming exasperated at the continued interruptions.

The juror who answered before spoke up again. "It's the street noise. We still can't hear."

"Close the windows and pull the shades," Goff insisted.

Groans sounded in the room. The oppressive heat got worse. Lottie watched Goff. He wasn't scholarly, but what he was good at was manipulating the environment to suit him. Oddly, the worse the circumstances became, the more he seemed to be enjoying the proceedings. Nothing seemed to break his cool.

Whitman pulled at his collar, showing he was also affected by the heat. Lottie saw his glance at McIntyre. She could guess he was thinking he could outlast the older, obviously overweight man. Whitman may be uncomfortable, but he had the Justice on his side and wouldn't object to anything he put into place. She glanced over at Becker and saw he seemed to be holding up in the heat. What she could see was the tension radiating off of him, his jaw was tight and he stared straight ahead.

She looked over at the audience. If it had been the general public, the complaints would be expected to be loud, but this audience was filled with reporters. They were affected by the heat, but they wouldn't leave without their story. Justice Goff watched the audience each time he made a ruling. His ego was wrapped up in their coverage of him in their papers. She knew Chris would bring them in each morning for him to check for his name. Goff kept a collection of the clippings in his office.

*It's already been a long day*, she thought. *Especially with the Justice only allowing 15 minutes for lunch and 30 minutes for dinner*. She had to make sure his meal of crackers and milk arrived on time. He could be sustained on very little, unlike members of the defense and prosecution. The rest of them had to figure out how to survive through this trial.

The witness interview continued with Brady; McIntyre stood up yet again. "Objection!"

Lottie watched the Justice's interactions with McIntyre. *Stop objecting*, Lottie muttered. He just kept at it, angering the Justice.

Goff looked at the attorney fiercely. "I will have you removed from the court if you keep objecting."

McIntyre shut up. Even Whitman was shocked by that instruction. Court continued.

Lottie noticed Becker's wife in her seat behind him. The jury seemed enthralled with her, and she gave them all of her attention. She wore soft colors and coiffed hair. As she put her hand up to pat it, she would send a smile toward the jury. *Goff won't like that*, she thought, and she was right.

Goff did take notice. "Madam, you will move to the other side of the court," he instructed her.

Mrs. Becker looked shocked but stood to follow his direction. Becker's concerned glance followed her. It wasn't just Becker watching her; the entire room paid attention as she was relocated.

When that was finally settled, the witness testimony continued. Jacob Hecht, a waiter at the Metropole, was next.

Lottie checked her notes. This one should be fast. He only saw the pistol, not the person holding it.

"You saw the person lifting the pistol?" asked Whitman, confirming that the gunmen were there.

"I didn't," Hecht confirmed.

The next witness was Louis Krause, another waiter at the Metropole.

"The night in question, did you see who shot Mr. Rosenthal?"

Lottie had read his statement and knew he hadn't seen the shooter.

"Yes, I can identify each person." He named two of the men unhesitatingly; Lefty Louie and Gyp the Blood

Lottie was shocked, and it showed on her face. She made notes frantically. That wasn't the answer he gave before. *Will McIntyre catch that?* she thought. She watched him scribble fiercely in his notepad. *Ahh, he caught it also.*

"Can you tell me what you saw after the gunmen had run off?" Whitman asked.

"I saw Jack Sullivan turn the body over," Krause said. Jack was easily identified; he was infamous in Chicago as the "King of the newsboys".

"Did it appear that Sullivan was trying to offer assistance?" Whitman inquired. He knew Sullivan was a defense witness and, if he could cast some doubt on his character, he would.

"No, once the body was turned over, Sullivan laughed, like he was happy that 'ole Herman was dead," Krause said.

"Laughed?" repeated Whitman, letting the word hang in the air. The jury didn't like that and frowned heavily at Becker, blaming him for Sullivan's reported misdeeds.

Lottie checked her list and saw Krause was one of Becker's witnesses. McIntyre may have to rethink that interview.

It was McIntyre's turn, and the first thing he addressed was the contradictory statement. "Sir, that's not the statement you gave to the police previously."

"Yeah, well, I remembered it later," Krause said defiantly.

"Are you sure you gave a true statement?" McIntyre asked forcibly. He was trying to push the man into admitting the statement was a lie.

When the attorney tried to push him again, Goff spoke up.

"Asked and answered. Move on with it."

Lottie checked her notes and saw that Louis Krause and Jack Rose shared a lawyer. He had also identified Bridgey Webber running from the hotel after the murder had taken place.

McIntyre had made note of it and asked his next question. "I see that you and Jack Rose share a lawyer."

Krause looked quickly at Whitman and then at the Justice. "Do I have to answer that?"

The Justice shook his head. "No, I don't think so. Let's move on."

Lottie gave Whitman a long look. She had also wondered about the shared lawyer between Krause and Rose and practiced statements. It appeared the witness had been coached.

McIntyre looked down at his notepad and asked a few further questions. He tried to circle back to his original question but was halted again by Justice Goff. Lottie noted the interference in her notes.

Another witness, Smith, a loiterer outside the Metropole, had identified one gunman.

"You were standing outside, and you say you saw everything going on?" Whitman asked.

"Yes, that is right."

Whitman got what he wanted. "That is all I have."

McIntyre stood up with his notebook. Lottie watched him and thought, *This is a very deliberate man.*

"You testified you were able to see him clearly?" McIntyre asked though it wasn't really a question.

"Yes," Smith replied.

"You wear glasses."

"I do."

"Did you have them that night?"

"Well, no."

"How far can you see without them?"

"Well, they're strong, I need them most times to see distances."

"But that night you didn't have them?" McIntyre pressured.

"No."

"Did the prosecutor pay you $2,500 for your testimony?"

Whitman jumped up. "I object!"

"Sustained," Goff said to Whitman. He turned to McIntyre. "That is disallowed," he said forcefully. "It will be stricken from the record!"

Lottie and McIntyre shared the same expression of disbelief while Whitman smiled and sat down.

# Chapter Thirty-Three

Lottie entered the office after a long day and evening in court. She found Chris just where she thought he would be, at his desk. Jumping up as soon as she entered, he ran over to take the heavy files from her.

"Hard day in court?" he asked, noticing how wilted she looked.

She rolled her eyes at him. "It was a very interesting day."

"What do you mean?" he asked as he moved the files to his desk for them to sort. They still had a lot of work in front of them to prepare for the next day.

"I'm not sure, but I took notes on all of it." She slumped in her chair and pushed her matted hair off her forehead. "I don't see the point of this trial, Chris. It's a case for appeal."

"Appeal? You've seen enough for that already?"

"Chris, when McIntyre objected—and rightly so—Justice Goff told him to shut up," she told him in exasperation.

He looked shocked. Goff wasn't a learned man, but he normally upheld the rules of court. He didn't comment, waiting for more details.

She gave him the rundown of the day's events.

"It's such an odd trial. We haven't even heard Becker's name mentioned yet."

Chris frowned. "Really?"

"Yes, but we've gone through quite a bit of testimony. I don't think the Justice is coming back here tonight."

"No? Then let's get organized and head home."

"Let me change first."

He nodded. "Go ahead."

She changed quickly, washed her face, and walked back into the room. They pulled the witness list for tomorrow and the evidence that might be presented. As they finished, she sat on the edge of his desk, swinging her legs, the sound of her boots scraping echoing in the room. They sat for a moment, listening to that grating sound.

Finally, Lottie spoke up. "Chris, it's so strange. It's like someone got to the other witnesses." She paused. "Either Whitman, which could lead to a lot of trouble down the road for him, or someone else already knew who the witnesses were. There's supposed to be no surprises; depositions should have been a repeat of previous testimony, but people are changing their testimony as they sit on the stand."

Chris looked at her with a brooding expression. "That is a pretty heavy accusation and not to be made lightly."

"I think it's obvious something funny's going on. I'll continue to note the issues," she promised as she got up to move the files to the secured room. She didn't notice Chris' frown as she cleaned up.

They headed downstairs. "Do you want me to go with you to get your cycle?" Chris asked.

"No, I'm okay."

She watched as he called for a cab. It was too late to walk home.

"See you in the morning," he called.

"Bye, Chris."

She waited until he was inside the cab before retrieving her bike. The attendant had waited for her.

"The Justice is requiring long hours," he commented.

"Yes," she said, bending down to crank the cycle. "It's been a very long day. I appreciate you waiting for me."

"It wasn't a problem. I'll see you in the morning," he said, and he pulled the door down and locked it behind her.

She got on her cycle and headed home. The cool air kept her awake, she slowed the bike and looked around the city as she tried to sort out what had happened in court that day. Oddly, though the trial had begun, she had received no more blackmail threats, she had expected them now that the trial had begun.

She didn't know what to make of it; the wait was increasing her tension. *Is it better to have not received a demand? Are things progressing the way they wanted them, without my help? Tomorrow will be another long day.*

# Chapter Thirty-Four

*I*t's a parade, Lottie thought. *How many times do we need to see the gunmen?* It was also apparent that the prosecutors wanted the jury to get familiar with these men. She watched as the Lennox gang: Lefty Rosenberg, Whitey Lewis, Gyp the Blood Horowitz, and Dago Frank Cirofici were brought in again, the jury's gazes alternating between them and Becker. *Are they trying to make him part of the gang? Guilt by association?*

It sometimes had the opposite effect and scared the witnesses into changing their stories. That happened when the taxi driver assigned to the Metropole, Thomas Ryan, was so scared of the men, that he refused to identify them. Whitman had played this one out too many times.

With each witness, McIntyre pushed the Justice again with objections, and at one point, Goff leaned over his bench and growled at him, "I've overruled you before this; you might remember that next time." McIntyre knew there was nowhere to go once that statement had been made.

Morris Luban was the next witness. Lottie looked at her

notes. He was a petty thief and forger. They had to bring him in from a New Jersey jail to be in court that day. She watched Becker closely; she knew Morris had appeared on his list first. He was added to Whitman's later. *Why had this changed? Did Whitman make the better deal?*

Whitman went first. "Mr. Luban, you were at the Metropole that evening when Mr. Rosenthal was murdered."

"I was," Luban said shortly.

"You indicated you could identify three of the gunmen there that evening?"

"Yes."

Whitman paraded the gunmen in again, and Luban didn't change his story.

Whitman got what he wanted and moved on to his next questions. "You indicated that you were in the Lafayette bathhouse three weeks prior to the shooting. Could you tell the court about that meeting?"

"I saw Jack Rose," the witness paused for effect, "and Lieutenant Becker together."

Lottie was watching Becker. He clenched his jaw harder as he glared at Morris on the stand.

"Could you tell us if you heard them say anything?" Whitman asked.

Luban nodded over at Becker. "He said, 'If that bastard ain't croaked, I'll croak him myself.'"

*That's it*, thought Lottie, *the first evidence directly linking Becker to the Rosenthal killing.*

McIntyre saw this also and asked him about it when it was his turn to question him. "You identified three of the gunmen," he said, looking at Morris.

"Yes, I did," Luban said confidently, staring back at Whitman.

McIntyre seemed to be okay with that answer and went on. "Hmmm. Why were you at the theatre?"

"I was there with a girlfriend to see a movie at Hammerstein's."

"Hammerstein's, you say? What movie would that be?" the defense attorney asked, absently looking down at his notes.

"I'm not sure."

McIntire looked up abruptly and met the witness' eyes. "Well, Mr. Luban, I am sure. I checked the schedule for Hammerstein's. Would it surprise you to find it was not open that night?"

Luban faltered when confronted with that. He didn't have an answer.

Lottie thought, *Finally, McIntyre won some points.*

McIntyre continued. "Mr. Luban, did you contact my client and tell him you would help him with this case?"

"Well, uh...."

McIntyre didn't wait for his response but pressed on. "Didn't you, in fact, send four different letters to my client offering to exchange testimony for less jail time?" When Luban didn't answer, he continued "When he didn't do what you wanted, you then offered yourself to the prosecution. You are trying to frame my client!"

The witness looked over at Whitman and then at McIntyre. "I expect a fair trade for my being here on this stand."

Justice Goff saw that McIntyre had demolished Luban's testimony. He immediately said, "We'll call it a day. Mr. Whitman, will you be ready in the morning?"

"Yes, Judge," the district attorney said quietly. He sat with his head bowed, thinking.

# Chapter Thirty-Five

"What are you doing here? It's barely evening," Chris asked as Lottie entered the office. He immediately went to help her with the heavy files.

"Thanks," she said. For the first time that week, she was tired but not exhausted.

"You wouldn't believe it, but McIntyre got ahead this afternoon," she stated as she sat on her office chair.

"How did Goff and Whitman handle that?" he asked, sitting on the side of his desk, watching her.

"There was a concern, hence the shorter day," she commented sardonically.

"Interesting. Was it important testimony?" he asked.

"It was, but it shouldn't have been."

Chris frowned. "Why?"

"Morris Luban contradicted his prior testimony," she stated simply. It had been going on throughout the trial.

"He changed it? How so? Did McIntyre catch it?"

"He didn't object. Instead, he went after him on cross. It

244

was smart. Goff wouldn't have let him question him later if he had objected."

"Well, what was the testimony?" he asked expectantly.

"There were two parts—the first one, he said he could identify three of the gunmen."

Chris frowned. He knew the prior interviews as well as she did.

She caught the look and said, "Exactly. Before this, he claimed he didn't see anyone."

Chris continued to frown but stayed silent.

"The second part was when he said he had witnessed a meeting at the bathhouse between Becker and Jack Rose. He claims he overheard them talking about the murder."

"The first link to Becker," Chris said. "How did the jury react?"

"I hope they paid attention to McIntyre and didn't believe Luban."

"So, it depends on who they decide is telling the truth," he stated, somewhat shakily.

"Yes." She looked over at him. "Chris, are you okay?" He looked a bit lost. He was normally so cheerful and confident; this wasn't like him.

"Yes, of course. Just a long day."

Chris stuck his hand in his pocket, crushing the note he had received from Jake Luban, Morris Luban's brother. It could help destroy Luban's testimony. The letter was clear, his brother and family do not believe he had seen the shooting, and that he had never been to the bathhouse.

"Who's up tomorrow?" Chris asked casually, leaving his hand in his pocket, wrapped around that note.

"Jack Rose," Lottie said, handing him the list.

"Only one name."

"Yes. I expect it'll be a much longer day than today."

# Chapter Thirty-Six

D .A. Whitman must have felt threatened at that point and pulled out the big guns. It was time for Jack Rose to be called in. *This one will be rehearsed,* thought Lottie. *Whitman will have wanted everything perfect for his testimony.*

She had pulled up her files the night before to refresh herself on his prior interviews. Initially, Jack Rose and his fellow conspirators, not including Becker, had been the ones who were going to be charged for conspiracy to kill Rosenthal. It was Whitman who had decided there was a connection between Jack Rose and Charles Becker. He directed the investigation, independent of the police, to prove it.

Whitman believed the police had proven they couldn't be trusted. He monitored the investigation closely after the murder and felt their actions showed a deliberate refusal to follow the facts. These facts included no clear identification of the gunman, even with six officers within 100 feet of the area.

The first break in his case had been the chauffeur, William Shapiro, who drove the conspirators to the Webber's gambling house and the gunmen to the Metropole. Shapiro finally gave in to the pressure and gave them some of the conspirators' names, Harry Vallon, Bridgey Webber, and Jack Rose. Initially, the papers reported that all three would face their own trials and be charged with conspiracy in Rosenthal's murder. *I guess Whitman had another option and chose to lay it all at Becker's feet.*

Lottie checked the files and realized the D.A. had Rose and the other conspirators stashed locally for weeks. On the way to court that morning, she tried to broach the subject with Goff.

"But, sir, the D.A. has had the men stashed locally, probably rehearsing their testimony for weeks."

The Justice didn't spare her a glance and said dismissively, "It's not important."

Nodding, she knew when to stop pushing him. *Another item for the appeal pile*, she thought, going ahead of him into the court to set up his files. She was just walking to her chair when he entered.

"All rise."

Justice Goff sat down behind the bench. He said, without looking up, "You may be seated. Let's get on with this. Mr. Whitman, did you want to redress Mr. Morris' testimony from yesterday?"

"No, sir. We'd like to have our next witness, Jack Rose, brought into the court."

Goff waved his hand at Whitman, indicating for him to begin. He then turned to the bailiff. "Close those windows and turn off those fans!"

As the bailiff did as he was asked, Jack Rose, also known as Baldy Rose, entered the court. Lottie watched him come in and saw that he was perfectly styled and dressed in a pressed blue suit. The man was in custody, but he didn't appear to have suffered any hardship. The other witnesses had been in bad condition and were delivered from prison the same morning they testified. *Not Baldy Rose,* she thought. *He looks well-rested.*

She watched him carefully as he sat down in the witness stand, noting how cool he seemed. Glancing around the hot room, she saw the jurors had rolled up their sleeves and were fanning themselves. Looking at the gallery, she noticed more seats had been added and thought, *It looks like an additional 100 more people have been squeezed into the room.*

She looked back at Rose. He removed his hat; no sweat beaded on his impressive head. *He must have shined it for court.*

His prior testimony covered his working relationships with both Rosenthal and Becker. The information he was set to provide on the graft and his ongoing work with Rosenthal rang true. *But that was the best way, bury the lies in a pile of truth.* She watched him, wondering what he would say.

Frank Moss, working with Whitman as an assistant prosecutor, took up the interview. As Rose was questioned, his tone conveyed no emotion as he explained how he had worked with Becker to collect graft. He then detailed his work with Herman Rosenthal. That work had been in one capacity or another for the last twenty years.

Lottie and the rest of the court listened intently. The lower Rose's voice became, the more the court strained to hear him. She also noticed Goff was on his feet, leaning over toward the witness. That gave an air of authenticity to the proceedings.

She heard the careful questions given and the ease at which Baldy Rose answered them. It was obvious his testimony had been rehearsed.

Moss continued asking him to detail the relationship between Rosenthal and Becker. "Mr. Rose, you have testified previously that Rosenthal and Becker had a personal and working relationship."

"Yeah, they were partners in Rosenthal's club. Rosenthal needed money and Becker knew it."

"How would you say they got along?"

"Becker went out of his way to socialize with Rosenthal. Rosenthal wanted reassurance that his club would be spared any more raids. He thought it would be best to have a deal with Becker to protect his interest."

"Did something happen to that relationship?"

"You could say that. Even with the partnership, Becker couldn't stop the raids. Rosenthal was losing money with each one. He was getting frustrated and took that out on Becker."

"What did the frustration lead Mr. Rosenthal to do?"

"He started talking about taking Becker down. He'd finally had enough and notified the authorities about the graft."

"Did Mr. Becker ever say directly that he wanted Rosenthal dead?"

"Yes, many times," Rose said quietly.

"Did anyone else witness these conversations?"

"Yes, Vallon, Webber, and Schepps were included in the planning."

Lottie listened to the testimony closely. She knew the three men he listed were the other conspirators on the witness list. Given their location the last few weeks, corroboration of Rose's testimony would be guaranteed. *It'll keep them out of jail. It seems that it's Becker or them.*

"Can you describe where these meetings took place?" Moss asked.

Lottie thought, *He needs the jury to take Baldy Rose's testimony as fact. Otherwise, there's no other motive for Becker to kill Rosenthal. That the conspiracy occurred was not in question; what was in question was Becker's involvement.*

"Was one of the meetings at the Lafayette Bathhouse?" Moss asked, leading the witness.

"Yes," Baldy Rose confirmed.

*Morris' statement is back in,* Lottie thought. *They have corroboration now.*

"Were there other scheduled meetings?" Moss continued.

"Becker had a scheduled raid of a crap game on West 124$^{th}$ street. He wanted to meet then, outside in an empty lot."

"When was this?"

"June or July, sometime."

*Moss didn't question that; did McIntyre catch it?* She watched the defense attorney closely. He gave no indication that she could read. Lottie made note of that discrepancy. *Baldy Rose could remember all of the details from that meeting, but couldn't be sure of what month the meeting happened?*

Once again, the newspapers that morning were ahead of them, already writing articles on that meeting, calling it The Harlem Conference. She looked at Becker and thought, *Who would arrange a murder in the open in a lot where anyone could see them? That just didn't seem likely for a police officer who knows that, if anyone saw them together, they could be a witness.*

As Becker listened to Rose's testimony, he seemed to change into stone. The only thing that showed he was human was the sweat pouring down his face.

Baldy Rose continued with his testimony. He stated that he followed Becker's direct orders to hire a hitman and organize the conspiracy.

Lottie thought, *All this proves is a connection of Rose to the gunman and the conspirators. It is just his word that Becker was involved. Why is his word deemed more important than that of a policeman?* She paused. *Patrick,* she thought. *He said that policemen who became involved in criminal activities were no*

*better than the criminals. Does Whitman believe that Baldy
Rose's testimony alone will convict him?*

She and the entire court sat through four hours of Baldy
Rose's testimony with no breaks. McIntyre tried to object
repeatedly. None of which were sustained. Lottie made
another note for the appeal files. The Justice would not allow
for any conflicting statements to be presented.

Lastly, as Moss wrapped up his questions, Baldy Rose said
there had been a follow-up meeting, after the killing, with the
crew, where Becker had congratulated them for their work.

Lottie watched the jury. They believed everything this
witness was saying. They were even nodding in agreement
with his statements. Worse, Baldy Rose's initial deposition
didn't seem to matter. All of a sudden, there were details that
had never been shared before, such as instructions from Becker
on how to kill Rosenthal.

McIntyre could not object that morning, but he was ready
for his turn that afternoon. He had pages and pages of data on
Baldy Rose's background and his misdeeds. There was plenty
to show that past crimes, depravity, and that, by his very nature,
he was not a good person.

Lottie watched as McIntyre approached the witness stand
to start asking questions. Question after question, it became
obvious McIntyre didn't have a chance. Whitman and Goff
might as well have been working off a script. Every question out
of his mouth, everyone that could have led to evidence of Baldy
Rose's character was objected to and sustained. *He might have
won some points there*, she thought, *if Whitman hadn't been
allowed to object to every question.*

Lottie leaned forward and rested her chin in her hands.
Even if Whitman and Goff weren't involved, Rose slowed the
process so much; that it almost didn't matter what the question
was. It took 20 minutes of questions just to find out that he was

from Poland. McIntyre was part of the problem, he allowed himself to be pulled down the path. After a while, even Lottie wanted him to move on more quickly; this frustrating waste of time didn't give any points to Becker.

He was trying to prove Baldy Rose had a personal grudge against Rosenthal and that Becker was not involved. The testimony drug on into the night. Lottie watch McIntyre with concern; his health seemed to be deteriorating in front of them. The later it got, he seemed to lose more and more color in his face. *Is Goff trying to kill him?*

# Chapter Thirty-Seven

After Rose's testimony was finally completed, Lottie and Chris were discussing the case after the files were put away.

"Chris, you wouldn't believe Goff's behavior toward Baldy Rose today. It was like he was a respected member of the community. He's a murderer, scoundrel, and miscreant, but the jury is being manipulated into believing everything the man says. In that court, you'd believe the world had been tilted on its axis; the gangster is the good guy and the policeman is the bad guy.

She folded her arms and laid her head on her desk. She turned her head toward him and said, "Just when it looked like McIntyre had something that would show the jury who Baldy Rose really was, the Justice interrupted and told Rose to take the fifth. Any answers that may have been given were stopped, that was it for McIntire."

She stood up and slammed her fist on the desk. "I can't stand watching this day after day."

"It'll be over soon," he said quietly.

253

She looked over at him and said, "I thought McIntyre was going to have a heart attack today. When he was about to collapse, he asked for a delay to rest. He's overweight and unhealthy. Goff turned a cold eye toward him and said, "No.""

"No! Chris, it had been four hours. We weren't even allowed food or restroom breaks."

"What happened?" He couldn't help but be fascinated.

"He couldn't go on and Goff took advantage."

"What did he do?"

"He told McIntyre that he was forfeiting the three hours of cross-examination and he wouldn't be able to call Rose again."

"Wow," he whispered. He hadn't realized this had gotten so far out of hand.

"Chris, McIntyre didn't even get to question Rose about the Harlem Conference. There's no way Becker's getting a not guilty verdict. Goff has made sure of that."

"What's the Justice like in court with Whitman?"

"Oh, they're pals. Goff may as well move to the prosecutor's table. He and Whitman are together at every break whispering, and not including McIntyre in any of it."

"He's definitely on their side," surmised Chris.

"Do you know what they call Becker in court, in front of the jury?" she asked.

"No," he said.

"Grafter," she stated.

"The Justice allows that?" he said incredulously.

"He does and he's part of it. McIntyre tried to tell the court that Rose and the other conspirators had an easy time in prison, but Goff stopped that as well," she explained.

They heard a scraping on the floor and Chris put his finger to his lips.

She nodded and they both watched the door as Justice Goff came in.

"Sir," said Chris, coming around his desk. "I thought you'd gone home."

"I will soon," he confirmed. "I needed a few things from the office. It's going very well, I think," he said with a self-satisfied smile and walked to his office.

"Sir," started Lottie as she moved toward him. "I'm concerned that the defense has grounds for an appeal."

That stopped him cold. He turned slowly and, for the first time, put his steely blue eyes on her. "And just what do you mean by that?"

Lottie refused to be intimidated. She took a deep breath and stated, "The defense hasn't been able to put forth an adequate defense. Your repeated overruling of his questions lays the groundwork for this." *Among many other things,* she thought.

For the first time, he seemed to have heard her. He didn't deny it, but responded with, "I'll take that into account tomorrow." Goff turned and walked into his office, slamming the door behind him.

Chris whispered, "Well done."

"Thanks. I don't know what help, if any, that will provide to McIntyre or Becker. At this point, there should be a mistrial," she continued in a low voice.

"That won't happen," he stated, wishing this trial could be over.

"No," she agreed as he helped her organize her files for the next day. She would have to bring everything over, realizing Goff could take them in any direction.

Chris walked her downstairs and noticed her hands were shaking.

"Will you be able to get home safely?" he asked, concern in his voice.

She started to respond when she saw a car parked just

outside of the door and a man leaning against the hood. Her frown turned into a smile when she saw who it was.

"Frank!"

He straightened as he saw her.

"Hi, Lottie. I heard it was a long day and thought you might need a ride home."

Chris sent her a crooked smile. "Looks like I can leave you in capable hands." He waved to Frank and walked off.

Frank went up to her and traced the circles under her eyes. "You look tired."

She didn't deny that. "Do you have room for my bike?" she asked. She didn't want to leave it overnight and would need it to ride to work in the morning.

"I think I can help with that." He reached into the back of the car to pull out some rope.

"A planner, I like that," she said.

She went to the garage to get the bike. He hurried to help her roll it out. They lifted it together and tied it down. Once that was done, they climbed into the vehicle.

She looked around at the damaged car and asked him dryly, "New?"

He patted the rather rackety dashboard and said, "It's a project." His other car had started out the same way. It was his hobby.

"Where did you get it?" she asked a bit dubiously.

"Junkyard."

"I couldn't tell." She laughed.

"It'll take some work, but I think it'll be worth it."

"You could be right," she replied, thinking that nothing of value came easily.

He reached into the back of the car and pulled out a pail, handing it to her.

"What is this?" she asked, bewildered.

"Open it," he invited.

She did and saw chicken and rolls inside.

"Food! I feel like I haven't eaten in weeks."

"I can tell. You've lost some weight. The hours you're working are too much." He had kept up with the trial through the papers.

"It won't be much longer now," she said, her mouth full of chicken.

He nodded remembering her mentioning Goff's vacation. He let the topic drop and the rest of the ride was quiet. As he pulled up in front of her apartment, he looked over and saw she was asleep, holding a half-finished drumstick in her hand. He smiled and stroked her cheek. "Lottie, wake up."

She blinked slowly and realized where she was. "Oh, I guess I am more tired than I thought."

"Do you have your key for your storeroom?"

"I do." She opened her purse, pulled out the key, and handed it to him. "Do you need some help?"

"I've got it," he said. He went out to untie the bike, set it on the ground, and rolled it to the storeroom. He put it away and locked the door behind him. Coming around, he helped her out of the car; she swayed into him.

"Can I help you upstairs?" he asked.

"Please," she said.

He put his arm around her waist and escorted her to her door.

When they got there, she pulled out her keys. "Would you like to come in?"

"I would, but do you need company this late?" he asked, checking the time. It was past midnight.

"I'd love you to stay over," she said simply, as she opened the door

"I think that can be arranged," he murmured and followed her in. "Why don't you go get ready for bed?"

"I'll do that."

She washed up quickly in the bathroom, put on her nightgown, and called out, "I'm out if you want to use it. I have an extra toothbrush in the cabinet."

He stuck his head in the door and raised an eyebrow at her.

"My brother Patrick," she explained. "He's always forgetting his at home."

He smiled and went in to wash up. The lights were off when he left the bathroom. Smiling, he made his way quietly to the bed and climbed in. As he pulled her close, she sighed deeply and they went to sleep.

Lottie woke and looked over at the clock. *How did six o'clock arrive so quickly?* She was still exhausted and started to get up.

"Hey, where are you going?" he asked, pulling her to him.

She thought, *I should say no, but I want this.*

He kissed her deeply and pulled her on top of him.

A little while later, she pushed her hair back. "Now, I really have to get dressed. I have to be in the office soon!"

He watched as she hurried to the closet to get her pants and shirt for the ride over and a dress for the courtroom before she headed to the bathroom.

She looked at herself in the mirror and made a face. *What have I done? I'm attracted to him, but not in love. It's not fair to him.* She put it out of her mind. There wasn't time to think about this now. She bathed quickly and put on her makeup. Exiting the bathroom, she was fully dressed and brushing her hair.

Frank came into the bedroom with a cup of coffee. He walked over and handed it to her. "This is for you."

"Thank you," she said, taking it gratefully.

"I'll be quick. Can I drive you to work this morning?"

"No, I'll be faster on my own," she said, gulping the drink down. She headed to the kitchen as he got dressed. He was hurriedly putting on his tie as he joined her.

"I wanted to ask last night, but you were so tired. Have you received any other threats?"

"What?" she asked distractedly. She was trying to get organized to leave. Realizing what he said, she replied, "No. And you know, it's odd."

"Maybe the case is going their way and they don't need help," he supplied.

She grimaced. "That could be. There does seem to be someone leaking information; the papers know who the witnesses are at the same time I do. It's just odd."

"No word from Rose?"

"No, and I have to admit I'm relieved. I have enough drama with the trial."

He caught her hand as she was crossing the room and pulled her to him.

"Frank!" she protested. "I have to get to work."

"I enjoyed spending the time with you," he murmured into her hair.

"Frank, we'll have to talk when I have more time," she stated, trying to pull away.

"Talk?" he asked as he let her go. "Why?"

She didn't want to go into it now but said, "I am attracted to you, but I don't think there's more than friendship here."

He dropped the hand he had on her arm. "I guess I was trying to make it more."

"Frank, I needed a friend, and you were here for me. I won't forget that." She glanced at the time again and said, "I have to get going."

He understood this was not the right time. "I would like to spend some time with you after all of this is over."

"Frank, I just don't have time to answer that now," she said as she grabbed her hat and bag. Opening the door, she found Patrick there. "Patrick!" She jumped into his arms.

"Lottie," he said, hugging her back.

"I can't talk Patrick. I'm late," she said as she pulled away and rushed out. She called over her shoulder teasingly, "Lock up when you leave."

Patrick watched her leave and finally noticed someone else in the room. He turned around slowly and said, "Hello, Frank."

"Hello, Patrick," Frank said in the same tone.

Patrick looked at him. "Why are you here so early?"

"Is it early?" Frank asked, stalling.

Patrick made his way to the bedroom and knocked the door open, the bed was not made, and there were men's shoes nearby. He looked pointily at Frank's feet. "Yeah, it is."

Frank felt at a disadvantage and went to get his shoes. He slid them on and came out into the living room.

"I'm in here," called Patrick from the kitchen

Frank followed his voice and found him raiding Lottie's pastries.

"Hey, save some of that for me," Frank protested, reaching for one.

Patrick let him take a pastry and they sat at the table.

"Are you together?" Patrick asked neutrally.

"Me and Lottie? No. I don't think we are," Frank said, thinking of their conversation this morning.

"Then what are you?"

"Friends. I brought her home last night. She was too tired to drive after her day in court."

Patrick raised an eyebrow at that. "I heard the Becker trial was going long hours."

"It is and I appreciate your coming back. We need the help."

"What else has happened?"

Frank went into the details of the blackmail and the possible tie-in with the Becker trial.

"Who's on your list of suspects?"

Frank handed Patrick his notes.

"Yes, I expected these names. I'm here to offer assistance."

"Good."

# Chapter Thirty-Eight

Lottie arrived at the office and entered quickly. Chris saw her. "Hurry and change," he said. "I'll help you move the files over."

She nodded and ran to the hall closet to change into her skirt. When she came back, Chris was waiting beside a tall stack of files.

They each took a pile and made their way to the courtroom. Chris set his files down and watched her. "Do you know his plans today?"

"No, not at all," she commented. "Hence the files."

"Do you mind if I watch for a few minutes?"

"Nothing at the office this morning?"

"No, it should be quiet."

Justice Goff stood in the doorway.

"All rise," the bailiff called.

Justice Goff entered and sat at his bench. "Mr. McIntyre, come to the bench, please."

McIntyre walked up. "Yes, Justice Goff?" he asked.

"I'm going to allow you time this morning to recall any of

the two witnesses and question them. You may ask any of the twenty-nine disputed queries from the previous days."

McIntyre looked at him with amazement. "That won't work. It will be entirely out of context."

"You are turning down the opportunity I am giving you?" Goff asked in a rough voice.

"The answer would have to be no, sir," he said firmly.

When he got that response, his gaze moved to the prosecutor's table. "Mr. Moss, I would like you to step up and ask the questions for Mr. McIntyre." Goff had made up his mind on the matter and sent a pointed look to Whitman. Whitman got the message and waved Frank Moss over to ask the defense questions.

Moss looked very confused as he was handed a list of defense questions to ask various witnesses on Becker's behalf. It was a confusing part of the trial for both the jury and the witnesses. Chris rolled his eyes and left the court by the side door after this was completed.

Clearly, Justice Goff thought he had fixed his issue with an appeal. He smiled triumphantly as Moss finished the questions, then he immediately moved on with the trial.

"Mr. Whitman, you may begin your witness interview."

The witnesses on the list for the day were known conspirators to Jack Rose. They were there to corroborate his statements.

Bridgey Webber was the first to take the stand and confirmed everything in Rose's testimony word-for-word in what appeared to be a rehearsed statement.

McIntyre stood up for his cross-examination. Lottie watched and waited for him to ask if the Harlem Conference had taken place. She listened to the questions and thought, *He made several mistakes. He's never disputed the Harlem Conference took place. He needs to convince the jury that this meeting never happened. It's a bit of a miss; the jury could assume that McIntyre accepted it as a real event.*

Next was Harry Vallon; his testimony was similar to Webber. He was there only for corroboration of Rose's testimony.

*Funny,* observed Lottie, *all of these people attending the so-called Harlem conference, and yet no one seems to be able to pin down when it happened. What about the chauffeurs? They indicated they were driven there. Why hasn't anyone asked about who drove these men to that location?* She made a note for her files.

The third conspirator to be interviewed was Sam Schepps. She sat up straighter in her chair to watch as he was brought in. This was the most important witness in this trial. Not even Jack Rose was as important.

*You wouldn't think it looking at him,* she thought as she watched him enter the courtroom. He seemed to be doing well as a prisoner/witness. He looked nothing like what he was, a man known for his fake jewelry and other cons. Today, he looked like he was a businessman on a lunch break. He wore a tailored suit and nicely combed hair.

What was the reason he was so important to the court? New York law clearly stated that the evidence of a crime was not admissible when all persons were a party to the crime. Schepps was in a precarious position; he had to show no apparent involvement with the killing, but also, he had to be able to corroborate what the other prisoners were saying.

*Why pick him for such an important role?* thought Lottie. She thought about that and pulled up the files she had on him. *He was the last one picked up. There was no one else who could play this role. Could it be that simple?*

She checked his current location and confirmed he was put with Webber, Vallon, and Rose in prison. *Time enough to get their stories straight,* she thought, casting a look toward Whitman. *How's he going to work this?* Jack Rose was clear in his early deposition statements, Schepps was the money man. Schepps had admitted giving Zelig $1000 to secure the Lennox gang for gunman services. That was Whitman's first problem. Before the trial, an altered statement was submitted that removed Schepps and replaced him with Jack Rose as the one who paid the money to Zelig.

And then there was William Shapiro, the chauffeur of the Packard who drove the conspirators to Webbers Gambling establishment and picked up the gunmen at the same location on the same night. He refused to name the gunmen, but he could identify some of the conspirators, Vallon and Schepps, as being in his car earlier that night.

She continued to watch Schepps, noting his grin. *That grin is disconcerting,* she thought. *He seems to think everything's under control. If it was me, this should have been the focus of the entire trial. This one thing could take Whitman's entire prosecution down. McIntire needs an admission that Schepps played an active part in the conspiracy.*

As McIntyre stood up with his notebook open, she shifted her gaze to Whitman. She noticed he looked unconcerned; he didn't seem to think the witness needed his help. He watched but didn't object to the question being presented by McIntyre.

Lottie pulled Jack Rose's deposition when McIntyre referenced it.

"You were there when Becker and Rose were discussing the murder?" McIntyre asked. He was trying to prove this witness was part of the overarching crime.

"I was there but I never heard anything," Schepps stated.

"How is that possible?" the attorney asked incredulously.

"They whispered in each other's ears when I was around," he said, preening a bit at his own importance.

Following up on that, McIntyre next asked, "You indicated you were with the group other times when they met. What did you do when they were talking?"

"I walked outside by myself."

"How long?" McIntyre demanded.

"From lunch until the evening."

McIntyre shook his head. "Your trip in the car with Jack Rose on the way to Webber's place and then with Harry Vallen on the way to the Metropole the night of July 15," he continued. "What did you talk about?"

Schepps said musingly, "Oh, the sun came up and the clouds were in the sky and things like that."

McIntyre had enough. "Were you a deaf and dumb partner?" he shouted.

Schepps just snickered at him.

"How often have you socialized with Becker?" McIntyre asked as he looked down at his notes.

"I hardly ever was with Becker. I only met him a few times in my life."

Lottie knew Schepps was lying. In earlier interviews, he had stated that he had been invited to Becker's home more than once.

McIntyre tried again to show he had contradictory testimony.

"Is it true, that in your prior statements you confirmed you have been to my client's house and that you were on friendly terms?"

"That question is disallowed, and the statement is inadmissible as evidence," Goff shouted.

McIntyre tried again. "I have a record here that says you had him in your home."

"I do not remember that."

Goff interrupted, "Move on, it has been reviewed."

# Chapter Thirty-Nine

"It got so bad," Lottie told Chris that night after court. "Schepps was noticeably laughing at McIntyre during his testimony."

"Did McIntyre notice?"

"Yes, it was horrible. He told Schepps, 'You're treating this matter as a joke!' And yelled at him to stop."

"Did he?"

"Sadly, no."

"What did the Justice do?"

Sighing heavily, she said, "He did the same as always, nothing. He doesn't do anything that might help the defense. Though I do think Whitman talked to Schepps at the lunch break."

"Why do you say that?"

"When Schepps got back on the stand, he stopped with the extraneous details and just stated the facts."

"Did McIntire get any questions in about the Harlem Conference?" he asked, hoping something good had come out of the day.

"No, but that is the question I wanted to be asked. Each time it has come up in the trial, no one can remember the actual date. It is clever. Becker cannot provide evidence he wasn't there if there was no definite date." She leaned her head back on her chair, staring at the ceiling.

"So, is that it? Are we done?" Chris asked.

"We are finished with Whitman's side. I think, if Becker would testify, they could generate some good feelings for him. He just sits there like a large statue. There is no center to the defendant's case, no heart and no one to root for. Also, the main person in the case, Schepps, came off as a corroborator and not a conspirator. The jury could tell he wasn't respectable, but they think Becker is worse."

"So, it is finally going to be McIntyre's turn to present his case. Lottie, get the witness list." She got it and handed it to him. He eyed the long list and asked, "How many?"

"Forty."

"About the same as Whitman's list. This will take more than a week," said Chris, continuing to review the list.

"It should be longer," she said scoffingly. "McIntyre still needs to prove Becker was not at either meeting at the baths or the Harlem Conference."

"Okay, so we will see what happens. Ready to head out?" Chris asked, helping her up.

"Yes," she said and headed home for some sleep.

# Chapter Forty

Chris and Lottie hadn't had a chance to talk after court during McIntyre's witnesses' testimony. Justice Goff was omnipresent in the office during that week—before and after the trial. He had his hands in everything, including McIntyre's witness list. He immediately began making changes by removing two people who could have helped Becker's integrity as a man and policeman. They were Will Travers Jerome, former district attorney, and Police Commissioner Waldo. Both could speak to his police record but were disallowed. Lottie glanced at Chris, and he shook his head, knowing she wanted to say something to Goff.

That final night of the trial, she was organizing the information into files to be locked away. At the same time, she was wrapping up the details of the week with Chris.

She shook her head and said, "I thought McIntyre might finally have a chance."

"What happened?" asked Chris.

"Fred Hawley, a reporter for *The Sun*, said there was no

way Becker could have been at the Murray Hill Baths for the meeting. He stated that he was with him the entire time that meeting could have taken place."

"We didn't have that in our depositions," Chris said, pulling the file.

"No. When he was asked by McIntyre about that, he stated he didn't want Whitman to know what he was planning to say."

"That sounds like a win. How did Whitman react?" Chris commented admiringly.

"He jumped up and said that was the most insulting statement he had ever heard in an American court. Then he demanded to take the stand to be interviewed by Mr. Moss."

Chris frowned. "Whitman made himself a witness? To be interviewed by his co-chair? This is a farce."

"Yes."

"What did he say?" Chris had to know.

"He contradicted the statement made by Hawley about his character."

"Who did the jury believe?"

"Whitman, of course," she said shortly.

"Just odd. Who was next?"

"Jack Sullivan. He was at Webber's gambling establishment with Rose, Schepps, and Vallen."

"Did Whitman have him under control also?"

"No, that one wanted to talk. He has stated since the beginning Becker was innocent."

"Wasn't he pulled in on this as a possible conspirator or murderer?"

"He was indicted," she confirmed. "Whitman's keeping him in jail to put pressure on him. They can't get him to flip on Becker, and he has no apparent ties to the case."

"What did he testify to?"

"He implied that it was a conspiracy to get Becker. Whitman didn't like him; Sullivan wouldn't bend to his will and change his story about Becker."

"That sounds good for McIntyre," suggested Chris.

She looked over at him and said, "It would be, but who to believe? Jack Sullivan or Jack Rose?"

Chris looked down at his list. "Wasn't the chauffeur, William Shapiro, next?" he asked.

"Yes. He was McIntyre's last chance to get Becker out of this mess. He needed him to help prove Schepps was an active member of the conspiracy and not just a collaborator."

"This has been the key all along. He was the chauffeur of the gray Packard that transported the hitman to the Hotel Metropole to kill Rosenthal. He also transported Jack Rose and Sam Schepps that same evening. His knowledge of their conversations could discredit both witnesses for the prosecution, if handled right."

"And it should have," Lottie said quietly. "McIntyre started his questions and what happened?"

"What?" asked Chris, fascinated by the events.

"You know that ponderous way he has of asking a question?"

"Long delays and lead-up?"

"Exactly. When he looked like he was finally going to ask the hard question, Whitman called for an immediate adjournment. Goff, of course, allowed it."

"What? Right then?" Chris was on the edge of his seat.

"Yes. And during the adjournment, Whitman and Goff got together to get a grand jury organized to look into police corruption. They had Shapiro called as a witness. Whitman watched as Shapiro was served in court and chose that time to offer him full immunity."

"Whitman knew Shapiro's testimony could have Schepps removed as a corroborator and negatively affect his entire case."

"Yes. Shapiro took the immunity offer and, in effect, switched himself from a defense to a prosecuting witness. They pulled him back up to the stand and what do you think happened? He recanted his earlier statements and said that Schepps was nowhere near the murder car."

"Wow! How did his summation go?"

"For McIntyre? Not well. He basically said, if Becker had been involved, he would have done a better job at planning the murder. He didn't bring up facts I thought were pertinent, specifically those involved in the Harlem meeting. He had testimony that could exclude the bathhouse meeting, but he should have gone harder on the Harlem conference."

"Who closed the prosecutor's case?"

"Frank Moss. Whitman watched with a self-satisfied expression. Unlike McIntyre's summation, Moss did go over each point in the case: confirming the four gunmen who fired upon Rosenthal, that Jack Rose was a puppet for Becker and scared of him, that Schepps was an accessory after, and a few statements mentioning the graft, without McIntyre saying the word."

"Concise," commented Chris.

"Interestingly, Moss did lie directly in the summation."

"How so?"

"He said Jack Sullivan had changed his testimony from the grand jury. I thought McIntyre was going to attack him on that one."

Chris muttered, "Tomorrow's the day the Justice will charge the jury."

Both of them frowned. Even the little bit of chance Becker had, could be killed by the charges to the jury. A judge could sway the jury to vote one way or another just by the instructions given.

"Will I see you in the morning, when Goff makes the charges to the jury?" Lottie asked.

He nodded. "I'll be there. I'll be happy to see this whole thing done."

# Chapter Forty-One

They walked over from Goff's office to the courtroom after lunch the next day. Chris seemed to be lost in his thoughts. They entered the courtroom and went to their table to await Justice Goff.

It wasn't long before he appeared. He carried his instructions with him; he had not allowed Chris or Lottie to have access to them before that day. She looked back over at Chris; he was staring down at his hands. *What is wrong with him? He's upset about something.*

Goff looked at the jury. Lottie knew he should explain how the jury should act in deciding the case. He should also give examples of how to evaluate the evidence. Example: If you believe one set of facts, you must find for verdict "A"; if you believe in another set of facts, then you must find for verdict "B". The concern was that the Justice could influence which evidence the jury should consider more seriously.

She watched him begin. He started strong with formal instructions on the points of law. As she watched him deliver his instructions, he discussed points about evidence, but only the evidence that belonged to the prosecutor.

She whispered to Chris, "He's giving a recap of the prosecutor's case and not the defendants."

Chris didn't look up at the comment. She frowned and turned back to listen to the Justice. She flinched when he went over the Murray Hill Baths and Harlem Conference as actual and not just suspected events. Even Morris Luban was given additional credibility for his testimony involving the locations of the event.

When it came to Jack Rose, Goff read from his testimony, again treating it as fact. Schepp's role as a witness with no foreknowledge of the murder was reinforced. Lastly, Goff said, "Charles Becker must be held responsible for actions that came from his direct orders."

*Orders*, she thought. Nothing was proven. It was all conjecture based on men who only wanted to protect themselves. She shook her head. *These are instructions to find Becker guilty! How is this justice?*

It had been three hours of instructions and the jurors were finally released at 4:30 pm to begin their deliberations.

# Chapter Forty-Two

Lottie walked back to the office with Chris. They both dropped into their chairs. Goff had stayed behind to talk strategy with Whitman.

"That does it," Chris stated. His voice was curiously devoid of emotion.

"Yes," she responded, frowning to herself. She wondered again about his mood. A strangled sound came from Chris's direction, she looked over and realized he was crying! He had laid his head back on the chair and tears streamed down his face.

She rushed to him, knelt, and asked frantically, "Chris, are you ok? What's wrong?" She had never seen him so emotional; he was usually so professional.

"Lottie," he said, grabbing her hands. "Lottie," he began again, "it was me."

"What was you, Chris? I don't understand."

"I gave them the witness list. I also gave them any updates you gave me each day. They knew everything that would happen in court."

She was nonplussed and didn't say anything. Her mind was racing. *Why?* she asked herself. "Chris, who did you give the list to?"

He tried to pull himself together. "I don't know. I had to leave the information in the park each night."

She frowned at this response. "Why did you do it?" she asked, trying to get to the bottom of it.

He turned red at the question. He looked like he didn't want to answer.

"Chris," she said more firmly, "you have to tell me."

"Pictures," he said miserably.

She understood immediately, but she wanted him to explain. "Pictures? Pictures of what?" He had to be talking about pictures like hers. She couldn't imagine anyone could find anything on him.

Chris pulled his hands from her and turned away. She didn't think he would answer and watched as he pulled open his desk drawer, removing a familiar envelope.

She stopped him. She knew from the way he held it that it contained intensely personal information. "Chris, I don't need to see them. I know what's in them."

He paused and looked at her like she was the enemy. "What do you mean, you know what's in them?"

She decided to tell him everything. Sighing she moved to the seat facing his desk and sat down. "I got my envelope a few weeks ago."

His expression changed and he looked defeated. "You got one also? Can you tell me what they were pictures of?"

"Yes," she confirmed, "the pictures were of me and Rose in an intimate position. They included a threat that my job and my family would receive copies if I didn't follow their direction. Chris," she prompted, nodding at his envelope, "what's in those pictures that they felt could make you do this?"

"I'm not ashamed," he said in a loud voice, and then immediately lowered it. "It was just what we do and where we work that puts us at risk for this type of threat." He paused, looking toward the windows, and finally said, "The pictures include a male friend, someone who wouldn't want the information out in public."

A male friend. So, she and Chris had even more in common. "Is he aware of the pictures?"

"No. I've been trying to protect him."

Lottie wasn't shocked at this new information; she hadn't known Chris was homosexual, but she lived in the village where these relationships were common. Chris didn't live in the area and didn't normally socialize with her, so she had no idea who he spent his private time with.

He had his face in his hands. "I've ruined my career! I've been unethical!"

"To protect yourself and someone else," she reasoned.

"Yes, but it's more than that. I also withheld evidence." He reached into his pocket and pulled out what appeared to be a letter.

"What is that, Chris?" she asked hesitantly.

"This is from Morris Luban's brother. It says their family knows Morris is lying about being in the bathhouse, that there was no way he could have been there at that time." His hands were shaking as he handed it to her.

She was quiet as she read the letter. She finally looked up and said, "I don't think the Justice would have allowed it anyway."

"That isn't a good enough reason! Lottie, have they asked you to do anything?"

"No. I must be a backup to you. If you didn't do it, I assume more pressure would have been applied to me."

He realized something and looked frightened when he asked, "Lottie, what did you do when you saw the pictures?"

She didn't want to make him upset, but she wanted to be honest with him. "I looked into it. I found the photographer."

"You did!" he said. He was shocked that she had information like this.

"I did. We had the photos and negatives destroyed."

"Did you know about mine?"

"No, but I'll make sure they're destroyed," she promised.

"You can trust them to do that?"

"Yes," she said with certainty.

"Lottie, were you scared of your family finding out about your life choices?" he asked, looking lost.

"My family would support me no matter what," she said softly.

"Then you're lucky. I don't have that kind of family," he said bitterly.

"They live in Boston, right?"

"Yes, and they have a conservative law firm there. They would disown me if this came out."

*Yes,* she thought, *this could cause a family to cut off all communication. This is why relationships like this are hidden away outside of the village.*

"Chris, I was more scared of losing my job. Being a woman here is hard enough, but being known as a lesbian lawyer... I was afraid I wouldn't be able to work."

He nodded, understanding. "What should I do? Should I turn myself in? I've tampered with witness lists and evidence."

"I don't think what you did made any real difference. I was in that room every day, and everyone wants to take Becker down. McIntyre is facing a tremendous battle. Goff and Whitman are obviously working together."

"Do you think Whitman is behind the blackmail?"

"I think Whitman's not playing fair, but this sounds like the gangster side of the equation."

She paused. "Chris, look at me." When she saw she had his full attention, she continued. "This case is a losing one, no matter what Becker does. There are too many people wanting him to take the fall."

"I should turn myself in," he said again.

"No, you will not," said Lottie emphatically. She stood and paced a moment. "Chris, I think what we should do is put together the letter for the appeal. We can send it anonymously to the appellate court and McIntyre." She thought about Frank. *I need to send a note to him about the threats to Chris. It may open up more suspects.*

He went silent, thinking. "Lottie, that's the right thing to do."

"After this is over," she promised. "For now, what you will do is go home and get some rest."

"You're sure?" he asked. He wanted someone else to make the decisions for a while.

"I am," she said firmly. She pulled him up. "Get your things. We need to get home. It could be hours before we have to be back."

He allowed her to move him around; that, in itself, was concerning. Normally, Chris was the leader.

He stopped abruptly before leaving and said, "Lottie, thank you. I don't know what I would have done without you."

She realized this could have gone very badly. "Chris, I'm always here for you. Don't hide parts of yourself from me. I won't judge you."

His eyes teared up again, and he hugged her quickly. He seemed more himself. "Let's go, and lock the door. The Justice is going home straight from the court and isn't expected back until the jury has finished their deliberations."

The man listening at the door heard them and moved quickly to a pillar opposite them. Staying in the shadows, he puffed on his cigar as he watched them walk by. Studying them closely, he thought about what he had heard: how they were going to organize a letter for appeal. This information had to be given to the right people. They would know what to do. He started to step from behind the pillar when he saw Lottie stop just down the hall.

Lottie hesitated. "Chris, I forgot my purse. You go on, I'll go back for it."

"Don't forget to lock back up," he said, heading out of the building.

As she turned back toward the door, she glanced over and saw Bob King standing in the hallway by the pillar.

"Bob?" she asked.

He looked a little frightened at her appearance.

She stepped toward him. "Is there something you need from the Justice's office?"

"No, no," he hastened to assure her. "I was just over on another case."

"Okay. You're sure you don't need anything else?"

"Yeah, I am sure," he said as he watched her unlock the door and go into the office. She came out quickly, nodding to him as she passed. The next stop for her was the courier's office, Frank needed to know about Chris' pictures and Bob's unusual behavior.

# Chapter Forty-Three

The jury was out, and Lottie was glad it was over. Chris had gone home, and she was on her way home to get some rest. As she turned the corner to enter the village, she heard a BANG. The bike slid to the side of the road, and she rolled to the ground. Her head hit the pavement; as the blackness started to overtake her, she heard voices.

"Get her," a hard voice called.

"What about the cycle?" another asked.

"Leave it," the first voice ordered.

"All right," the other said regretfully and picked up Lottie, putting her into a waiting car. They drove away quickly.

Jojo came out of a local store and saw Lottie in a car. "Lottie!" he called, trying to wave her down. When the car departed without Lottie waving back, he shrugged and started to head home. That was until he saw her motorcycle laying in the street. He knew she wouldn't have left it on purpose. Walking over to it, he stood it up; the front tire was flat. He bent down to examine it and saw a large hole. Was this related to the gunfire he had heard earlier? *What happened here and why did she leave in that car? She would never leave her motorcycle.*

He rolled it home and brought it into his apartment.

Annabeth walked out of the kitchen, wiping her hands. "Why do you have Lottie's cycle?" she asked, concerned.

"Ma, I think she's in trouble. Look at this," he said indicating the tire."

She bent down. "Looks like a hole."

"I think it was made by a gun," Jojo offered. "I heard something that sounded like a shot before finding the bike."

"Where's Lottie?" she asked, looking at him. She was suddenly very concerned for her friend.

"I don't know, but I think we need to get Frank involved."

"You're right. Do you still have his number?"

"Yes," he said.

"Let me see it, please," she requested, holding out her hand

He reached into his pocket and handed it to her.

She read it over. "Have you seen Joseph around lately?"

"I haven't had a chance to call Frank, but I have seen Joseph hanging around Rose's place this week."

"You stay here. I'm going to JP's house to use their phone." JP's house was a few blocks outside of their area, but she had borrowed her phone before this.

"Lock the door behind me," she called as she left.

She walked quickly to JP's and knocked on her door. It opened quickly. "Annabeth, are you okay?" she asked when she saw Annabeth was out of breath.

"I'm fine, but I think Lottie might be in trouble. Can I use your phone?"

"Of course." JP knew Lottie from the tearoom.

Annabeth picked up the handset, cranked the handle, and spoke into the phone. "I need a number please." She gave it to the operator and waited. As the phone rang, she thought about that bullet. *I pray she's still alive.*

"Hello," a voice answered on the other end.

"Is Frank Griffin there?"

"Just a moment," the voice said. "Frank!"

There was silence, then a familiar voice came on the line. "This is Frank."

"This is Annabeth."

"Oh, hello. What can I do for you?" He hadn't expected to hear from her, but it was a nice surprise.

"It isn't about me Frank. Someone's taken Lottie." She told him about Jojo finding her cycle.

He was silent. "I received a note from her a little while ago. I hadn't followed up yet, but I will now."

"Will it help find her?"

"Yes, I believe so. Thank you." He hung up the handset and thought about who he knew might have information. He got dressed and headed over to his mother's house. She opened the door, and she could tell something was wrong.

"What has he done now? she asked, exasperated.

"I think he's involved in a kidnapping."

She shook her head. She spent most of her life pulling her second child out of problems. "This stops now!" She got her coat and hat and said, "Let's go!"

Frank nodded. He and his mom were very similar people. Jacko was much like his father, talented but not responsible. The only person Jacko was fearful of was her.

They made their way to his apartment. Frank banged on the door.

"Who is it?" a low voice called.

"Jacko, it's me. Let me in," demanded Frank.

"NO! I won't. Go away," Jacko said in a louder voice.

Frank looked at his ma and cocked his eyebrow.

She took over from there. "Jack William, you will open this door now!" Her tone was clear. There would be consequences if he didn't follow her directions.

The door opened immediately. Jacko looked pleadingly at his ma. "I didn't do anything," he whined.

They walked in. Jacko glared at Frank. "Why did you bring her here?" he whispered furiously.

Ma sent him a hard look. "You will sit down and answer Frank's questions."

Jacko looked mutinous as he sat down and waited for Frank to begin.

Frank and his ma continued to stand.

"Did you work with anyone else to take blackmail pictures?" Frank started.

Jacko didn't answer. Instead, he looked at his mother and quickly away.

"Answer, Jack," she demanded.

"Yes," he muttered.

"Who of?" Frank continued.

Jacko looked sullen and didn't say anything.

Frank answered for him. "It was of Chris Burnes and another man."

Jacko didn't respond. Instead, he turned red and sank further into the chair.

"Lottie indicated they were taken in Chris' apartment. How did you manage that?" Frank asked, acting genuinely interested.

"Window. I found a window that was open and took the pictures that way. He has a ground apartment," Jacko muttered.

"Did you go in?"

"Only partway. I needed to open the window and make sure I wouldn't be seen from the inside."

"So, breaking and entering and blackmail, plus assorted other crimes."

"What do you mean?" Jacko screamed.

"What he means, Jack," said Ma, "is you either go to jail or you come home. You're causing far too much trouble on your own."

Jacko looked at her beseechingly. "But, Ma," he whined, "you said if I could support myself, I could stay in my own apartment."

"If you will remember, Jack," she corrected him, "what I said was, if you could support yourself through legal activities, you could live by yourself. I think we can all agree that what you have been doing breaks that agreement." She looked over at Frank and he nodded.

"Will I be able to come back?" Jacko asked, looking around.

"Only if you finish with Frank's questions and enter into an agreement with me."

Jacko looked resolute and asked, "More questions?"

"Yes. Who told you to take Chris' pictures? Was it Rose?" She had yet to be found.

"No," he said. "I haven't seen her since that morning. It was Joseph Bancroft."

"Lottie's Joseph?" Jojo had told his mom he had been around the neighborhood a few times.

"Yes."

Frank pounced at that. "When?"

"He contacted me at the same time Rose wanted Lottie's pictures."

"Did he say anything else?"

"No," Jacko said shortly. "He isn't in the habit of talking to me."

Ma stood up. "Jack, you need to get some things to take home. You won't be coming back here for a while."

"Oh, Ma..." he began to whine. At her sharp look, he cowered. "All right," he said dejectedly.

Ma looked at Frank. "Did his information help you?"

"It did. I also confirmed something else."

She looked at him curiously. "Where to now?" she asked.

"Bancroft has a house on the north side. I'll gather some men up and head that way. Jacko," he warned, "do not mention this to anyone! People could be hurt or killed."

"I'll keep an eye on him," Ma promised. "He won't be seeing anyone."

"Do you need help getting him home?"

"I have it under control."

"I need to get to a phone and head over there." Frank left them there.

# Chapter Forty-Four

Lottie slowly woke. She realized she was sitting up. Her body ached and her head hurt. She took a moment to think before opening her eyes. *My motorcycle. Did I crash?* She opened her eyes slowly. *Where am I?* The room was dark and there wasn't much visibility.

She heard a question come from her right. "Are you okay?"

Turning toward the voice, she saw a slender blonde woman tied to a chair.

"Are you okay?" the woman whispered again. "They carried you in earlier." She didn't mention she had thought Lottie was dead and it terrified her.

"I think so. Sore." Lottie moved as much as she could with her legs tied to the chair and her arms tied behind her.

"There was a young man taken also. I think they called him Chris," the other woman whispered.

"Was he all right?"

"He appeared to be."

Lottie squinted at the woman. "Lissette?" Joseph's wife.

"Yes."

288

"What's going on? Why are we here and tied up?"

"Did you get a set of pictures?"

Lottie thought about that and answered, "I did. I have your pictures and negatives."

"You've seen my pictures?" Lissette didn't seem embarrassed that Lottie had seen them.

"I have. I found Rose's stash. I also found the photographer, so I have the negatives from him."

"What did you do with them?"

"I hid them. Don't worry," she said when she saw Lissette frown. "They won't be found. No one else but me has seen them."

"Good."

"You are married to Joseph?" Lottie asked tentatively, confirming her thoughts.

"I am."

"When were your pictures taken?" Lottie asked as she tried putting the pieces together.

Instead of answering, Lissette asked her, "Are you aware that Rose is Joseph's sister?"

Lottie was shocked. "No! No, that's not true!" *That would mean . . .*

Lissette watched the emotion cross Lottie's face and said in a kind voice, "I know it's true. I've known them for a long time. Rose's secret life was found out and she was forced to leave home about five years ago. There was no contact between her and her family after that. That is until Joseph moved there."

Lottie was shaking with emotion but tried to think back. *Have I ever seen them together? Side by side? No, not once.* She thought that was because Rose was angry at her for being in a long-term relationship, but was it because the relationship was with Joseph?

Lottie asked, "How did your and Rose's relationship start?"

"Joseph set it up," Lissette said with a bitter tone.

"How so?" Lottie asked, shocked.

"Joseph's family and mine have always thought that he and I would end up together. So, when he came back from Harvard and, instead of coming home, he went to the village, naturally they were disappointed. I was relieved. I'd heard about you and thought that it might stop the push from our families for us to marry."

"Why were you against marriage?"

"I had my reasons," she commented softly. "Then, one day, Joseph came by on a Sunday and asked if I wanted to drive around. I said yes. We stopped by Rose's apartment. He asked me to go up to get a note from her." She looked at Lottie. "It was a setup."

"What happened when you saw Rose?"

"You know how she is."

Lottie nodded.

"Her raw sexuality. I hadn't experienced that pull before. Before I knew what was happening, I was in her arms. Something happened to me. Electricity."

"There was more than the one time?"

"Yes. I came back on my own several times after that."

"You think they set it up? Together?"

"I do and, when I got those pictures, I knew," Lissette muttered darkly.

"How did you receive them? Was it by mail?" Lottie asked, thinking of hers.

"No. They were hand-delivered by Joseph."

"Was he angry, jealous?"

"No, if anything, he was self-satisfied. He gave me an ultimatum. I had to marry him or the pictures would be sent to my family."

"They wouldn't have liked it?"

"That's putting it mildly. What happened to Rose, being sent away, would've happened to me. My money was locked up in a trust until I reached 30 or I was married. I'm not sure how I'd have gone on."

"So, they knew they had you. What happened next?"

"Joseph said I had to marry him."

"Why the push for marriage?"

"He was aware of how my trust worked and he needed a business to funnel their money through. They needed my family's companies to do this."

Lottie frowned. "I thought they were bankers."

"No, his family owns some of the gambling houses that that police officer, Becker, was targeting."

*Finally!* Lottie thought. *A connection. They had to get Becker out of the way.*

"So, you were targeted for the money? Were Chris and I targeted for information on the trial?"

"Oh, I can answer that," Joseph said as he and Rose walked in. They brought Chris in with them. He was tied up. They sat him in the chair and Lottie mouthed to him, "Are you okay?"

He nodded.

She looked back toward the front of the room and, for the first time, she saw Rose and Joseph side by side. It was impossible not to notice the similarities in their faces. The cheekbones and the shape of their eyes. *Why didn't I see it?* she asked herself.

"See it now, do you?" Joseph asked and smirked. He could always read her.

"Yes." She looked at Rose and said, "And I'm disappointed in both of you."

"Oh, that hurts," remarked Joseph, grasping his chest dramatically.

"Was any of it real?" she asked, letting some emotion into her voice.

Joseph didn't seem to know how to answer that. He stayed silent.

Lottie continued to watch him as she asked, "Why do all of this? You could have been a writer and stayed in the village." *With me.*

"No," he said. "I tried that life. It was time to go back."

"Papa died," supplied Rose. "He got the chance to run the business his way. He didn't want to be a writer; he just didn't want to be told what to do."

"Joseph, what is your involvement with the Rosenthal murder?" Lottie just had to know.

"I needed to find a way to get the raids on our gambling houses stopped. We were losing money," he said simply.

"And you couldn't stand that," murmured Rose.

He looked at her knowingly. "We both have a love of money, don't we, sis?"

Rose shot him a frown, not responding.

"What did you do to stop the raids?" asked Lottie. They were willing to talk, and she hoped a delay would give them a way out of here.

"I made the first call to report Becker's graft," he said.

"The anonymous one?" asked Chris, talking for the first time.

Joseph answered, not removing his gaze from Lottie's. "Yeah, then I went to see Herman. It wasn't hard to convince him to go to Whitman."

"Did you murder Rosenthal?" Lottie asked.

"No. Didn't have to. Jack Rose and that bunch took that on," he said simply.

"Do you know if Becker was involved?" Lottie continued.

"I didn't care one way or another. The results are everything I could have wanted. I was just hoping to get him out of the way on graft charges. I couldn't have predicted they would go after one of their own. Once Whitman decided Becker was behind it all, we just greased the wheels as necessary. I didn't have to do much; they can't move fast enough to execute Becker," he said. "Oh, and Officer Bob mentioned the appeal. You will not have an opportunity to see that through."

There was a question Lottie wanted to ask. "Rose, what was your role in this? Why would you take private pictures of people in a very vulnerable moment?"

Rose finally looked at her. "I needed money. I had to figure out a way to pay the bills."

"Why not get a job?" Lottie asked.

"Doing what?" she jeered. She sent a disgusted looked at her brother. "My family wouldn't help me."

Joseph was silent during this discourse; he decided to take control. "The trial is coming to a close, and we'll need to get rid of anyone who knew of our involvement."

Lottie was the first to say something. "Get rid of! Are you going to kill us?"

"Yes," he said simply. Rose didn't seem to realize he was serious about that, until that moment.

He looked at the three contemplatively and said, "I think Lottie should die first. After all, she meant the most to Rose and me."

Lottie tried to delay him. "Really, you cared for me? Then why did you marry her?" she asked, nodding at Lissette, goading him.

"Lottie, I had to do that for my family. I couldn't marry someone who's broke and a lesbian," said Joseph.

"The only difference between her and me," said his wife, "is that I have money; I have the same sexual background that she does."

He looked at her nonplussed. "You're normally such a quiet woman."

He suddenly realized what they were doing and raised his gun. "You're distracting me! Lottie first." He pointed his gun at her.

Lottie took a deep breath and closed her eyes, expecting the worst. When the shot didn't come, she opened her eyes and saw Rose struggling with Joseph for the gun.

"Rose, let go!" Joseph yelled.

"NO! You won't kill Lottie! You promised!" she yelled back.

"Well, I take it back! Let go!"

He slammed her against the door, trying to get her hand off the gun. Lottie watched them and used the distraction to get her hands out of the ropes. She reached down and untied her legs. Next, she went to untie Lissette, she heard multiple gunshots from further in the house and running feet.

Joseph and Rose were too wrapped up in their fight to realize they were about to be discovered. Suddenly there was a BANG, the gun had fired. Chris, Lottie, and Lissette watched, unsure who was shot. Rose's face mirrored Joseph's in horror. She stepped back and watched as Joseph fell to his knees and collapsed face down.

Rose still held the gun. She screamed and dropped it. The door was kicked open. Patrick and Frank rushed in, leading other men into the room.

Patrick checked Joseph first. "Dead."

Frank looked at his men and said, "Take her into custody."

Rose had curled up into a ball and it took two men to remove her.

He went over to Lottie. "We were a bit late. I got your note and put it together with the information Patrick and I had gathered and headed here."

"You were just on time, according to my thinking."

They finished untying Chris and Lissette.

Patrick looked closer at Lottie. He saw bruises and scratches on most of her body through her torn pants and shirt. "I think you might need to see a doctor."

"I can help her," Lissette said.

"And you are?" Frank asked.

"The wife of that one," she said, pointing at Joseph.

"I'm sorry for your loss."

"I'm not. I'm glad he's dead," she said shortly. "Can I take Lottie upstairs to patch her up?"

Frank looked around. "Yes. I'll need to question you to fill in some of the blanks."

As Lottie walked by Chris, she muttered, "Say nothing about the trial."

He nodded, he understood the need for his silence.

Lissette walked Lottie to her room and into the bathroom. "Sit down on that chair. Can you take off your shirt?"

"Yes." Lottie unbuttoned it and pulled it off. She sat in her chemise.

"You'll be sore. Take a hot bath tonight." Lissette started on the cuts and scrapes on her back and, in a few minutes, Lottie was able to put her shirt back on. She rolled up her pant legs and got the same treatment.

"I'm sorry Joseph hurt you," Lissette said.

Lottie grabbed her hand. "You have nothing to be sorry about. He used you as much as he used me. I'm very sorry you didn't have someone you could talk to about what was happening."

Lissette looked at the hand holding hers and said, "Thank you." They stared at each other for a long moment.

"What will you do now?" Lottie asked.

"The marriage has opened up my trust. I will take a bigger role in my company. I'm an accountant."

"I didn't know you had gone to college."

"I know," the other woman said ruefully. "Most people see me as a little princess. I went to Harvard at the same time as Joseph."

"I believe you can do it."

"You've worked in law for a while now. Do you enjoy it?"

"I enjoy working for the clients. I don't think my clerkship is the right direction for me."

"So, we're both moving in new directions."

"Yes."

Frank called from the hallway, "We need to get some questions answered."

"We're coming out," Lissette called back.

They finished up. Lottie buttoned up her blouse and pulled her pant legs back down. They met him in the hallway and accompanied him downstairs.

As they sat down with Frank and Patrick, Chris was already in the room. Frank looked at all three and began.

"We'll keep this simple. Joseph had a breakdown, and went after his wife and prior girlfriend, threatening to kill them both. Chris got taken because he was with Lottie when Joseph kidnapped her."

The three of them noticed the pictures and blackmail weren't mentioned.

"Yes, that is the simplest," said Lottie. "What about Bob King?" She did remember seeing him at the crash scene.

"He is being charged with kidnapping and assault. He knows better than to open his mouth," said Frank.

"Frank, what'll happen to Rose?" asked Lottie.

"It depends," he said slowly.

"On what?" she asked. She didn't want to be in a relationship with Rose any longer, but she didn't want anything bad to happen to her.

"What happened exactly?" Patrick asked.

"Joseph went crazy," Lissette said. "He said he would kill us all. Rose tried to stop him, and they got into an argument. They began struggling to get the gun."

"The gun went off during the struggle," Lottie finished.

"I'll take her in on manslaughter," Frank said. When he saw her expression he continued, "She can claim self-defense."

He could tell Lottie was already thinking of Rose's defense. "You can't defend her."

"No. But I can recommend the right person," she reasoned.

Lissette looked at her and said, "Why do you care about what happens to her?" She wanted nothing to do with that family ever again.

"We're not friends anymore, but I think she should have representation. Frank, can I see Rose for a moment? Alone?"

He studied her and finally said, "Okay, but don't take too long. She's in the sitting room." They stood and Frank walked her there. "You have a limited time."

Rose jumped up when she saw Lottie enter the room, she was halted by the young officer guarding her.

"Lottie, thank goodness! Will you be representing me?"

"No, I won't," she said. She looked over at the officer. "Can you step out for a moment? She won't get away from me."

He looked over her shoulder and saw Frank, who motioned him to the door. It was closed softly behind them.

Rose looked so let down. She dropped down into a chair and said, "What will I do?"

"I'll have someone meet you at the police station to handle your case. It will be pro bono. Free," Lottie explained. "He owes me a favor. Have you been read the charges against you?"

"No, I haven't."

"It's manslaughter. You will plead self-defense. Lissette, Chris, and I will be witnesses."

Rose frowned. "Are there no other charges?" She thought of the voyeurism and blackmail.

"No one wants any other charges presented."

Rose looked relieved. "Does this mean I might not have to stay in jail?"

"I think it might, but don't get your hopes up. Rose, once this is over, what are your plans?"

"I think I'll take Lily and go to Paris," she stated firmly.

"So, you did have her with you?"

"Yes. Lottie, I'm sorry for all of the trouble."

Lottie was quiet for a long moment. "You and Joseph. Was it a sick game involving me?"

"No," she said quickly. "It just turned out we were both attracted to you. You saw how angry I was that he took you away from me."

"Yes," she mused.

"He was always doing that. Taking away people I loved. First, it was Mama and Papa. He told them I was a lesbian and that destroyed our relationship. He took my money and then finally he took you."

"If that was the case, why did you help him use me to try to sabotage the Becker trial?"

"Money," she said simply. "I always needed more. Joseph knew that and used it to involve me."

"Rose, I found the money and I'll be sending it back to those women you blackmailed."

Rose looked like she wanted to argue but instead raised her chin. "Now that Joseph is gone, I can sell the business and this house. I'll have enough to get by."

Lottie took her hand. "I care about you and only want the

best, but please don't make the same mistakes you made here. I won't be there to help you."

"I understand."

"Also, treat Lily better than you did me."

Rose laughed suddenly and sounded surprised when she said, "I think I love her."

"Just her? No cheating?"

"It's been just her for a while, and I have to say, I've enjoyed it."

"Rose, I hope it works out in Paris for you both."

"Me also."

# Chapter Forty-Five

By the time they reached the police station, word had been sent that the jury had reached a verdict.

Chris and Lottie hurried over to the court. It was still closed, with access only allowed to the press. *That's that,* Lottie thought until she saw a dozen very pretty women in brightly colored silk gowns and large hats sitting in the gallery.

Chris looked around. "The windows are open and the blinds were drawn up."

"Well, it is a party," she said sarcastically, nodding at the ladies.

"Who are they?"

"Not sure," she muttered, but she suspected they were there at the invitation of Justice Goff.

"Hmm."

The jury was brought in.

"Uh oh," Chris muttered.

"What?" she asked, looking around.

"They aren't looking at Becker."

"Oh, no." She knew that normally meant the news was bad.

Justice Goff entered and confirmed she was right about the ladies. He nodded to them as he got down to business.

"Mister Forman, do you have a verdict?"

"We do."

"Please read it."

"We the jury find the defendant, Charles Becker, guilty on all counts."

The Justice turned to Becker and said, "The jury has said you are guilty. Mr. Becker, you will die in the electric chair." He preened as he delivered his perfect closing to his perfect trial.

Lottie stared at Becker during the pronouncement. The man who sat like a stone during the trial sucked in his breath noticeably. He appeared to struggle to hold himself together as he was walked out by the sheriff.

# Chapter Forty-Six

## A few months later

"Lissette is responsible for this?" Rose asked, indicating the ticket in Lottie's hands.

"Yes. She purchased tickets for you and Lily. There's also a fully paid apartment arranged for you in Paris. She sold Joseph's house and set up an account for you. There are conditions," Lottie cautioned. "She doesn't have to help you. That being said, she does not want any contact from you. Do not send any personal letters or ask for more money. It will not be provided."

"So, that's it, I guess. I'm on my own."

"It is. I have a cab waiting. I'll help you pack and take you to the ship's dock to meet Lily. You'll depart this evening."

"I'm to leave town as soon as possible?"

"Yes. Rose, look at this as a positive thing. Paris is a more open place to live."

"Yes, I have always wanted to live there," she said quietly. "You know I never meant to hurt you."

"Hmm," Lottie said, not believing her. Rose loved the thrill of the threats and the response of her victims. She picked up her pace, marking boxes to ship over or what could be donated or trashed.

When the packing was completed, Rose sat. "That should be it," she said.

Lottie handed her a glass of water and they sat quietly, drinking. "You know, I was thinking about divided lives," Rose started.

"Oh, Rose, not that again," Lottie said. She thought Rose was going to criticize her once more.

"No, not you. It is me, as it turned out. I was never honest about who I was. My life here was a lie. Maybe I can change that in Paris." She looked over and saw the necklace around Lottie's neck. "You found it," she remarked, motioning to it.

"Yes. Why did you leave it behind?" Lottie asked. She made no move to give it back to her.

"I thought you would see it and come to rescue me like you did Joseph," she said, looking away.

"I did search for you; it turned out you didn't need to be rescued."

"No, no, I guess I didn't."

Lottie and Rose rode together to the ship, and she accompanied her to the stateroom to her room. Rose knocked on the door and Lily answered. She saw Lottie and put her hands up around her neck. Lottie watched her and stayed where she was. Looking at Rose, she said in farewell. "Good luck. Have a good life."

Rose nodded, watching Lottie leave the room. She held out her hand to Lily and pulled her in close. They went out to the deck to watch the ship leave the dock.

Lottie didn't turn back, what she did was take the necklace off and tossed it off of the gang plank as she walked down. That part of her life was over. She hailed a cab and told the driver to take her to Greenwich Village.

After she paid him and got out, she looked at the building before entering. A smile slowly turned up the corners of her mouth as she pushed the door open and went in.

Patrick and Papa were adding shelves behind where the desks would sit.

"You're back!" they exclaimed.

"I am."

"Did Rose get off okay?" asked Patrick.

"She did." She looked at him. "Thank you for arranging for Lily to get to the ship."

"Sure, it wasn't a problem."

Papa walked up and said, "You're just in time. Chris," he called, "bring that sign."

Chris came out of the back. "Here it is," he said proudly.

She ran over to him. "Let me see."

He held it up for her to read. It was a beautiful sign that said: *Chris Burnes, Lottie Flannigan, Attorneys at Law*

"It's perfect," said Lottie.

"I agree," he stated.

Papa had installed hangers outside the office. They all went outside and watched as he climbed up the ladder and put it in place.

"That is wonderful," she said, looking up at it. She glanced at Papa. "Thank you."

"It is nice," said Chris. He looked at Patrick and Papa. "Thank you both so much for helping us get the office ready."

Chris and Lottie had resigned their clerkships after the trial. After it had finished, they sent an anonymous letter to Becker's lawyers, laying out their notes on his appeal. It contained a statement that Charles Becker deserved the chance to defend himself and that didn't occur in Justice Goff's court.

Some of the items included:

Calling Mr. Becker a "grafter"; a term used by the prosecutors and the Justice.

The conspirators were kept in the same location and allowed to corroborate their testimony.

The Harlem Conference was not supported by the driver's testimony to the events. There was also no information provided about the driver's identification.

McIntyre was unable to question these individuals and to allow the jury to hear the testimony.

No specific dates could be submitted to allow Becker the chance to give evidence he was not there for either the Bath House meeting or the Harlem conference.

The location of the Harlem conference was extremely questionable to be out in the open and at a vacant lot, late at night.

Justice Goff also offered the Harlem Conference and the Bathhouse meeting as fact in his closing and not supposition.

Justice Goff treated the defendant and his attorney with open hostility, which was apparent to the jury and interfered with their ability to weigh the evidence properly.

Justice Goff's continued favoritism of Whitman; was apparent with each and every ruling for the prosecutor.

The final line of the note stated, "We do not think the defendant had a fair trial. We think he suffered grievously from the erroneous disposition both of questions of law and discretion."

# Chapter Forty-Seven

That evening, Patrick and Lottie were having a quiet dinner at her apartment. Papa was spending the evening with Henrietta and Danny.

She looked at Patrick and asked, "You were asking about Joseph before the Becker trial started. Why?"

"Just a feeling. I didn't trust him."

"What were you looking for?"

"Initially, I was just checking him out. This person who treated you so badly. He did have an important name, but the family's money wasn't in banking like you mentioned."

"When did you realize he must have been part of the gambling establishment?"

"When I came back, during the trial. My contacts confirmed he owned one of the locations Becker was targeting. It was buried under another business. I finally found it under Lissette's company name."

"Joseph made the first anonymous call to Whitman that started this whole mess. It's also probable that he pushed Rosenthal to go through with the grand jury testimony."

"But why?"

"Get rid of the competition. He probably figured he could ride it out."

"Interesting," he responded.

"What was your plan?"

He said, "I was working undercover, helping bring down some of the bad cops."

"You were part of that large contingent?" The New York Police Department had brought in more than 40 officers to clean up their precincts.

"Yes, but I couldn't share that with you."

She understood and let it go. "Did you know Frank before that morning at my apartment?"

"Yes. he was my contact when I was here assisting in the Becker investigation," he admitted. "He requested I come back to assist him. I didn't know it would also involve you. He told me about the pictures and blackmail."

"I figured as much," she said ruefully.

"Jojo confirmed Joseph was hanging around Rose's place about that time. Frank was also able to find out Rose's last name. We planned to meet over there to question him when Frank found out you'd been taken."

"And you arrived at Joseph's house."

"We saw Bob King hanging around outside and grabbed him. He told us you were there."

"The way I see it, it was perfect timing."

"What've you done with the pictures and money?"

"I destroyed them," she said simply. "Then I contacted each woman and returned their money with assurances their ordeal was over."

"That's good." Patrick looked at her. "Do you think she will try it again?"

"I watched her closely in the last few weeks. She does seem different and committed to Lily."

"That may just be a consequence of being in quarantine with her. Once she's back in a social scene, she may revert to her past ways."

"I hope not."

"I thought we'd be eating with Frank tonight."

"No, not tonight," Lottie said. "I believe he's spending all of his time with Annabeth and Jojo."

"I didn't realize they were seeing each other," he said in surprise.

"For a while now," she confirmed. "What about you? Are you heading home soon?"

"I'm thinking about staying here. Frank asked me to join his team, permanently."

"Will you stay?"

"I think so."

"That's wonderful," she said and hugged him.

As they settled back, he asked, "Are you seeing anyone now?"

"I might be," she said with a small smile.

"Anyone you can tell me about?"

"Yes."

# Chapter Forty-Eight

## A month after Rose left town

Lottie was working with a new client and Chris had gone to court for a trial. As she wrapped it up and walked the client out, she heard a voice call softly, "Lottie."

She turned and saw Lissette walking up the sidewalk toward her.

"How are you?" Lottie asked warmly and walked up to kiss her.

"I'm good. I have lunch if you'd like to share with me?" Lissette asked, holding out a basket.

"Let me close the office and we can go to my apartment."

"That would be lovely."

Lottie looked around the office, then at Lissette. Her life was no longer divided into two parts; she no longer hid who she was in her law career or her private life. Everyone in her life accepted her for who she was.

# Rosenthall Murder flow sheet

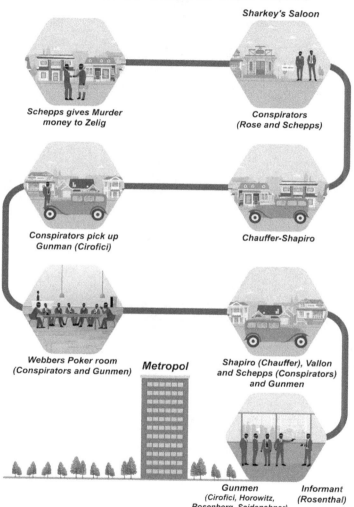

Sharkey's Saloon

Schepps gives Murder
money to Zelig

Conspirators
(Rose and Schepps)

Conspirators pick up
Gunman (Cirofici)

Chauffer-Shapiro

Webbers Poker room
(Conspirators and Gunmen)

Metropol

Shapiro (Chauffer), Vallon
and Schepps (Conspirators)
and Gunmen

Gunmen
(Cirofici, Horowitz,
Rosenberg, Seidenshner)

Informant
(Rosenthal)

# Becker Trial Conspirators and Gunmen

## Informant/Murdered

Herman Rosenthal, a small-time bookmaker, and gambler; was murdered at the Metropol in 1912.

## Accused conspirators:

Charles Becker, Police lieutenant, head of the special squad, and charged with conspiracy to murder Herman Rosenthal.

Jack Rose, conspirator to murder Herman Rosenthal. aka Baldy Rose. Mob informant worked with Rosenthal and testified to conspiring with Becker.

Harry Vallon, conspirator to murder Herman Rosenthal. Gambler and mob informant.

Sam Schepps, a conspirator to murder Rosenthal. Schepps was identified by coconspirators as the "paymaster" of the plot to kill Rosenthal. This statement was later rescinded and he was changed to a corroborator, a key person in proving conspiracy.

## Accused Gunmen (Members of Lennox Gang)

Francisco Cirofici, a gunman, shot Herman Rosenthal. aka Dago Frank, not a regular member Lenox gang.

Harry Horowitz, a gunman, shot Herman Rosenthal. aka Gyp the Blood, a regular member of the Lenox gang.

Louis Rosenberg, **a** gunman, shot Herman Rosenthal. aka Lefty Louie and Louis Marks, a regular member of the Lenox gang.

Jacob Seidenshner, **a** gunman, shot Herman Rosenthal. aka Frank Muller and Whitey Lewis, a regular member of the Lenox gang.

**Webber Gambling establishment owner:**

Bridgey Webber, Provided the location for the gunman and conspirators to meet. Gave details on Rosenthal's location to the gunman.

**Driver of conspirators and gunmen:**

William Shapiro, Chauffeur of Conspirators and gunmen. Was not involved in the conspiracy. Identified Conspirators but would not name gunmen.

**Money man and head of Lennox Gang:**

Jack Zelig-leader of Lennox gang, Gunmen worked for him. Listed on both prosecution and defense witness list. He was murdered just prior to the trial starting.

# Author's take

***Do I think he did it?*** *I don't think I can say for sure if he was innocent or not. I think he wasn't given a fair shake in his first trial and the retrial was justified. Unfortunately, the second trial appeared to be politically skewed as well.*

The appeals court found fault with the evidence. One of the main issues was using Sam Schepps as a corroborator. The justices concluded that he was definitely a conspirator.

Because of this, in the second trial, Whitman changed his strategy of using the conspirators (Vallon, Rose, Schepps) as the main focus of his trial. Whitman's case had relied heavily on Schepps as a non-conspirator but at each meeting to provide corroboration. It was obvious to the appeals court he was part of the conspiracy. Active as the bagman for the gunmen and in the car with conspirators on the way to the poker room.

Whitman needed a corroborator that must not have any association as a conspirator. He also needed to prove the Harlem conference happened, he did that with the help of a young black man named James Marshall. He was finally able to fix the date of the Harlem conference to June 27, one thing the first trial did not do.

James Marshall was on Becker's payroll as an informant and who had been present when Becker ordered Rose and the others to kill Rosenthal. He was a more credible witness than Schepps and was able to show no apparent involvement with the killing and provide corroboration. Incidentally—Marshall testified to the date and the men at the Harlem conference but did not address what they were discussing. Vallon's testimony was used to confirm what was said.

The second trial was only longer than the first by a matter of two days. The judge had his own political aspirations and followed Goff's example by accepting almost all of the prosecution's argument.

It was so upsetting to Becker's council that he stood up after the instructions were delivered and said, "I object to the whole charge on the grounds that it is an animated argument for the prosecution."

The jury already privy to the first conviction took even less time to convict Becker and sentenced him (for a second time), to be electrocuted.

Becker's last hope before going to the electric chair was a governor's pardon. Becker's bad luck continued when he applied to the governor for a pardon. Whitman had been elected Governor of Illinois in the time between the second trial and the scheduled execution. As expected, he did not pardon Becker. He was executed on May 22, 1914.

The gunman had been executed between Becker's 1st and 2nd trial. The conspirators were released without any charges.

# About the Author

K.R. Mullins is the author of historical fiction books. She holds a BS in Biology and a MBA in Business. She lives in Texas with her husband and son. When she is not writing she is working as a Process Safety Engineer at a large chemical company. You can connect with her on her website www. kimberlymullinsauthor.com.

*Photo Credit: Blessings of* *Faith Photography*

 twitter.com/kremullins_kim

9 798985 993080